D0299653

PRAISE FOR *GOOD SAMARITANS*

'Irresistibly dark and deviant' Eva Dolan

'I loved this book. Dark and at times almost comical, a great blend of crime thriller and the darkest imaginable domestic noir. Actually, like domestic noir on LSD' Sarah Pinborough

'Totally addictive. Like *Fight Club*, only darker' S.J. Watson

'Beautiful, gripping and disturbing in equal measure, a postcard from the razor's edge of the connected world we live in' Kevin Wignall

'Possibly the most interesting and original writer in the crime-fiction genre. I've loved his books for years. *Good Samaritans* is his best to date. Dark, slick, gripping, and impossible to put down. You'll be sucked in from the first page. Buy it!' Luca Veste

'Ridiculously brilliant. A deliciously dark five-star read' Lisa Hall

'Black-hearted noir. Disturbing and brilliant' Tom Wood

'Sick … in the best possible way. Will Carver delivers a delicious slice of noir that will have you reeling' Michael J. Malone

'A twisty, devious thriller from a sick mind … Thumbs up!' Nick Quantrill

'*Good Samaritans* is dark, edgy, disturbing, shocking and sexy. It's also highly original and one of the best thrillers of the year. Cancel all plans when you start this book and warn those around you: any interruptions may cause them harm. You need to read this book' Michael Wood

'A dark and addictive novel that felt deliciously sexy to read, like I should read it where no one could see' Louise Beech

'Forget "snap, crackle and pop" this is more like "crash, bang, wallop", so twisted, so enjoyable and so flippin' clever! This book is GENIUS' The Quiet Knitter

'Quirky, cool and dark as sin, *Good Samaritans* will rock your reading world' Liz Loves Books

'Sick, twisted, depraved, but oh-so f**king intelligent! If you are looking for something that is going to blow your mind away and offer you a unique and intense experience, then pick up *Good Samaritans* and hide yourself away from the world, because, believe me, you are not going to be able to put this down! I felt as though the pages were laced with a substance that served to hook me ... like a literary crack cocaine. One hit and I was powerless to resist!' Chapter in My Life

'*Good Samaritans* is sexy, dark, explicit and graphic in places, so certainly not for the fainthearted. It's twisty and twisted too. Is this a love story? Oh yes, but not necessarily in the way you think. It's certainly a tale of lust, obsession, control and desperation. The book kept me guessing and certainly kept me engrossed, with many laugh-out-loud moments and pages read with a gasp ... I'll never look at bottles of bleach in quite the same way again' Off-the-Shelf Books

'*Good Samaritans* is quite different to anything I've read before – it has the thrilling plot I look for, as well as a sexy and daring pulse throughout. If you're looking for something that speeds up the heart rate in more ways than one, I highly recommend Will's new novel!' Once upon a Book

'Ultra sexy ... a raunchy and deviously enthralling treat' Nic Parker

'As the story unfolded and events started to take shape in a way I was not expecting, I began to wonder. I wondered and wondered and wondered ... and was left gobsmacked! *Good Samaritans* is a rodeo drive in the city in a family car. It looks safe and harmless on the outside. Scrape the surface and discover one of the most intense and haunting novels' Chocolate 'N' Waffles

'Well, throw in roughly three bottles of bleach, a crazed wife, Maeve, and two other bodies and you have yourself one hell of a plot. With twists and turns to throw you off course, this will capture your mind, heart, and soul' Donna Hines

'He's best known for the January David series, which ended in 2013. Now Will Carver is back with a standalone that takes good deeds to a whole new level. Sleep and Seth Beauman don't get along, so he stays up late, calling random strangers and hoping to make a connection while his wife sleeps upstairs. Then one night he gets a crossed line. Hadley Serf is suicidal and thinks she is talking to the Samaritans. It's the start of a strange relationship that can only end in tears...' Crime Fiction Lover

'My book of the year ... hands down' Waterstones bookseller

'Bloody brilliant ... unlike anything I've ever read' Laura Rash, Goodreads

'Twisty, turny and downright OMG' The Book Trail

'Once in a while an irresistible book will come along that is so dark, twisted and dangerously addictive that it leaves you feeling absolutely filthy! *Good Samaritans* is exactly that book, and his detailed descriptions are clear, evocative and certainly unforgettable. Will Carver has a very unique writing style, original, modern and wholly daring. Highly recommended' Miriam Smith

GOOD SAMARITANS

ABOUT THE AUTHOR

Will Carver is the international bestselling author of the January David series. He spent his early years in Germany, but returned to the UK at age eleven, when his sporting career took off. He turned down a professional rugby contract to study theatre and television at King Alfred's, Winchester, where he set up a successful theatre company. He currently runs his own fitness and nutrition company, while working on his next thriller. He lives in Reading with his two children.

Follow Will on Twitter *@will_carver*.

GOOD SAMARITANS

WILL CARVER

**ORENDA
BOOKS**

Orenda Books
16 Carson Road
West Dulwich
London SE21 8HU
www.orendabooks.co.uk

First published by Orenda Books 2018
Copyright © Will Carver 2018

Will Carver has asserted his moral right to be identified as the author of this work in accordance with the Copyright, Designs and Patents Act, 1988.

All Rights Reserved. No part of this publication may be reproduced in any form or by any means without the written permission of the publishers.

A catalogue record for this book is available from the British Library.

ISBN 978-1-912374-37-3
eISBN 978-1-912374-38-0

Typeset in Garamond by MacGuru Ltd
Printed and bound by CPI Group (UK) Ltd, Croydon CR0 4YY

This is a work of fiction. Names, characters, places and incidents are either products of the author's imagination or are used fictitiously. Any resemblance to actual events, locales or persons, living or dead, is entirely coincidental.

For sales and distribution, please contact *info@orendabooks.co.uk*

For Tuesdays

'But a Samaritan, as he travelled, came where the man was; and when he saw him, he took pity on him.'

—Luke 10:33

'When you have insomnia, you're never really asleep. And you're never really awake.'

—Narrator, *Fight Club*

It doesn't get you clean. Not that much bleach. Sure, there are face creams that you can buy that will help with dry skin or dark patches left from overexposure to sunlight and they're clinically proven to help. But it's a trace amount.

And, for those suffering with eczema, a bleach bath may be recommended. Your dermatologist will tell you that the bleach can significantly decrease the infection of Staphylococcus aureus, a bacterium prevalent in those who are plagued by this skin condition. Still, it is recommended to use no more than half a cup of bleach in one half-filled bath of water.

Because it won't make your skin sparkle like it does your toilet basin. It will burn. It will blister. You will bleed. It will hurt like hell.

Unless you're already dead.

It's the moment before that hurts like hell. That drowning sensation you can sometimes experience when somebody much stronger than you forces their weight down against your windpipe. It's the gasping for air that will hurt, not the bleach.

And then there's that weird buzzing in your ears as you die, and your face is discolouring, which makes it easier for coroners to determine the cause of death, though the compression marks on your neck are a huge giveaway. And the way your eyes are now protruding. They won't know for sure about your tingling muscles or vertigo, and the bleach will take care of the blood that came out of your ears and nose.

But don't worry about the bleach, the six bottles of bleach poured into a bathtub topped up with hot water that you are dumped into and left for days. The one where you are scrubbed inside and out as the chemicals burn your entire body and strip your hair of any colour. That part won't hurt.

So there's no need to run your skin under cold water or wrap your wounds in plastic. But that will still happen. You will still be taken care of. And your fingernails will be cut and your teeth will be brushed, just in case you bit or scratched when you could still feel pain.

And you won't be cold when you are dropped in a ditch or a field or some undergrowth with only the plastic to protect your modesty and cover your mottled skin. Of course, your body will be cold, but you won't feel it.

It will be okay. You can just lie there. Rest.

Hope a dog-walker wanders by, or an overamorous couple lie down in the wrong place or a kid goes searching for a ball near the wrong tree.

Wait for that Good Samaritan to find you.

They will find you.

THAT WEEK
SUNDAY

1

I was troubled. There was no doubt about that. The list of things I hated about myself was long and easy to compile. And, like so many people who need the support of others around them, who need to be able to talk without fear of judgement or ridicule, who need love and encouragement and positivity, I was alone. Everyone had given up. Even those who were still in my life were waiting, counting the days until that phone call would be placed to say that I'd finally succeeded and they could all get on with their lives now without Hadley Serf getting in their way.

I'd tried to kill myself before.

I'd tried a lot.

That first time – well, what everybody thought was the first time – was a classic wrist-slashing attempt. Poorly thought out and badly executed as it was, people started to sit up and listen.

I was in my flat, alone, and I'd had enough. I took a razor in my right hand, placed it on my forearm, pressed it into the skin and swiped downwards through my wrist towards the palm of my hand. I would have gone across the wrist but I'd watched a film that had very clearly stated that it was the wrong way to do it. How embarrassing to be found dead having cut your wrists the wrong way. I'd never live it down.

I only cut the left wrist, a good four-inch line in my arm, and then I called my boyfriend, who came to get me and take me to the hospital. Then he dutifully and diligently called my friends to let them know.

And they rushed from wherever they were at that point to come and see me.

And they didn't understand it.

And it was awkward.

And it still is. Because they haven't really bothered to dig a little deeper.

To understand just how much I can't stand me. And that ever-growing list of things that I don't like and can't seem to fix.

They talk amongst themselves, saying that it is my father's fault. He has always suffered with depression but won't admit it to himself. He has always belittled Hadley. That's what they say. And they say other things, 'I don't know what she's so depressed about, her parents have loads of money.'

They yawn. They wheeze. They spit.

Of course, I don't care about my family's apparent wealth. I thought about my father and my mother and my younger brother before I ran that blade through my skin, unzipping a dark-blue vein that released a beautiful crimson worm. I thought about them and how much they would hurt if they found out I was dead. I thought about my boyfriend, too. And all my friends. It wasn't a decision I was taking lightly. But I figured that, in the long run, their lives would genuinely be better, richer, without me. And I figured mine would be infinitely improved if I was no longer getting in my own way.

I cry.

I fake.

I bleed.

I had tried to explain this to my friends and they had tried to understand. They were supportive for a couple of weeks, then they thought I was fixed and they got on with their own lives again.

My boyfriend called it all off a week or so after that.

2

'Samaritans, can I help you?'

That's how it always started. It was his third call that night. Nobody suicidal; that was a common misconception. It was just late. People often called because all of their friends were asleep and they had nobody they could talk to. About the difficulties they were having in their relationship, or the questions they had about their sexuality, or the fact that they just felt so lonely.

And sometimes, not a lot, it's a prank. Somebody who doesn't need to talk, who doesn't need help, who has no questions burning inside that they have no outlet for. Who, instead, think it is funny to waste somebody's time. To interrupt the precious seconds of those in true need of assistance and companionship.

He'd had three calls already. None of them were a waste of time. Not to him. He was helping. He was there for those who needed it most.

Trying to fill that hole inside of him.

Trying to get himself clean.

His name was Ant. He was twenty-five. He had finished university and travelled around Australia, New Zealand and Fiji with his friend James. Two months into what seemed like their greatest adventure, Ant found James hanging from the back of a bathroom door, a leather belt around his neck and his dick in his hand.

It had looked like an accident, as these things so often do. And the trip was cut short as Ant helped with paperwork to get the body flown back to the UK. And, just as he was getting closer to finding out what he wanted to do with his life, Ant became lost.

Impure and hopeless.

It changed everything. From that point on, Ant just felt so god-damned dirty.

In an effort to deal with what had happened, he volunteered with the Samaritans. And now he was here, still, years later, listening to somebody who possibly wanted to go the way James had and, this time, he could help.

And when he did, in just that moment, he felt a little less dirty, a little less lost.

3

Mostly, they'd just hang up the phone.

Whoever they were.

Seth didn't know.
He was just dialling a random number.
Hoping for some connection.

It goes something like this.

There are two sofas in the lounge. One for Seth, with two seats, that he sits up in. One for his wife, with three seats, that she lies down on and then invariably falls asleep – halfway through the programme that she has insisted they watch. This is called marriage. Routine. Settling down. Settling in. Settling. He tells himself that she has no idea they're unhappy. Because it's too pathetic to think that they both let this happen.

She misses the second half of the TV show. He watches it to the end just in case she wakes up and finds that he's turned over to something that doesn't turn his brain to a liquid he can feel dribbling out of his ears. What he wants to do is turn it off. Read a book. Do some exercise. Masturbate. Take one of those floral cushions from her sofa, one of the ones that really ties everything in the room together, and place it over her face, holding it down tightly so that he never has to ingest another minute of *The Unreal Privileged Housewives of Some American City He Doesn't Give A Fuck About*.

He wants some warmth.

To feel loved. Needed. Wanted.

But he sticks it out. He watches it while she snores. He doesn't remember the names of any of the characters, just like he can't remember anything his wife likes anymore, or the reasons he fell for her in the first place.

It gets like this.

The credits roll. He wakes her up. She apologises. He says something like, 'Don't worry, babe. You didn't miss much.' Then she goes to bed. She used to kiss him goodnight but that stopped a couple of years ago. He's pleased it did. It felt wrong. Forced.

Then he's alone. With his thoughts and ideas and anguishes. And nobody to share them with. No one to lighten the load.

He wants to pick up the phone now and dial a number. But it's too early. That's like admitting defeat. Tonight could be the night. He could fall asleep. He could stay asleep.

He doesn't fall or stay.

That's how it always goes.

It's been like this for eighteen years.

His evening continues.

He flicks through the channels with no real purpose. Perhaps the small hope that he'll stumble across a movie where a woman is showing her breasts, because he can't always rely on his imagination when he wants to grab hold of his cock. They don't have sex anymore. He thinks that, maybe he'll feel sleepy after he has come. He just feels pissed off, though. The pleasure lasts for a second. Maybe. He used to be able to control the ending, prolong it, make it last. It seems too much like work, now. It's not about pleasure anymore.

It's truth and nothingness. That moment when you come, when you can't deny the pleasure of orgasm, no matter how short it is, there is an inescapable nothing. Everything in that instant is true. And he'll take that, because all the other things in his life seem to be a fucking lie.

Seth can't sleep. And that's a problem. It affects everything in his life. And everything in his life affects it.

Afterwards there is a come-down. The inevitable low. Because there isn't a thing that will top that half-second of joy. Seth's shitty day is about to get so much worse.

Could he try harder? Should he have to? Things aren't unpleasant. They don't argue. She puts him down from time to time but he guesses that's just to make her feel better about herself. He's heard that marriage is about compromise. He figures that's what he's doing here. Compromising. Occasionally, he lets her make him feel like shit and, sometimes, in return, she goes to bed early.

He has ideas. They are far beyond his incredible lack of talents, but he thinks about things. All those things that he could do but tells himself he doesn't have the time. He could leave his life. He could get out and start anew. He could pick up his clarinet and fly to New

Orleans and play it on the streets. He could read more. And not the two hundred contemporary novels that his wife ingests every year on her commute to work and that she forgets within seconds of finishing. Important books. All those Americans that lived in Paris in the twenties who wrote things that should be read. He could learn a language. He could do anything. He has the time. He's awake so much. It's the state of mind that stops him.

Heart is up. State is low. Brain is racing. These three simple ingredients are enough to now keep Seth awake for the next six hours. Quarter of a day of doing nothing. He feels tired. Exhausted, actually. But somehow ultra-responsive. Stimulated. Yet with no impetus to do anything. He just wants to sleep. And he can't.

Is this who he is now?

Who was he before?

Was he kind? Is he still?

He gives it three hours of tapping his foot and flicking through channels on the television. Half watching a programme before changing again.

Finally he concedes and picks up the phone. He flicks through the phone book, his homemade phonebook, made from a database of thousands of customers who had ordered from DoTrue, the computer company where Seth works. He found the file while fixing an error on his boss's laptop.

Seth stops at a random page. He dials a number and waits. It rings seven times. A man picks up. He has an accent that is about seventy miles north of Seth's home.

'Hello?' he asks.

'Hey, it's Seth. I can't sleep. Want to talk?'

'Go fuck yourself, freak.'

He slams the phone down at his end.

And so it begins.

Another night.

4

It was a cold night in Warwickshire but Theresa Palmer couldn't feel a thing.

She'd been there for a few days, tucked away between four or five trees. People would eventually tell the tale of how she was found in the woods, because it romanticises the story; it somehow makes it darker, creepier. The local and national news, however, would flit between the use of undergrowth and copse.

The grave was pretty shallow. You'd have thought she'd have been found by now. It wouldn't be too long. Whoever had left her there must have been in a rush. Or maybe they were simply lazy. Cocky. Didn't want to get their hands too dirty.

It wouldn't be long before a man would enter the woods/undergrowth/copse with a plastic bag rolled over his hand, thinking he was only going behind that tree to find a small pile of beagle shit.

Not long until that man's body would turn cold and he would inhale nervously and knowingly.

Not long until he let out a short scream that only his faithful dog would hear.

Not long until he would call the police to inform them that he had found a body, bleached and bloated and wrapped in plastic.

It really wouldn't be that long until Detective Sergeant Pace would discover that the woman who had been reported as missing was dead. And that she is the second person to be found like this, miles from home. Alone and dead.

Detective Sergeant Pace is a shadow.

Detective Sergeant Pace is paranoia.

Detective Sergeant Pace is losing.

5

Pills. It was pills the next time. It's good to try new things.

Pills can be a great way to go. Have a drink. Swallow enough tablets to stun a small elephant. Drift off into a pain-free, eternal slumber.

When you don't get the pills thing right, though, it is horrific.

I did not get the pills thing right, either.

My friends would say things like, 'If she really wanted to die, she could do it properly. Get a gun. Jump off a really tall building. This is a cry for help.' They were wrong, but that's what they wanted to believe. Yet, still they don't help.

I had a new boyfriend. I always thought that it would help. He was so much better than the one who had left me when the first sign of challenge presented itself. My friends liked him. I loved him. And he seemed to love me.

I was thinking about him as I popped another pill in my mouth, sitting in the driver's seat of my old Fiat. I reminisced about our holiday to Rome, where we had crept out of our window onto the roof of the hotel and made love under the dark Italian sky with traffic buzzing around below us. I remembered him going down on me and the sound of my climax being drowned out by the horns of a thousand mopeds working their way around an unmanageable one-way system.

I recalled our smiles and laughter and his white teeth and dark skin and those muscles in his shoulders that I loved to squeeze in my hands as we kissed. And I decided that he would be better off without me in his life, dragging him down.

So, I swallowed a pill and took a drink. Swallowed a pill and took a drink. Swallowed and drank. Swallowed some more. And my eyes felt heavy. And the music on the radio was not worth listening to. Not worth dying to. So I opened the door and got out of the car but my legs were not working and they buckled beneath me. And I hit my right eye on the car door as I fell. Then my cheek grazed against the concrete where I landed. And the screen of my mobile phone cracked under the pressure of my body. I fished it out of my pocket and called my boyfriend to tell him what I had done and where I was. That boy who I loved.

Two fingers dug to the back of my throat and I threw up on the floor next to my face. Then I passed out. And that's how I was found. Completely beaten by life.

The hospital said that I needed an evaluation and sent me to stay somewhere for a few days to be viewed and prodded and diagnosed. Friends visited. They said things like, 'She got closer this time.' And, 'I can't believe she'd do that to him. He's so nice. She couldn't have been thinking about him at all.'

But those friends still stuck by me and watched out for me, calling me every day, talking about nothing, trying to behave as though everything was normal. But everything wasn't normal. It lasted about ten days. And that boyfriend who loved me so much lasted another three on top of that.

6

'When did you realise?'

'Where did that happen/what happened?'

'How did that feel?'

Ant had these three sentences written on a Post-it note that he would stick to the corner of his computer screen. It was his routine. He would write them down at the beginning of each shift – he wasn't always sat in the same chair. He knew them by heart. He remembered them. But having them there made him feel comfortable, like he was in control of the situation, the conversation. He had an out, if he needed it, which he never did.

He was drinking coffee close to midnight after a pretty tough call. He brought his own coffee in to work. He didn't like the vending machine. It was dirty. And his thermos would keep his drink warm enough for hours. And he knew it was clean. It was his. That was important.

His last call was a man in his twenties whose father had passed away. It wasn't sudden, the guy had been in and out of hospital over the years, always alcohol-related, but he hadn't gone to visit him. He wanted to. He'd hated his father. Hated him for who he had been and how he had changed. And he hated that he loved him. He wanted to visit but he couldn't.

He'd said, 'It would have affected my family that are still alive.' Ant wanted to push him on that but had left a short silence, hoping the caller would fill it with further information. He didn't fill it.

'What happened?' Ant asked, his eyes flitting towards the redundant note stuck to the screen in front of him.

'Liver. Of course. You know how much you have to drink for your liver to fail? A fucking lot of booze. He would do six bottles of wine in a day to himself. As a warm-up. It was ridiculous.'

Ant sat and he listened and that was all the caller really wanted. He obviously couldn't talk to his family about how he felt. He said he was faking it in front of them. Their hatred was pure, or it seemed pure. He was the only one who felt love towards the dead man. As wrong a love as it was. He needed a release. Ant was providing that service. He was helping.

But the call ended and Ant realised he hadn't really said too much. That was acceptable, every call was different and he had done his job well. But that caller, that estranged son with no outlet for his grief, he thanked the stranger at the end of the line for being there. That filled Ant with a warmth. A sense of fulfilment and purpose. He was cleansed.

And that caller told Ant that he would always regret not going to see his dad. Because closure was now impossible. As was confrontation with the rest of his family. He would have to live with that forever. But he was prepared and ready to do that. He would take the hit for everyone else.

Ant foresaw a caring man's encroaching nihilism. And he feared for his future. Like he would be a one-day call – for something more serious. Something that would require Ant to participate more. And the thought turned him cold.

And that coffee he had brought from home, that sweet, clean, dark caffeine hit, wasn't hot enough to change that.

He stood away from his desk for a moment and tried to push himself past his experience. His phone rang again. He sat back down, placed the headset over his ears and hit the button to answer.

'Samaritans. Can I help you?'

7

After the first rejection, Seth liked to regroup in the kitchen. Clear his head. Make a coffee. He's so fucking tired but he knows he's going to be awake most of the night, so why not be a little more alert, a little more awake. He knows it is counterintuitive. He knows it makes no sense. But insomnia makes no sense.

It's not that he doesn't ever sleep, although that has happened – he's had days where he couldn't switch off and that stretched on for half a week. Being awake that long does things to you. For Seth, it begins with his vision. He starts to see everything in close-up. He could be on the couch, staring at a programme he doesn't want to watch and all he can see is the television screen. His entire view is a 42-inch image of botoxed women flouncing around shoe shops. His wife, if she were awake, would see the screen, the TV stand that it sits on, some of the coffee table, the walls behind, part of one of the curtains. He just sees fake lips and fake breasts as he fakes interest.

The second sign that he is too tired involves a break somewhere along the wire from his brain to his mouth. Things that he's thinking in his head come out. And things that he thinks he has said to people have only been thoughts in his mind. His wife secretly loves this phase because she can tell him that he never mentioned something and, even if Seth is sure that he did, he can't really be sure. And, because sleep consolidates memories, he can't truly remember. She could say anything and he has to believe her. She makes him sound like a sociopath.

It's another compromise. She accepts that his mind is a mess sometimes, and he accepts that it could be her that is messing with his mind.

When people say that you should fight for your marriage, these are the things they are fighting for. Seth is exhausted and his brain isn't functioning properly, but he knows that advice is horseshit. And he convinces himself that he did exactly that. He fought. But he's just existing through it.

Seth's particular form of insomnia is not about getting no sleep, it is about poor sleep. It does take him a while to get there. And the more frustrated he gets about not dozing off, the less likely it is that he will. He usually does, though. But never for long. He wakes up. A lot. Sometimes for fifteen minutes every hour. Sometimes he sleeps for two hours and then he's awake for three before falling into a terribly deep sleep between the hours of six and seven in the morning.

He always beats his alarm. But he leaves it on, anyway. Because he still has hope. It's all a dream. Even though he hasn't really dreamt for years. He mostly does that when he's awake.

In short, he can't get to sleep but he doesn't really feel as though he is awake, either.

Anyway, coffee helps.

The kettle whistles on the stovetop and he imagines his wife's eyes rolling. No wonder the idiot can't get to sleep. He makes a black coffee, no sugar – that stuff is no good for you – and he lays it down on the coffee table and he picks up the phone again.

He flicks through the phonebook once more. This time, he stops on M. F. Marshall. She lives west of his house. Around nine miles away. He's had less hostility from the calls when his voice vibrates along a wire in that direction.

It rings four times.

'Hello?' She sounds awake.

'Hey, it's Seth. I can't sleep. Want to talk?'

'I'm sorry, who is this?' Her voice is older than his. A couple of decades, at least.

'My name is Seth. I'm having trouble sleeping. I have nobody to talk to.'

'Oh, dear. There are numbers you can call for that sort of thing. I'm not sure I'd be any help in that department.'

A man's voice shouts something in the background. M.F. Marshall ignores it.

'Just a chat,' he pleads, trying not to sound desperate.

'I'm sorry, I think you have the wrong number.'

M.F. Marshall doesn't hang up. But then a male voice snatches its way into the conversation.

'Who is this?' it asks.

'It's Seth,' he says. 'I can't get to sleep.'

'Well, you're upsetting my wife, Seth. So would you kindly fuck off?'

He hangs up and Seth highlights the name on that page in the phonebook so he doesn't trouble them again.

8

I'd been drinking. Alone. Again. Even though it never makes me feel any better at all.

The cat jumped in through the flap on the back door, stood in the lounge, looked at me, rolled its eyes, and moved on upstairs. I never wanted that thing. My last boyfriend bought it for me. Some kind of companionship, he thought. A replacement for the children I'd never had and he never wanted. Perhaps.

A kind gesture or a consolation.

Still, I fed it, watered it. It made its mess outside the house. We lived together but there was no companionship, no connection, no love. It was a marriage without the paperwork. Each of us waiting for the other to die.

And the cat had more chance of coming out on top.

I poured more white wine into my mouth and rolled my eyes. The drink was vinegary at best. A bottle brought to my house by a friend for a party. It had probably been left at their flat before it migrated to mine. You'd have to be really desperate to drink it.

I'm great at desperation.

I was in the frame of mind that had visited me on numerous occasions before. I began to think of all my friends, their individual lives and how they bettered mine. Then I told myself that I added nothing to theirs but trouble and hassle and too-much-effort.

And this is how it always started. And, this time, I had no boyfriend to think about. That was different. I always had someone. Hopping from one man to the next. Fucking up another life. As many as I could.

I know I'm pretty and smart, smarter than I let on, and when I feel good, I feel really good. I'm outgoing. Funny, even. But nothing was funny that night.

My friends were whispering to each other in my mind, looking back over their shoulders, shaking their heads in disappointment. I knew what they truly thought about the things I had done in the past. None of them had really spoken to me about it. They didn't try to understand. They thought they knew it all.

They bitched, they sighed

And I drank some more. But there were no blades around or pills. No rope, hanging languidly from a roof beam, casting a shadow across the stool beneath. The bath was empty. The toaster was on the kitchen worktop where it always sat. Knives were in the rack. I don't own a gun. I was on the first floor, the jump would only bruise me.

All was as it should be. But I still wanted to die.

I placed the empty wine glass back on the side table next to my purse, which I unbuttoned, unfolded and rifled through to locate a crumpled card wedged between two store cards I was nowhere near paying off.

I picked up the phone and dialled the number.

I waited for the ring tone.

It never came.

'Hello?'

9

Seth's homemade phonebooks are thick with a rainbow of fluorescent rejections. Lines and lines from weeks and years of this idea, this hope that maybe somebody will talk back. Somebody might listen.

He stops on a page full of Turners. One is even highlighted in blue. There are three more Turners left to call. But that won't happen tonight because he is only going to flick through to the letter S.

He drinks his coffee and looks at the television. The volume is turned down to zero and he can see enough of the area around the screen to know that the night is still young.

He flicks the pages of the book. Stops. His hand hovers above the page and his finger drops down to D. Sergeant. He runs the tip of his finger across the paper until it reaches the number he has to call. He exhales and starts to hit the numbers on the keypad. It starts to ring but he's startled as his mobile phone vibrates in his pocket.

'Give it a rest for one night and just come up to bed.'

He tells himself that she means well. But she doesn't realise how unproductive that would be for him.

And then he worries. Has it really been that long? Has that six or eight weeks passed by already? Things come around so quickly when you don't want them. Seth didn't quite remember the last time he was intimate with his wife. Each time had blurred into one. The same old moves. And it hadn't been intimate for a long while. Not for Seth.

And he wondered whether she even really wanted to have sex with him because she just laid there and turned her head to the side. Or moved onto her stomach so she was comfortable and didn't have to look at him. And he thought that it was just another thing that they half did together that neither of them wanted to be a part of but were somehow too scared not to do.

And he thought that she still got the better end of the deal because he just wanted to cry. And he was relieved that she wasn't looking at him. He felt so sick. And he somehow had to make himself hard on his own, with his hand, to get the condom on, then he had to get it inside her as quickly as he could before she realised that he was already unaroused. And he wondered whether she could even feel him in there.

And then he stopped caring.

She had walked back up the stairs alone. And, even though he really needed to go up to use the toilet, he'd wait. Because he'd been caught out before with no escape. A duty-bound woman, lying on a bed, offering him the opportunity to fuck a naked cadaver.

If only he could cry himself to sleep.

Things changed. They rearranged. But it all stayed the same.

Seth waits a few minutes. There hasn't been another call, another text message.

He's not wanted.

And he's thankful. But he knew that was the case.

He treads carefully up the stairs, avoiding the parts he has memorised that creak under his weight. He hits the top step and peers through the open door. She's already asleep. Or she's pretending. There was a time he would look at her sleeping and think it was beautiful. He'd tell himself that he loved her. He'd tiptoe in, turn the bedside light off and kiss her softly on the forehead. He'd say 'Goodnight' even though she couldn't hear him.

He can't remember when or why that stopped happening. He used to think that would be his forever. But he knows now that it is this. Sneaking past a woman he no longer knows or wants. Knowing that he doesn't belong there but has nowhere else to be, though anywhere else would surely be better.

Or maybe he does want this. Maybe it's the tiredness talking. Maybe that takes a positive man and makes him negative.

Creeping like the idiot he undoubtedly is, he uses his phone screen to light the bathroom so he can determine the best place to aim his urine. But not straight into the water like he usually does. Against the porcelain for volume control. He pushes the flush quickly so that enough water enters the bowl to wash away the worst but with minimal noise. Then he wets his hands with just enough water and completes his spy mission with a quiet descent back to the lounge.

He flicks through the page of another phonebook, his hands still a little wet, and his finger drops on a new name. Ms Hadley Serf.

It's late. The clock tells him that. He needs the clock. His body always thinks it's time to sleep, his mind always disagrees. He dials the number and hopes Hadley's demeanour is as beautiful as her name.

10

'Hello?'

She was drunk. Ant could hear it in her voice.

These are the calls he fears, but wants. The calls that people assume are every call he receives. They're not. Most suicides are men in their thirties. And they rarely call. Because they don't know how to talk about whatever it is they are going through – grieving the loss of a loved one, separation from their wife, losing contact with their kids. The woman on the phone was suicidal.

And Ant wasn't going to let her die.

That's why he was there.

He could feel the sweat forming on the hairs of his armpits. He looked at the corner of his screen. The few prompts everyone in that room had memorised stared back at him. He wiped at his eyes, the sweat was relentless.

'Have you been drinking?' he asked.

'Of course I've been drinking,' she answered, but it wasn't aggressive. 'It makes everything easier. It makes doing this easier.'

'It makes calling me easier?' Ant knew that wasn't what she meant; he was averting her focus.

There was a pause while she thought about what he said.

Ant covered the mouthpiece of his telephone headset and breathed deeply. He had seized control of the conversation. The thrum of noise in the room of all the other phone calls dissipated in a subtle buzz before disappearing into insignificant blur.

'I wanted to end it.'

Ant was already confident of a resolution after hearing the caller use the past tense.

'I've tried before, you know?'

'What happened?' He didn't need to look at the note on his screen. But he still did.

'Which time? I've tried a lot. I can't even get that right.'

This was fairly common. Low self-esteem was utterly debilitating. Ant witnessed it every week in some form or another. And he'd started to hate the health industry and the way that doctors so frivolously handed out antidepressants. And the way that pharmaceutical companies were creating problems with their drugs that they would then fix with other drugs that they had also produced. And he was sick of the way social media had made people less sociable and how the great art of conversation had seemingly been lost somewhere between your latest faux-humble bragging status and your next hashtag.

And he knew that what he was doing meant something, it had a place in the world. Because people were now so busy talking that they had forgotten how to listen.

Ant knew how to listen.

He knew how to watch.

The woman on the phone went on about her difficulties, how she had attempted suicide before, how she had found a card and called him and she didn't know why. Ant knew why. He was making her clean again.

She apologised for being lame. She must have said sorry thirty times. Her friends made her feel like she was a burden. Her family had probably done similarly while she was growing up. So everything that was wrong made her feel ungrateful, like she was moaning, like she shouldn't be doing that. Ant told her it was not the case. It was not moaning, or complaining. It was not self-indulgent. And, mostly, he told her that she had nothing to apologise for.

And she needed to hear that. Deep down, somewhere, she knew it, herself.

'Thank you. For listening. For not judging. I need to go now, though.'

'I'm here. There's always somebody here. What are your plans, now?'

'Don't worry. I'm not going to do anything stupid. I'm drunk and I'm tired and I just want to lie down and shut my eyes and wait until the morning.'

'And that's what you're going to do?'

'That's what I'm going to do.'

Ant smiled, shut his eyes for a second and nodded. And breathed. The noise from other calls started to fill the room once more to let him know that he was safe. He saw the time on his screen and realised he had been listening for over twenty minutes. His T-shirt was a couple of shades darker through uncontrollable perspiration and he felt dirty. His lips pursed. He wanted to wash. To get changed. He had deodorant in his bag and three clean T-shirts. He was prepared.

'Good night.' The caller offered.

'Sleep well.' Ant waited for her to hang up then did the same.

He fell back into his chair; his back was wet. He unhooked his headset and turned his phone to divert. He needed to wash his entire torso. He needed it at that moment.

Ant picked up his rucksack from beneath his desk and walked over to the disabled toilet. There, he ripped off his T-shirt and threw it into the container meant for female sanitary products. He had brought his own bar of soap. There were three in there. He scrubbed his entire body, rinsed it and threw the soap away, too. He dried with one of three hand towels zipped in a separate compartment and tied it up in a plastic bag when finished. He sprayed himself and put on a new T-shirt that looked exactly like the old one. Dark, grey, unbranded and anonymous.

And he looked at his face in the mirror. His eyes were tired but he was pleased with himself. He had prevented tragedy. He had helped. It was one of those calls.

But it wasn't Hadley Serf. He would not save her life.

Not tonight.

11

Hey. It's Seth. I can't sleep. Want to talk?

But the phone never even rang. So he didn't get to say what he always said.

Seth dialled the number as it was written on the page. He put the phone to his ear and waited. There was nothing. Several clicks.

Then a woman spoke.

'Hello?'

It threw him.

She asked again: 'Hello?'

Her voice was soft. No hint of a regional accent. It was one word but she sounded nervous.

'Hello.' It was all he could think of to say.

'Oh, hi. The phone didn't even ring. You guys are fast. I guess you have to be, right?'

'You want to talk?'

'Is that how it works?'

'Conversation? Usually.'

She laughed. It was absolute innocence. He'd caught her off guard. She didn't know what to expect but she wasn't expecting that.

'That's funny. I thought you'd be all solemn and serious.'

'Why would you think that?'

'Well, I guess you hear a lot of shit over the phone. Some messed-up stuff.'

'Mostly just people telling me to fuck off then hanging up.'

She laughed again.

Seth felt himself smile and relax into the sofa a little.

'I've never done this before. Is this what it's usually like?'

'Not at all. Every call is different. I'm just glad you're still here.'

'I'm still here. I've been low tonight.' She paused and Seth filled the gap she had left.

'I'm sorry to hear that. What's going on?'

He felt genuinely concerned. This girl, this woman, this wonder-fully bright light in his otherwise dreary night was oozing melancholy from that very first hello. He sensed it. But she still had the decency to stay on the line and talk to a complete stranger. And she was being open and responsive. He wanted to know her.

'Same old shit. You know? Some days are worse than others. My boss is annoying me. I screwed up at work a little on Friday. So did he. But it all gets shovelled downwards and I'm taking all the blame. I don't even really like my job, but it's the principal of it all. He expects me to just lie down and take it. Part of me wanted to fight my corner but the other part cares so little about what I do for a living that it seemed a waste of energy. That has lingered over the weekend.'

Seth found himself nodding in agreement. Then there was a silence.

'Go on,' he prompted.

'Well, I just ended up taking it. Like I always do. It probably was my fault.'

She reeked of low self-esteem. It was different from his own. Seth had an issue with self-like, hers was self-worth. She hadn't asked him about himself yet, but the dynamic already had the fragrance of code-pendence. And that gave him a buzz because it seemed that nobody actually depended on him.

She continued.

'Then I spilled coffee on my shirt at lunch and I'd forgotten to charge my phone overnight so I had hardly any battery to call or text my friends. The train home was late. Blah blah blah. It's all stuff that everyone goes through every day. Who am I to complain?'

'You're you. You are allowed to complain. Everything you have said is a genuine irritation. I'd be annoyed if I dropped black coffee on my clothes and my journey home was lengthened because of a leaf on the track or some other avoidable reason. If it upsets you or annoys you, you can say that you are upset or annoyed. You can talk about it.'

'Thanks. You know, you're very easy to talk to. You're good at this.'

He couldn't see her over the phone, obviously, but he knew she smiled at that moment.

'Good at talking?'

'Yes. And listening.'

There was a silence. Comfortable.

'My name is Hadley, by the way. I'm not sure I'm supposed to tell you that.'

'Hadley, have you never used a telephone before?'

She could hear the smile in his voice and she breathed out her own.

'This is not how I expected this conversation to go. At all.'

'Well, it rather dashed my own expectations, too. I thought I'd be awake for another four hours, staring at a wall, wishing I could just drift off for a few minutes.'

'Is this how you usually talk to people?'

'I'd like to say "Yes" but I really try not to lie.'

'I must be special,' she teased.

'I'd like to keep talking to you. I'm actually wide awake right now. How was the rest of your day?'

She continued her yarn. Flitting through the mundanities of life and imbuing them with significance and poignancy. Dropping money in the road, for most, would be an inconvenience, a mild irritation. To Hadley, it was a metaphor for the decay in society and the toll we all pay for valuing those things with a price tag.

Everything was bigger than it was. Everything was heightened. Little things were important. Seth understood that.

He liked that about her.

He liked her.

This stranger who had been at the other end of the telephone line, talking about herself like he was some kind of agony uncle, like they were friends.

Friendship. Such a novelty. It might be easier if he could believe that his marriage simply lost its passion. That the spark was blown out and they were left with the friendship they had built.

When Seth met his wife, he was attracted to her physically. That's how it starts, isn't it? You see something you like, something shiny, and like a magpie, you want to grab it, whatever it is. You're not friends when you start. You are putting forward your best face, showing them the absolute best of you. Seth had long forgotten what the best of him was. And he has no idea what it is now. Maybe his new friend Hadley is right, he's a listener. He absorbs the troubles of others. That's exactly what he was doing with Hadley Serf. Only, he didn't know it at that point.

He just thought that she was beautiful. He was attracted to her, physically, even though he'd never seen her.

She told him she had drunk an entire bottle of wine that a friend had left at her house.

'Probably on purpose. It was horrid for the first couple of glasses.'

Seth laughed.

Then he told her his name.

'I'm Seth, by the way.'

12

Detective Sergeant Pace is alone.

Detective Sergeant Pace is disturbed.

The case isn't moving forward. He has suspected the stepfather and the long-term boyfriend. These cases are often domestic. But the very nature of the disposal is incongruous to that train of thought.

It is calculated. Deliberate.

Barbaric.

The bleach is everywhere.

Outside and in.

To Pace, that denotes a coldness to the killer, something removed. Perhaps, even some pleasure.

He has interviewed co-workers, family, friends. Standard. Nothing is coming up. Not a bad word has been said. That is usually the case; people don't like to speak ill of the dead. People are superstitious. But there is always somebody who will speak out, who will hint at something negative, but Pace hasn't unearthed that person, yet.

This seemingly friendly, helpful, thoughtful and loving young woman was never late for work, hardly ever ill and volunteered for those less fortunate within her local area.

That local area is Bow, East London. And the authorities are drawing a blank about the possible reason her body has been found a hundred miles away in a park in Warwickshire.

News coverage has started to fade.

The public has started to move on, to forget.

Detective Sergeant Pace is not giving up.

13

'Wow, Seth, eh? You really are a maverick. I think it is okay for me to tell you my name but I'm not sure you are supposed to tell me yours.'

'I assure you, it's customary.'

'It's my first time. I really wasn't sure whether I should pick up the phone tonight. I've seen a couple of therapists. Obviously. And they just sit there. They're supposed to be listening, but it's not two-way. You don't feel like there is a dynamic between you. It seems more like judgement. You know?'

I worried that Seth was overwhelmed at the ease with which I was sharing my story, my information. But he seemed unworried with the conversation, pleased almost. Not watching the clock, slowing down its movement.

'And how does that make you feel?' he joked. Putting on his best therapist voice, which was essentially his own voice but posher, and a bit creepier, and he elongated the last couple of words.

'Exactly.' I was smiling again. I looked into my empty wine glass. I wanted a drink, but not to numb my pain or help me sleep something off, or lose some inhibitions so that I had an excuse for the bad decisions I was undoubtedly going to make with the guy across the bar.

I felt good. And I wanted to feel even better.

'Would you hold the line for a moment? I'll be right back.'

'I'm not going anywhere.'

I rested the phone receiver on the arm of the sofa and flounced my way towards the kitchen.

I felt a little lighter.

14

Seth waited a couple of minutes. It was silent. He couldn't hear anything going on in the background. But there was no dial tone. She was coming back. He felt sure of that. The anticipation was exciting. He could feel his heart in his chest. It was quiet, he felt it beating in his ears.

'Hey. Still there?' She was out of breath.

'I'm still here. All sorted?'

'Yes. Thanks for waiting. I was fixing myself a gin and tonic.'

'How lovely.'

'Well, you say that, I couldn't find any lemon. Or lime. And I'm fresh out of tonic water.'

'Straight gin, then.'

'Well, turns out I'm also out of gin. So I've been turning the kitchen upside down.'

'Kitchen spray and Coke?'

'I wish. Ended up with a miniature bottle of *limoncello* that I brought back from Italy years ago. I was going to give it to my boss but he breathed in the wrong way that day, so I kept it. For an occasion such as this.'

'Makes sense. Although dissolving some laxatives in there and giving it to him could have been a much better use of your time.'

'Oh, Seth, if only I had known you back then.'

'Can you hold the line for a moment? Don't go anywhere.'

Hadley agreed to afford Seth the same courtesy he had given her. He placed the receiver down on the warm leather where he'd been sitting. The phone was cordless, he could have taken it with him and continued to talk but it would just be his luck that he'd wake his wife and have to cut off the first person to engage with him properly in months.

He entered the kitchen; the tiles were cold beneath his feet. He could see two bottles of red wine in the rack, along with a bottle of mulled wine left over from last Christmas. It would be out of date before the festive period came around again but he still couldn't bring himself to throw it out.

He was always hanging on to the things he didn't need.

There was a bottle of Prosecco in the fridge. He knew that. It was opened on the weekend and not finished. It would be flat by now. He wasn't even the biggest fan when it was teeming with bubbles.

It would have to be wine, he thought. But then he spotted his old hip flask, resting on a space built for a wine bottle. He picked it up, shook it, heard that there was liquid in there and he opened it. It smelled amazing. He wanted it. He poured all of it into a glass, added a dash of water from the kitchen tap and slunk back to his seat.

'I'm back,' he announced in a half-whisper.

'Where have you been, I was starting to get worried?'

'In the kitchen, grabbing a drink. I thought I'd join you.'

15

'You know?' I asked at the end, repeating myself like a nervous, dependent dummy.

I didn't know if Seth had been joking again about the drink or not. I didn't care.

'I wanted a *limoncello* with ice and water. But there was no ice in the freezer. And I've never bought *limoncello* in my life. So I settled for the water. With a little whisky.'

We talked for another forty-five minutes. It moved on from my

wonderful brand of woes to my thoughts and likes and fears and hopes.
I spoke of the present but never the future and rarely the past.

And Seth listened.

My own personal agony uncle.

'Just in case. You know?' I anxiously questioned again, sucking the
rhetoric from my sentences.

'You know?'

He knew. Of course he knew.

He said he knew.

And I believed him.

16

Seth was overwhelmed. He had done the same thing every night for
months. He watched mindless television while his wife dropped off
on a separate sofa to his. He would then flick through the channels
until he was positive that she was sleeping soundly upstairs. He'd masturbate and make a cup of late-night coffee – not always in that order.
And he'd flick through his special phonebook, calling people he didn't
know, hoping they would talk to him, stave off the demons of another
sleepless night. If only for a short while. But tonight was different.
Hadley was different.

She was a distraction.

She was a rush.

Talking to her seemed to mean something. And he had forgotten
what that felt like. He had worth. His company was being enjoyed.
And, while that gave his ego a boost, his mood was already slumping as
he envisioned the moment the phone would be placed down and her
voice would go quiet. He hadn't spoken too much about himself but
he started to wonder why she would want to continue the conversation
when she realised how boring he was. How nothing he was.

Seth thought about lying, telling her that he taught a class for children with special needs or that he worked in research for a disease he could come up with when that information was requested. But it wasn't in him to lie. Not to Hadley. He faked his way through life too much. With Hadley, he just had to be himself.

He wanted that.

He needed it.

Connection.

Then she said, 'I've had a card for the Samaritans in my purse for a long time. A friend gave it to me. Not to be pushy, you know? Just in case. You know?'

You know?

Of course, he didn't know. It took him a while to register what was happening.

Then Hadley cut through the silence with her third you know?

So Seth lied.

17

Ant needed routine. The structure. The regime. It kept him calm to do things the same way over and over again.

Before Australia he had worked for a month in data entry. Moving numbers from one column to another for eight hours a day. He did it for four weeks to boost his money for the adventure that lay ahead of him and his best friend. And he loved it. The repetition. The clinical cleanness of the process.

Ant left that evening in his third grey T-shirt – another difficult call later on. He'd thrown away another bar of soap and now had two sweat-drenched shirts in separate bags in his rucksack.

When he got home, he immediately threw his dirty clothes into the washing machine and placed them on a high-temperature wash. He threw away the two ripped plastic bags and hung his rucksack on its hook. He walked, naked, into the bathroom and opened a new bar of soap; he would need to buy more in the morning. He scrubbed his body in a shower that was as hot as the water that would tear through his clammy clothes.

And he rubbed at his pink skin with a fresh towel and cleaned his teeth in front of the mirror, which had steamed up moments before. Ant was pleased with himself. He had done his job well that evening. He felt proud. And useful. And helpful. And purified. And like he was exactly where he was supposed to be.

And he felt settled. And tired. And clean.

This was his life. A purgatorial loop that he was content to waste, one day at a time.

18

And it dawned on Seth what had occurred.

A great act of chance. Of serendipity. It wasn't Godly intervention or fates colliding. It wasn't destiny or astral influence. It wasn't predetermined or written in the stars.

No. This, like everything in life, was about luck.

Luck. And lies.

It had happened before. Not everybody hung up. Not everybody swore or called him a freak. He had talked to others. There's no way he would have carried this on if he'd never had a conversation with a stranger late at night.

And a couple of those had turned into something. Recurring calls. Regular conversations. And things can escalate quickly and go too far and before you know it you're doing something that you know you shouldn't do. And you're supposed to be married. And they know you're married but they don't seem to care. And that's not right. So it concludes. And never peacefully.

But Hadley didn't feel like that. It was different. This would be different, he told himself. Maybe something more. This time...

It was innocent. She had picked up the phone to make a call at the same moment Seth had dialled her number. It probably happens all the time. A crossed line, or whatever. She thought he was someone else, something else, but he was himself. He was just being himself. So it wasn't a complete lie.

He understood her story and how she felt. He knew what alone was like. She was interesting. He liked listening to her. So he let himself imagine future conversations with Hadley Serf and he told himself that she would understand him, too, because they had that connection. And she wouldn't push it and ruin it. Like others had.

Things weren't real, though. They were heightened due to fatigue and the rarity of an actual conversation.

So, maybe that was Seth hoping again.

He just knew one thing: he didn't want it to end like the others. It couldn't.

He was her Good Samaritan.

He was a hero.

That night, he didn't realise it, but Seth had saved Hadley Serf's life.

19

Hadley and Seth both slept that night. Deeply. Soundly. Hopeful and deluded.

She was full of vinegar and butterflies. A mysterious man she had never met had been sweet and attentive and funny. He'd relaxed her and made her think about things in a different way. A way that didn't seem as scary. And the litre of drink inside her helped the whole situation blur just enough around the edges that it made her feel she was awake inside her dream.

And Seth was somehow relaxed for the first time in a while. Though she had excited him with her honesty and openness, the tension had released from his shoulders and he slouched into the sofa cushions, his head dropping forwards, his chin against his chest, an unhealthy curl to his back. The last thing he saw was a close-up of his belt buckle before the darkness.

His mind had been emptied, while Hadley's had been filled. With booze and with ideals. And each had resulted in a delicate, quiet slumber.

The yin to the yang.

The woman to the man.

The charity to the desperation.

And she had been emptied of her loneliness and the contents of her stomach, while he was filled with the warmth of companionship he hadn't felt at home for a long time. And a sense of opportunity.

The black and the grey.

The half-truths and lies.

But both of them ended their nights with that something they'd been looking for and the nothingness they secretly craved.

MONDAY

20

The guy had a handful of dog shit when the police arrived. He hadn't wanted to put it down or throw it away. He didn't want to leave the body. Or his dog, who he was stroking with his free hand and consoling like the kid he'd probably never had. And he was worried it would be seen as tampering with evidence or disrupting a crime scene or something, if he left and threw it away.

He was in shock.

He was crouched down next to his dog when two of the local Warwickshire constabulary arrived.

'Sir? Sir?' The female officer asked. 'Are you Malcolm Danes?' She looked at the dog. The bag of crap swinging on the man's finger.

Her partner moved into the undergrowth. The body was obvious. He wondered how long it had been there and why it was only just being found.

It smelled clean and dirty.

Bleach and death.

The beagle had been sniffing around the body, there were plenty of tracks around it, and the dog had moved the plastic away from the dead woman's face, revealing what looked like blonde hair but was merely stripped of colour.

The young officers were smart and professional, but very local. Small town. The body that had been found nearby a few months ago seemed like something that would forever be chronicled in local lore as a one-off. But this changed everything.

He called his partner over. She finished with the beagle-owner and told him to stay where he was for a moment. Then she approached, stopping for a moment to look at the corpse in the copse.

'What's that guy's name?'

'Er...' she flicked through her notebook.

'Not the guy out there, who found her, the one from the news. Who's working on the other girl from near here.'

'The London one.'

'Yeah. On the news. Tall. Dark ... Really dark.'

'Detective Sergeant Pace,' she had to try not to smile at the thought of him.

'That's the fucker. He's going to want to see this.'

They were standing in front of another dead woman in another Warwickshire park and Pace was sitting at a desk in London. This was miles from his jurisdiction. But there was no mistaking that this was definitely his case.

21

Seth heard his wife leave for work in the morning. He was sure she slammed the door on purpose because he'd fallen asleep on the sofa again. He didn't know what her problem was – did she really want him next to her? Him. With his face. The first thing she would see when she woke up.

Hadley was on his mind as he brushed his teeth. Seth was wondering what she looked like. He thought about searching for her on social media. How many Hadley Serfs could there be? But the weight of his lie was already anchoring both of his shoulders. She was vulnerable and immature. She thought that he was somebody he was not. But she trusted Seth. Needed him, even. It would crush her to find out who he really was. That he was getting dressed to go out and sell some computers.

And then that thought started to suffocate him.

It seemed that he had uncovered himself as the predictable complication in a bad romantic comedy.

He was no longer brushing his teeth for Hadley. He was brushing them for the office. That oppressive basement with barred windows and no air-conditioning. And that five-foot goatee beard of a boss puking clichés and spouting business jargon despite being many years his junior. A fucking idiot zygote.

And his reflection in the mirror was no lie. The checked shirt, two sizes too big, with the middle-management pocket over his left breast. Another cog in the machine. He could call in sick today, try to sleep, but it's frowned upon in the office. They're not allowed to be ill. And that is supposed to make them feel important, like they'd be missed, like they contribute, but, Seth understands, it's his boss telling him that the company turning a profit is more important than an employee's personal health and wellbeing.

Seth's eyes don't lie, either. They are black and dead and ten years older than the rest of him. He doesn't know when the light went out. When he stopped feeling anything but removed and tired. When you don't sleep for as long as he hasn't, you are hypersensitive, small things become large things. Significant things. But you feel nothing.

He thinks about Hadley and whether he could cut himself like she had. Would that make him feel? Would that be a release? That's why people do it, right? He thinks.

Then he daydreams about punching his boss in the face. But he feels so numb. *Could I cut him? Would that wake me up? Would it be a rush? Would I suddenly feel like I was contributing something positive?* His mind wanders.

The thing with insomnia is that, even though you don't sleep properly and you're tired all the time, you're hoping that something will come along that will really wake you up.

Then maybe you'd get some sleep.

Seth thought that maybe Hadley would help him to rest. And maybe he would help her not want to kill herself. It was a stupid thought that made him worse; he was so tired. She wouldn't want him, he decided. His own wife doesn't really want him and they were best friends at one point. They were lovers. They bought a sensible car with space for dogs that they didn't want and children they would never have.

He pulls up in that same car outside his work building and the boss is smoking out the front with two of the external sales guys, whose suits hang ludicrously perfect on their less weary bodies. They're laughing together at a joke they don't think Seth would understand and his boss looks at his watch, exaggerating the movement to let Seth know that he's running late.

I could plough them all down and reverse back over them. And only they would care.

But he doesn't, of course. He pulls in to the space that isn't reserved for him but he parks in every day without fail.

Predictable Seth. But not reliable.

'Afternoon, Seth,' his boss chortles. He's seven minutes late.

'What happened? Shit the bed.' Both of the external guys laugh at that like it was W. C. Fields.

'That's what you say when someone is early for work.' Seth keeps his gaze forward and pushes past them, into the modest, grey foyer of DoTrue.

'Big enough to handle. Small enough to care.' That's the motto.

What a joke.

He has enough time when he arrives to make a coffee, start up his ancient computer and scroll through his emails before his 9:30 product forecast meeting. He rolls his eyes at the giggling bravado and nicotine left behind him and walks straight into the kitchen. Where Jones is stood, watching his cardboard pot of porridge oats spin in the microwave.

Seth needs his coffee. He doesn't need Jones.

'Ready for the meeting, Seth?' Jones asks in that annoying monotone of his. He doesn't even avert his gaze from his rotating breakfast.

Seth lifts the kettle, there's enough water in there for one cup of coffee but habit means that he adds just a little cold water from the tap so that he feels he has freshened it up. He saw something while flicking through the channels about losing vital minerals by reboiling. Which was almost definitely bullshit. But he doesn't need that right now.

So he clicks the kettle on and his tiredness makes the sound seem like the start of an applause. No matter where Seth looks in the room, he can see the red light that tells him his liquid is heating up.

He looks at the time left on the microwave. Eighty-six seconds. And he plays a game with himself. First, his kettle has to click off before

Jones' microwave beeps. Also, he has to say nothing for that time. Difficult, having just been asked a question.

'Seth?' Jones asks, this time turning around.

He spots the light on the kettle. Seth watches as his eyes flick to that side and he wonders whether Jones is now racing him.

'Are you? Sorted for the meeting?'

Seth nods. And shrugs his shoulders. He's still winning.

The morning isn't great for Seth. He's not even sure that he's really there. He could be on the sofa at home still. This has to be a nightmare.

The meeting will be an irritating waste of time. All the sales guys have to forecast what revenue they will bring in this month and how many units will go out the door. Seth is in charge of computer monitors. They each fill in a spreadsheet and send it to the product manager. He collates it, then they have a pointless meeting where he reads it back to them. Then the boss comes in at the end and tells everyone that they're not being ambitious enough so raises their targets and forecast amounts so that they work extra hard and he doesn't have to pay them any extra. Of course, his own forecast is low enough that he will receive a nice, fat bonus for all their hard work.

'Sent my forecast to Jim a couple of days back. Good month last month, as you know. Managed to sandbag a few deals.'

Seth watches the kettle. It's hissing but not spluttering as he would like it to. And he curses himself for topping it up.

Jones bends down to look through the glass and spur on his oats. Seth pictures himself kneeing Jones in the ribs as he does so, then opening the microwave door, pulling out his hot breakfast and pouring it over his face as he lies on the floor in pain.

Instead, Seth loses the game by humouring him.

'Yeah. The schools order. Set you up, eh?' He hates himself for doing it.

And the microwave pings loudly.

Then his kettle bubbles and the light clicks off.

'Yeah. A new month now, though. Clean slate for all.'

'Clean slate with some juicy sandbags.' And he pats Jones on the shoulder as he leaves for his desk. Like he's his friend and he's congratulating him on his deception.

Seth has no idea who he is in that moment.

So he spoons in two mounds of instant coffee and fills to the top with the water that boiled a second too slowly. Those minerals cost him.

Resting against the work surface in the kitchen, he holds the coffee to his mouth and blows cold air over the top, like that will make a difference. He thinks about Hadley's voice. She thinks he's some kind of Good Samaritan. And he wonders what it would be like to be good. To offer something of worth to the world. But he's jolted out of his reverie by the sound of the three hyenas strolling back towards the office, their lungs full of tar and their heads filled with an overinflated image of their own attractiveness and self-importance.

He hesitates for just a moment, not knowing whether it is best to get to the office before them or walk in behind, unnoticed. Of course, he ends up emerging from the kitchen at the same time they step around the corner.

'Take your time, Seth. You might even get your computer fired up by the time the meeting starts.' The boss snipes. His henchman laugh on cue.

'Ha! That ancient piece of shit?' It's another of those instances where he's tired and he thinks he's saying something in his head but he's blurting it out like the idiot he is.

There's silence. Awkward. Seth sees that his boss thinks about stopping to confront him on that remark. There's an almost undetectable pause. Seth sees it, though. Small things are big to him.

But small things are small to his boss. And they don't come much smaller in his eyes than Seth Beauman. The insignificant barcode.

They all walk on in silence. Seth thinks his boss was shocked that he'd answered him back. Maybe he's been getting it wrong all these years. Maybe it never even happened.

22

I wake up with a cheap-wine hangover. My first thought is the pain at the front of my skull. Then my dry mouth. Then the fact that I have to go to the toilet. I take one arm out from beneath the duvet. It's too cold. I can live with the pain in my kidneys for another few minutes.

The previous evening starts to drip its way back into my memory. The slow breakdown of my self-worth as I was crammed tightly like a barn chicken against a thousand other commuters all gasping for a glimpse of daylight.

Stepping into my one-bedroom flat and being hit by a stench from the kitchen I did not have the willpower to face.

Locating the aroma as a three-day-old thrown-out microwaveable Thai meal I hadn't eaten, festering in the bin.

Taking the bin out.

Replacing the black bag.

Opening the fridge.

Finding that shitty bottle of wine I didn't want.

Sitting on the sofa and wondering whether it would be the time I would get things right and take myself from this mortal coil.

Then taking that crumpled Samaritans card form my purse. Calling the number. And having what I recall as the best first date I'd never been on.

I thought about Seth and wondered what he might look like. He sounded tall, I told myself. A kind voice. A humble tone. He was funny. And attentive. And mysteriously unconventional. He seemed to like me. Of course, my low self-esteem kicked in to eradicate that thought.

That's his job, Hadley. He is there to make you feel good. He doesn't want you to kill yourself.

There's probably some Samaritans leader board where you can win an iPod for stopping the most pathetic people from ending it all. You're like those lonely guys who think that whores really love them and they're not just spreading their legs and moaning on cue for a handful of twenties.

I know I sound stupid and young, and I know it all sounds like it's happening fast, but, when you're alone, somebody listening to you can mean the absolute world.

I look at my alarm clock. It's due to beep, annoyingly, in two minutes. That's when I'll get up, I decide. A couple more moments of self-loathing.

My head throbs, my kidneys stab into my back, and my mind flits back to Seth. I liked him. He was there for me. Not like those last two idiots who had jumped ship when the going got a little tough. He would be there for me whatever I am going through.

I was desperate. I was the schmuck who believed that the stripper chose the lap dance, not the client. I was the lonely heart who wrote to the death-row inmate. I was the sad sack considering another call that very evening, where I would ask specifically for Seth. I wanted him.

The alarm sounded.

I hit snooze and pull the covers over my head.

23

She had slammed the door before she left the house. She knew that. She had wanted to wake Seth up. Not because she was annoyed with him for not coming to bed. Not because she missed him next to her, though a part of her did want him there, but because he was asleep in the lounge. He was asleep. Seth, the idiot insomniac who drank coffee at midnight and called strangers, was asleep. And she wanted to wake him up.

The car didn't start first time. Or second time. Maeve rolled her eyes and rested her forehead against the cold steering wheel and breathed a heavy sigh. She usually commuted by train but had to drive for a meeting at head office that day.

'Come on, you piece of shit. Not today.' She spoke softly, with her eyes closed.

And in that same position, she turned the key once more and pushed the accelerator into the floor. Something ignited and sparked the vehicle to life. It made a hell of a noise, which undoubtedly irritated Seth, and she smiled subtly to herself before leaning back over her right shoulder and pulling the seatbelt across her chest.

She pushed the clutch and jerked the gear stick into reverse. And she stared at the front door as if she was looking back on the past to a moment where she was happy, but her expression said the opposite.

Maeve, like her husband, had changed. They were both so numb now. The paths of their lives had been parallel for so long, side by side. And inevitably, as with any relationship, they had veered further and further apart. And it had become harder and harder to get them back close again. It was evident, to Maeve at least, that those paths managed to cross one another when faced with adversity. The untimely death of Seth's father brought them closer than they had been in half a decade. Maeve's own sudden illness had given them both a new lease of life they had almost forgotten was possible.

They needed trauma.

It focused them.

Then she got well again. And the relationship got sick. Since then, the adversities had all but dried up. With a couple of exceptions. But, most days, Maeve was left wondering just what it would take to get them back on track.

One thing she did know was that they definitely weren't going to get there if Seth was sleeping properly, if he was fully in control of his mental faculties, if he was making good decisions, if he could separate thoughts from the things he said aloud.

She knew what happened to him when the sleep deprivation got really bad, how his vision was compromised, how he saw everything close-up. When he was like that, she found herself staring at him a lot, watching what he did, how he moved, the shape of his lips as he spoke, but she hoped, desperately, that he would look back at her. Just at her. Because, if he was that tired, and he was looking at Maeve, Maeve would be all that he would see.

She blinked, took her focus from the front door and looked over her left shoulder to reverse from the parking space, revving more than she needed, hoping Seth was awake and tired. And even if he was thinking about what a noisy, irritating bitch she was, at least he was thinking of her.

Maeve threw the car into first and swung it round to exit the quiet little close, where all the houses were identical. The light was finding its way higher into the sky and would be a wonderfully bright British grey by the time she pulled into the office car park. She flicked on the radio and managed to find a line in each song that played that she could relate to her life. And it should've made her feel sadder or more hopeful or whatever emotion the songwriter was striving to convey. But the simple truth was that Maeve had forgotten how to feel the everyday. The small delights that life had a habit of throwing your way when you least expected. Everything was in the extreme.

And, that morning, as her engine rattled and a synthesised sound from the eighties vibrated the air in her car, as she drove further from the man she wanted to love inordinately, radically, dangerously, she felt lost. And isolated. And immeasurably dead.

24

You can buy skin-lightening creams online that contain only natural ingredients but there's no guarantee that they actually work. For a more powerful product, they would need to contain hydroquinone or corticosteroids such as hydrocortisone.

But in the UK you can only get these on prescription. They're usually used for people with visible birthmarks or other dark skin patches. The idea is that they suppress the concentration and production of melanin, which gives your skin its pigmentation.

The side-effects are obvious: skin inflammation, burning or stinging, itching and flaking. A small price to pay if your self-esteem has been affected by facial discolouring, it would seem.

As with any medical procedure, things can go wrong. Your skin can turn too light. Or too dark. It can thin. It can make blood vessels more visible. It can scar. And then there's the possible kidney, liver and nerve damage. And the birth defects if you're stupid enough to try such a thing while pregnant.

A step further would be a chemical peel. This involves the application of hydroxy acids, trichloroacetic acids or phenol, to remove skin cells, and can either be at a superficial or deeper level. It is used to even out skin tones or reduce age spots.

You won't get this on the National Health Service, though. It'll cost you £100–500, and the effects are not always permanent.

Again, expect swelling and redness and a freezing sensation of your face. It can burn. It can peel. A small price to pay.

Theresa Palmer was dead.

She had been left in a bleach bath for two days. Side-effects include the usual lightening of skin and hair. Burning and blotching. Itching that you can't feel because you are dead. Thinning layers of skin. And that caustic, bleach smell.

The broken nose isn't a side-effect. That was caused when her murderer punched her so hard that it exploded across her face, making her cry instantly and lose any sense of where she was in the room.

The marks on her neck have nothing to do with the bleach bath, either. Her killer had tied a leather belt around her neck and dragged her around for a while before pulling it so tight that oxygen could no longer pass from her lungs to her brain.

Had she been alive when dumped into that bath, undoubtedly her lungs and kidneys would have failed. She was lucky.

But she was dead. And she had nothing to do with that first girl, who was found a couple of months before with her pale skin and stripped hair and strangled neck. They didn't know each other. They hadn't met. Their paths had never crossed. But they both lived in London and were found, wrapped in plastic, in Warwickshire.

Somebody needed to find the thing or person that connected them together.

25

The thing is, it's just so boring. But that's what Ant likes about his job.

Ownership matters, they tell him. Something about physical material and e-material. If you have a journal or a book or a paper that somebody has written, it is there, it is yours. Publish something on the Internet and it is there, for everybody. Anytime. Everybody.

Ant doesn't care about that. He doesn't give a fuck about temperature-calibrated vaults in the Vatican. He never considers the different qualities of paper and how some pages of older books must be turned over with a spatula because fingertips contain destructive oils that can damage texts.

He wants to scan pages and copy information into a spreadsheet and not really ingest any of the information that his eyes could absorb and his brain could ingest. He wants that numbness that so many people are trying to escape. He wants to switch off. He feels too much. Because he spends his evenings so wired, tuned in to reality and humanity, he just wants the downtime. Turning handwritten words into digital text. Copying one thing from one place to another.

Cruising. Existing. No-difference-making.

Not thinking. Not about the girl who called him last night. How she wanted to not exist. How he helped her to choose existing. He doesn't even want to feel good about what he did for her.

He wants nothing.

To feel nothing.

To be nobody.

He scans another paper into the system that nobody has read, apart from the author when it was a physical entity.

That is exactly what he is.

A sullied facsimile of the man he once was.

26

'It all looks good,' Jim looked up at the projected image of various numbers in boxes.

Another meeting that could've been an email.

'Jonesy has still got some decent run rate this month from the schools deal, which will prop up all your margins so we can afford some high-volume deals at a lower mark-up, if need be.' He points a laser at one of my boxes as he says this. 'Should be a good end to the quarter. I'll get these numbers over to HQ and—'

On cue, in strolls the embryo in a pinstriped power suit and double-Windsor-knotted tie.

'Four thousand monitors, Seth? Get hold of the disties and ramp that up. This time of year they should be taking fifty percent more than that.'

He walked over to the laptop and changed Seth's total to six thousand. Seth's expression didn't alter. He didn't want to give him the satisfaction. But inside was his usual resigned anger.

He did the same thing to all of them, like he always fucking did. Jones smirked to himself, he'd kept some deals under the radar and under-forecast, like they all should. Like they all did. For some reason, Seth still let himself hope, too much. They were all sent on a course to help them forecast accurately so this kind of shit didn't happen. All it did was teach everyone to fumble with the numbers. Everybody but Seth.

With a smile on his ferret face, that tornado of torment twisted back out of the meeting room, telling them all to have a good day, to 'go do some good'. Seth watched as the boss jumped into his bright-red penis extension, which Seth would never be able to afford, and sped off, unquestioned, at ten in the morning. All nicotine and spinning tyres.

Seth lost himself out of the window for a minute. Thinking things that he knew were too awful to share with anyone. Hoping his boss's tyre blew out at a hundred miles per hour.

'Still with us, Seth?' Everyone was looking at him. He could see their eyes in close-up.

'Fuck, I wish I wasn't, Jim. You'd think I'd fucked his mother.'

He did it again. Said what was in his head. It felt right. So he stood up, grabbed his papers and his mobile phone and walked out.

He knew he wasn't at home on the sofa imagining this. It was real. Definitely happening. And that's what felt so great.

Of course, Seth couldn't just leave in his eight-year-old Ford, driving off to God-knows-where when he'd only just arrived at the office. He walked back to his desk, leaving them all in the boardroom, talking about nothing that mattered, laughing about nothing that was funny, squawking about his outburst and exit, blissfully unaware that today was like any other day where nothing important has really happened.

It still smells like Jones's oats and cold coffee, when he gets back to his worn swivel chair. And it's fucking cold. And dark because three of the fluorescent bulbs have died. It's been weeks. Maybe longer. It may be shorter, Seth is so tired that time is pretty irrelevant now. His days are longer than everybody's. And this place makes them longer, still.

But it's a break to be alone. He moves his mouse and the screen jumps to life, asking him for his password.

TH1S1SH3LL

Ha! Let's see them crack that when they want to know where the bodies are buried, he laughs to himself at his stupid joke. It always makes him smile as he types it in. Seth's silent protest.

And he dutifully opens his emails to see how many he has missed in the short time before that pointless meeting, then he pulls up the Internet browser and searches for Hadley Serf via the various social media platforms at his disposal.

There are only a few in the UK, but as he types the letters of her surname into the search box, the list of people gets shorter and shorter until all that remains is somebody called Serena Hadley, a mum of two boys, in her forties, from Boston. Both her sons – Tyler (eight) and Casey (six) – are big Celtics fans. They've been on holiday to Big Bear three years in a row. It looks beautiful. Snow will do that to anything it touches. She updates her status three to four times per day and often takes pictures of her baking. She wears thick-rimmed glasses, even at the beach, and used to work for a computer games manufacturer but cut her hours right down after Casey was born.

And she really needs to update her privacy settings because she has pictures of her boys in the bath together for any sicko to look at. And images of her holiday in Aruba at a time when she didn't piss a little every time she sneezed.

And then there is Hadley. His Hadley.

She is pretty. That much is obvious. Seth manages to scroll through thirty-four of her profile pictures with ease. Her security settings are enough to block photo albums of holidays and nights out with friends but he gets a pretty good idea about her from those. And he already knows she is smart from their conversation the previous evening.

Seth looks over his shoulder at nothing. They are still in the board-room, though they must have nothing left to discuss, but he feels on edge. He shouldn't be looking for her, whether he is a Samaritan or not. But he wants to know her more.

And now he knows what she looks like, how she wears her hair, the amount of make-up she uses, her frame, a rough idea of height. And he likes her voice. He knows some of her deepest secrets and darkest thoughts. She's not a stranger to him. It's not weird. But now he is the desperate one.

Seth looks back at the doorway again before zooming in on her face. She is beautiful. The kind of beautiful that would make other women say that she was too thin. But you can tell it is that natural waif phy-sique. And she is probably still at an age where she thinks that she can eat anything she wants without putting on any weight. It will catch up with her, of course. If she lives that long.

He scrolls through every picture once more. He likes an image where her hair is wet and tied up. That is his favourite. That is the Hadley he heard on the phone the night before. She is fucked up and suicidal and lonely and longing. And her hair is wet and tied up. Seth can see her in his mind. Her heels tucked up behind her, sitting on her side, drinking wine. She seems comfortable in her skin. Not like a person crying for help. The person she undoubtedly is.

A gaggle was building in the corridor as Seth's colleagues approached the office. He looked at the time in the corner of his computer screen. So much of the day still to wade through.

Jonesy dropped his weight into the chair diagonally across from Seth and smiled.

'Six thousand monitors, eh, Seth?'

The others sniggered.

His day was going to drag on longer than his nights.

He looked at the clock again. Twelve hours. Half a day to trudge through. In half a day, his wife would be in bed asleep and he would be able to open up the phonebook again, flick towards the back and call Hadley Serf once more.

He had no idea what he would say but he knew he needed to speak with her. And, he thought, maybe she needed him.

27

I was distracted at work. But not by my usual what-would-actually-be-the-best-way-to-kill-myself trail of thought. I was thinking about my stranger. The man who had saved my life and probably had no idea he had done so. That softly spoken, idiosyncratic Samaritan who listened and talked to me like I wasn't mad or damaged. I felt the overwhelming need to speak to him again. To thank him, of course, but also to hear his voice. To talk without judgement.

But you can't just phone them and ask for one of their operators by name. I was pretty sure of that. And I was certain that he wasn't supposed to have told me even that amount of personal information.

Maybe I could call and ask for Seth. Maybe that would get him in trouble. Perhaps it would be better to phone up and act hysterical, like

I am ready to kill myself right there and then unless I get to talk to the guy who had helped me the night before.

Yeah. That'll work. They won't have a choice. I smile to myself. My colleague, Melissa, sees.

'What's that grin all about, Had?'

'What grin?' My cheeks feel hot.

'The one that tells me you either got laid last night or met somebody.'

Melissa is nice. A nice gossip. Not in a malicious sense, she doesn't talk about people behind their backs, she doesn't bitch, but she just seems to know everything about everyone. She asks how you are in the morning and she means it. She wants to know. She is nosey, but in a caring way. And she smiles. A lot. I had always wondered how somebody could be that happy all the time. It looks so exhausting.

'Oh, Liss. I can't remember the last time that happened.'

I can. I was drunk at the pub with my friends. I got talking to a guy at the bar and was left there with him. We drank together a little – beer, tequila, more beer. We kissed at the bar. We touched each other a little. Then we went outside, found a car park where I bent over and pulled my underwear to one side so that he could fuck me.

It was carnal and spontaneous at the time. I'd even told him to finish in my mouth and it had felt like the right thing to do. But the next day, it hadn't felt as good. And the day after was a bit worse. And it's these things, coupled with my friends abandoning me, that get me into the position where I am drinking at home alone and thinking about razors and pills and ropes and bloody bathtubs.

I lean forwards and whisper, 'I did meet somebody, though.' Then I spring back in my chair excitedly and Melissa moves herself forwards, hungry for more information.

'Well? What's he like?'

'He's great. It's early days, though, you know? But he's smart and funny, a great listener.' Fuck, I'm so pathetic.

'What does he do?'

'Works in the public sector.' I shock myself at how easily that first lie emerged.

'Okay. And what does he look like?' Her eyes widened.

I went on to describe the Seth in my mind, with his dark, effortlessly styled hair and his height and his muscular physique, particularly those arms. And I even swooned a little as I made up more and more detail.

'And just one date?'

'So far. But we'll definitely go out again. Sometimes you just know straight away.' I look at the clock on my computer screen. 'In fact, I'm speaking to him tonight on the phone. So let's see where that goes.'

That was the first thing I'd said that was true.

28

And then he's home. Seth doesn't remember much of his day. That monitor on his desk was all he could see. The benefit was that Jonesy's smug face was in the periphery of his tired, altered vision. He was sat in that office but he wasn't really there. He didn't know where he was. It was like sleeping with his eyes open. Nothing really happened but the day still passed and he managed to send emails on impulse and drive his old Ford home on instinct.

He dropped his laptop bag at the bottom of the stairs and hung his coat up. Maeve hated that he dumped it there when he got in but it was habit, like his masturbation or her drinking. He picked up the mail from the floor and shut the door behind him. There were four letters for Maeve, two were from credit-card companies. He thought she only had one credit card. He started to worry that she was spending again. That was a particularly stressful time the last time she owned up to her secret debts. A difficult period. But they were closer as a result.

Drama meant connection.

One letter was for Seth from a charity. He'd got caught on the phone one time, he didn't know how the guy had even got his number but he listened to his story, just for somebody to talk to. He understood how easy it was, for the people he called at night, to say, 'Fuck off, freak'. But he didn't.

He couldn't. It was a troubling story to listen to. Something about poor kids and refugees and protecting people from being captured or made to live like battery hens. Seth couldn't quite remember. His memory was screwed. He accepted that. Like he accepted that his sleep was screwed. And his marriage. And all the other things he knew he needed.

He turned straight into the kitchen and placed the letters into the tray where another fifteen bank statements remained unopened. And he knew Maeve wasn't keeping an eye on her finances.

The fridge was stocked. He took out two chicken breasts, mushrooms, parsley, crème fraîche and Dijon mustard. He pan-fried the chicken then added the other ingredients to make a sauce. It went well with sweet potato wedges. It was one of Maeve's favourites. For Seth, like almost everything else, it just blended into the day and became something else completely forgettable. Another part of his routine that was leading towards a phonebook and a stranger's voice.

He made himself a coffee as the sauce bubbled away. Why not? *I'll be awake anyway*, he thought.

The latch on the front door clicked and keys jangled and feet stepped and wiped and stamped. Shoes were kicked under the rack. A coat was hung up. Then, a familiar voice.

'Oh, Seth, can't you find somewhere to put that bloody laptop when you get in?'

Cue sighing. And yawning. And the glazed look of apathetic surrender.

29

Maeve doesn't really care about the laptop that much. She's used to it by now. Seth wasn't going to change. It was too late for that. Moaning had become her habit. She didn't like it, but it was somehow easier.

She appeared in the kitchen doorway and smiled but Seth's back was to her as he stirred something on the stovetop.

'Ooooooh, is that what I think it is?' She closed her eyes and sniffed the air.

Seth turned around to greet her, a wooden spoon in his hand with a delicate amount of sauce coating it. He blew over the spoon in an attempt to cool it and held it to Maeve's mouth. She dutifully and graciously tasted and nodded her approval. To the neighbours opposite, if they could see through the kitchen window, the Beaumans looked like a couple in love. Tender and affectionate. Smiling and playful.

Maybe, in their own way, they were.

Maeve went straight to the fridge and pulled out a bottle of white wine.

'You want a glass?'

'I've just had a coffee.'

'Finished?'

'Yeah.'

'So you can have a wine.' She took two glasses from the cupboard above her head, unscrewed the cork and poured. She swigged half of her glass immediately and topped it back up.

'Cheers,' she clinked Seth's glass, resting on the worktop, as he stirred. 'How long until it's ready?'

'Go in, I'm about ready to dish up.'

They sat on their separate sofas and enjoyed the meal and the wine – the dining table was an ornament now. It would have been a good place for Seth to keep his laptop. And they watched the evening news.

It wasn't pleasant. The police had found a body. A female body. The second time this had happened, in this area, in the last year. They believed it belonged to Theresa Palmer, a twenty-something nurse from Reading. The body was found in Warwick. The Warwick police were urging anyone to come forward if they remembered anything unusual from a certain date and time.

The problem was, it was bleached and wrapped in plastic, just like the first body. This one had been found by a high-spirited beagle on its morning walk – but this victim was not from the Warwick area. This led the police to believe that whoever had killed these women had taken them back to their hometown to possibly engage in some fetishism before disposing of the bodies.

'Honestly, Maeve. Do we have to watch this while we eat? I'd rather watch one of your home makeover shows.'

She rolled her eyes but not seriously. 'Bit squeamish, all of a sudden?'

Seth forked in a wedge of sweet potato instead of answering.

'It's interesting, I think.'

'How is anyone supposed to remember what they saw on a specific date like that? It was months ago.'

They both finished their dinner. Maeve polished off the rest of the wine. They watched a show about a couple turning a windmill into a family home, an American crime drama and a Scandinavian crime drama. Then, part of the way through a celebrity pranking show, Maeve drifted to sleep on the sofa. Seth watched the clock. He stared at the phone, then his wife. He saw them both so close but he wanted the phone so much more.

Seth cleared his throat, loudly. Maeve flinched at the sound but, instead of waking up, she turned away from him and got more comfortable. She was settling in and it was frustrating Seth. He was thinking of Hadley. He needed to speak with her. About anything. Maeve hadn't even asked him how his day had been.

He watched to the end of the home design programme, half intrigued by the final reveal. But it never came. The house was incomplete. Why make the programme if there was no conclusion? It was a frustrating letdown. An anticlimax. A waste of his time that he blamed on Maeve, who was still stretched out on the sofa, long, languid breaths forcing her back up and down. She looked peaceful. Seth sighed.

And he stood up and walked to the kitchen. Then he put the kettle on and banged a few plates around, hoping to nudge his wife from her gentle slumber.

The kettle whistled and he left it a little longer than he should have. He poured the hot water into the cup but was startled and spilled it.

'Night, then.'

He jumped and turned around to the kitchen doorway.

'Fuck, Maeve. You scared the hell out of me.'

She half smiled. 'Sorry. I thought you knew I was there.'

They looked at each other for a moment, neither knowing what was appropriate to do or say. Should they kiss goodnight? Should he go up with her? Was it time to make love?

'It's late, babe. Don't have a coffee. Come on. Stay up for a bit, sure, but come to bed.' It was heartfelt. She was concerned.

Seth turned away, giving that look she'd seen a hundred times before. The one that said *You don't understand, stop saying that shit to me.* It was as if he liked feeling the way he did. But Maeve knew that before she spoke up. And it didn't stop her from saying it.

'I'll be fine.' He turned away, wiped up the water he had spilled and stirred in his coffee granules. When he turned around, Maeve was gone. The last three stairs creaked as she hit the top.

He had enough restraint to flick through the channels, aimlessly, until his coffee was cool enough to drink down in three gulps. He leant to the right of his sofa and grabbed the phonebook he'd used the night before. He flicked to S. The page had been folded at the corner. Hadley's number had been circled. He picked up the phone, paused, breathed deeply, then tapped in the number and waited.

He muted the TV.

He turned over his shoulder and looked at the empty doorway.

The phone beeped into Seth's right ear.

Engaged. It was engaged. Hadley was on the phone to somebody else.

He slammed the mobile phone down on the sofa and swore. He'd waited all day for that, built it up, and the final reveal never came. Another incomplete house.

And Maeve heard it all.

30

Daisy Pickersgill had been forgotten.

She was the first woman to be found bleached, wrapped in plastic and dumped in Warwickshire woodland.

But, in the two months since she had been found, there had been more political scandal over expenses and unrest between members of the shadow cabinet. A young radical had blown himself up and killed a bunch of children in the process. An opposing extremist had retaliated by driving his car into a crowd of peaceful worshippers. The national football team had been beaten by an opponent of apparently lesser skill and one of the players was being blasted on the front pages of the newspapers for drinking and fucking some young reality TV starlet who was not his trophy wife.

In that time, processed meats had been moved to a level one carcinogen alongside cigarettes. Long-range nuclear weapons were being tested and shot out to sea in what looked like an international pissing contest. There were two separate zoo incidents that saw animals mauling or killing their keepers. A NASA mission to photograph the storms of Jupiter was a huge success. Celebrities died. They had kids. They went to rehab. They gave to charity. Businesses went under. House prices went up.

And that sweet twenty-eight-year-old youth worker was pushed further and further back in the public's mind and agendas were forced forwards and adverts were consumed and society was scared.

And people felt like they cared about so many things, but it only meant that they ended up caring about nothing.

Detective Sergeant Pace still cares. He still remembers Daisy Pickersgill. He will make sure that she isn't lost again.

31

I picked up the phone.

'Fuck it.' I even said out loud. Then I thought, I'll just make it up as I go along.

I took the crumpled card from my purse and dialled the number again.

A man answered. My excitement was fleeting. There was the faint possibility I had lucked out. His voice was soft, with an even tone – maybe they taught that – but it wasn't Seth.

'I'd like to speak to Seth, please?'

'I'm sorry.'

'Seth. I spoke to him there last night. I was low. I was feeling low. He helped me.'

'Are you feeling low now?'

'I just want to speak to Seth. He'll understand.'

'Try me.' He persisted, softly, probably wondering what he would do if things escalated. Did he even know a Seth? I wondered.

'Look, I don't want to offend you, because you sound nice enough, but I need Seth. I spoke to him last night. And if I don't get to speak with him again, I don't know what I'm going to do.' I lied. And I felt bad. But what I was saying was true. I needed Seth. He understood me. Or maybe I just wanted him.

Grow up, Hadley.

'Okay. Okay. Listen, you're not alone. I am here. I will try to find Seth for you, Okay?'

'Thank you. I appreciate it.'

'I'm going to speak to someone here and see if I can find him. Please don't leave. If he's not here, you can talk to me. I will listen.'

I said nothing.

'I'm not hanging up and I'm not putting you on hold, I'm going to try to find Seth.'

I said nothing. He seemed genuine. Eager.

Then I waited for about three seconds, decided I'd completely lost the plot, and I hung up on that poor, sweet guy.

32

Ant placed his headset on the desk and scrambled over to a supervisor to explain the situation.

The supervisor chastised him for leaving a potentially vulnerable person hanging on the end of a lifeless call. Meanwhile, that potentially vulnerable person was telling herself that she was being an idiot for trying to get hold of Seth. And Seth was trying to call that potentially vulnerable person at that time but had received an engaged tone.

He had hung up the phone.

As did Hadley.

And, when Ant returned to his headset, he realised she had gone. His heart sank. The sense of the unknown turned him cold. What if he'd let it happen again to someone else? It was his fault.

Then he clicked a box on his computer screen.

Took down Hadley's number.

He would call her back.

33

Seth felt let down. They hadn't arranged to speak but, in his mind, they both wanted it to happen. Maybe she was on the phone to a girlfriend, talking about him. He just needed to kill some time before trying again. He wasn't going to call anybody else. He didn't need any more rejection.

He checked out Serena Hadley. She had updated her status twice since the morning. Once about her kids and the amount of driving she had to do to get them to their various sporting clubs, and once about how tired she was. 'How can I find the time to eat right?' she had asked her one hundred and eighty-six friends. Several mothers had sympathised.

Then he was clicking on photos of Hadley that weren't remotely suggestive but he managed to find suggestion in them. He ejaculated into the centre pages of one of Maeve's fashion supplements, folded it and threw it in the bin. He poured himself a glass of water, picked up the phone and redialled.

'Hello?'

'Hadley?'

'Yeeeees. Who is this?'

'It's me. It's Seth.'

'He found you.'

Seth had no idea what she was talking about. But he could hear her smiling. Then she explained. He just went along with it. That seemed easier, less desperate than him calling her of his own accord. But he told her that he'd wanted to. So that she would feel a little less embarrassed about what she'd done to get hold of him.

'So, how are you feeling? Did you want to talk to me about anything in particular?'

'I'm, actually, pretty good. I haven't felt like this in such a long time.'

'Well, that's great to hear. Why were you trying to get hold of me, then?'

'I just wanted to talk to you, Seth. Just you.'

Seth waited a moment and let the words sink in. And then he took a small risk.

'I just want to talk to you, too.'

He heard a noise overhead. Maeve had got out of bed. Next was the unmistakable click of the bathroom drawstring light switch. Hadley was talking but Seth was listening to the sound of his wife's piss ferociously hitting the water in the toilet bowl. He heard toilet paper rip. Silence as she wiped. Then the flush before she wandered back across the floorboards and into the bed they sometimes shared.

Hadley was still talking when he clicked back into the conversation. He didn't have to keep lying to her because he never really said that much. She obviously needed his shoulder and his ear more than she realised. Seth let her speak.

'Can we do this again? I want to do this again?'

It was bold but he knew she'd go for that.

'Same time tomorrow?' she asked.

'It's a date.'

He put the phone down and smiled. Then walked upstairs and got into bed with his wife, where he didn't sleep for the next three hours.

TUESDAY

34

It's all too familiar.

Detective Sergeant Pace feels sick to his stomach.

Detective Sergeant Pace is irrationally anxious.

Detective Sergeant Pace is back where he started.

This victim was taller than the last. Heavier, too. The killer didn't seem to have a type. Though they all ended up looking similar with their pale skin and white hair and caved-in faces and bruised necks.

The body of Theresa Palmer was discovered but he has no idea who she was. And there was very little to go on. Looking at missing persons in the Warwickshire area is going to be a waste of time but he would have to do that. Even though his gut is telling him that she would be from London. He'd have to cooperate with the locals.

He's looked at her body and there are no distinguishing features. Any scars or birth marks have been hidden by the bleach but the coroner would locate them with some closer scrutiny.

Identification would come down to dental records and a little bit of luck.

Detective Sergeant Pace does not feel lucky.

Things feel the same as they did when he received the call to say that Daisy Pickersgill's body had been located.

Confused. Let down. Like it is somehow his fault. Because everything he touches gets tainted and turns to shit.

Detective Sergeant Pace is dirty.

Detective Sergeant Pace is a trigger.

But he is determined to find the person that killed these two girls.

Detective Sergeant Pace cannot forget.

35

And the next day was the same and nothing happened until that night.

Ant had been restless all evening. Thinking of that girl who he'd left dangling on the phone. He rattled around in his tiny Coventry flat all the next day wondering what had happened to her. He'd told his supervisor that he could call her back, but his suggestion had been shot down, of course. It left Ant anxious for the rest of that shift. He felt like he wasn't really helping anyone. He wasn't helping himself.

He thought about Australia, the sunshine, heavy backpacks, beers, laughter and adventure. Climbing, sleeping outside, falling, eating well, and that hook, that fucking hook on the back of a bathroom door.

And the feeling that he had let someone down.

Ant didn't want to be responsible for another death.

It had to stop.

He drank some more wine. He'd been drinking most of the day. The pad he'd taken from his desk the night before was lying open on his coffee table next to the bottle of wine. It was placed purposefully so that two of its straight edges were perfectly aligned with the sides of the table. That always calmed him. Neatness. Cleanliness. Balance.

He called the number on the pad and waited.

The phone rang five times before being picked up.

'Hello?'

Ant waited. He needed more than that. There was nothing he could say. Was that the voice of the same girl from the night before?

'Hello? Who is this?'

He started to breathe heavily. Intrigue and excitement pawing at the rational side of his brain.

It sounded like her. But he couldn't be sure.

'Seth? Is that you?'

Seth again. What was with this Seth guy? There was no Seth, Ant had checked.

He felt relief. He had screwed up, he knew that much, but the caller hadn't hung up the phone and jumped in front of a moving train – she was there, talking, asking for Seth again. Maybe Seth wasn't real. Maybe this girl was delusional and did really need help.

His heart raced.

'Oh, go fuck yourself, you psycho.' And she hung up.

Ant did not like that. Not one bit. He only wanted to help. He was checking on her. Due diligence. Overdue diligence. And she had made things personal.

He put the phone down on the coffee table and knocked over his wine.

'No, no, no, no, no, you fucking idiot.'

Ant ran into the kitchen and opened up the cupboard beneath the sink. Everything was lined up perfectly in sixes. Six canisters of furniture polish, six bottles of bleach, six fabric softeners. Spare sponges and cloths were arranged neatly into baskets, as were the bin liners.

He took out one of the cloths and a bottle of carpet cleaning foam. And he scrubbed until it looked new. And he looked at his handwriting on the paper and he thought about that ungrateful girl who had called him a psycho. And he thought, *You don't know me*.

He couldn't let it go. And he wouldn't.

36

'Is this weird?' Hadley asked Seth.

'I don't know. I mean, people used to meet each other in bars and clubs and at university, now it's all online dating and putting up pictures of yourself from when you were much thinner than you really are and saying things like "I love travelling and the outdoors, I have a passion for music, blah blah blah", and it's not really real. But it seems to be the way now. And it's working, to an extent. So this ... no, this isn't weird, it's just another way that two people can meet.' He's not even sure where that came from but she bought it.

'You make a very convincing case.' Her tone was light, fun.

'Well, I thought about it for a long time. I wanted to get it just right.' Seth smiled.

'I have a friend, Angela, she's been with a guy for nearly two years. She met him that way. Well, not a dating site so much as a booty call app. One of those ones where you swipe in a certain direction if you like the look of someone and if they do the same to you, you can chat, hook up, and have sex.'

'You think that's weird?'

'I guess not,' she mused. 'People need people, right? And sex. There are still people meeting in bars and going home on the first night, I'm sure. This way you know up front that it's the reason you're there. I swiped you, you swiped me, let's fuck, kinda thing.'

The words excited him. He hadn't masturbated before their call like the other time. It was planned, this time. It felt like a date. You can't do that before a date. It's not right.

They talked for over an hour. Seth had forgotten that Maeve was even upstairs, asleep. He laughed on the phone, gasped, whispered. They spoke a little about sex and her job and her friends. He avoided talking too much about himself, speaking of the things he liked and didn't like more than the things he did and didn't do.

'It's so strange how close I feel to you, Seth. I mean, I've only known you a few days but I've told you things I haven't even told some of my closest friends. I feel so bloody comfortable and I don't even know what you look like.'

'I can send you a picture of me when I was much thinner, if you'd like.'

They both laughed. They had a connection.

A connection that was heightened by loneliness, desperation and sleeplessness.

'You know what I mean, though, right?' she said.

Seth paused to collect himself. Was he really going to go down this road again?

'I feel it, too. It's refreshing. I feel lighter, better just for knowing you. And I don't even really know you.'

'Yet...' she jumped in. It was suggestive and positive and Seth had been here before.

Only a couple of times. That tightrope of fidelity had wobbled in the past. Only twice. Two times. It's not about sex, just having the conversation constitutes an affair of sorts because he was wandering from the path that was the life he chose. His heart was being pulled in a different direction. It scared him.

Fear was the most powerful emotion.

But he didn't know where Maeve was one hundred percent of the time. She could be anywhere. With anyone. His two times could pale in comparison to her flirtations. But she was still with him. She hadn't run away with another man. So maybe it worked. Or maybe they stayed at the same level of broken. Either way, he wouldn't begrudge her a dalliance over that last decade.

'Yet...' he responded, adding some suggestion of his own. 'Same time tomorrow?'

'Oh, I can't. I'm out tomorrow night with some friends. The next day, definitely.'

'Yeah. No worries. The next day.' He tried to sound as relaxed as possible but his insides were shrivelling with anger and disappointment.

'Perfect. Speak then. Bye, secret stranger,' she teased. It would normally provoke a reaction from him but he was too pissed off. There was no way he'd sleep now.

'Bye, Hadley. Have fun with your friends. Maybe you should ask them if this is weird.'

'Oh, no. I won't say a thing. I want to keep you all to myself.'

She put the phone down and so did Seth.

He wanted to feel guilty. But he couldn't.

Then he found that forty minutes had passed. He'd been sitting on the sofa, his legs stretched out on the floor in front of him, feet crossed over one another, right over left. His arms were folded and his head had lolled slightly to the right. He'd been staring at the television screen the entire time and it wasn't even switched on. Time had moved on without him noticing.

He turned the lights off and went upstairs. He took a piss, brushed his teeth and got into bed with his wife. He pulled the corner of the duvet over his shoulder and turned his back to her as though he was ready to sleep. But he didn't. He just laid there in some kind of suspended animation until her alarm went off for work. Then he dropped off as soon as she got out.

Ninety minutes later, his own alarm sounded. It had been a solid rest.

37

Maeve hadn't been asleep. She had started by letting her mind wander to thoughts of the brooding Detective Sergeant Pace. Then she'd heard some laughter and strained her ears at the mumbling. She had been here before. Twice. Through the initial changes in mood to the standoffishness to the awkwardness. Then the distancing. To the eventual collapse and cleaning up the mess.

She knew it was coming. She could feel Seth not sleeping next to her. When it got this bad, he got reckless. Stupid, really. He made mistakes and stupid decisions. But at least it was interesting. For a while.

And it ended. It always ended.

And it ended badly.

But that's what brought them closer together. It was all she wanted.

She was tired, too. And irritated by the noise. And she was low, knowing that Seth was about to go on another of his misadventures. He'd found someone who would talk to him, who would listen to him talk. She wouldn't cry about it, she wasn't the kind. She was resigned. A living sigh.

But she was hopeful.

Expectant that it would all go wrong.

And she would get Seth back.

38

Theresa Palmer had brilliantly white teeth.

Perfectly bleached.

But with three fillings in her molars, one in a premolar and a half crown that she'd always hated the sight of, she was swiftly identifiable. And Pace had to travel to Kilburn to notify her family.

Kilburn High Road is a mixture of shops, restaurants, independent housing, luxury apartments, short-let flats and anything in between. A few years back, a man with a Samurai sword ran down the street and took some of his aggression out at a chain store before being detained.

Sally Palmer does not live in a luxury apartment. Neither does she rent one of the flats above Primark. The Palmers are average. Sally is divorced and living with her boyfriend. They've been together for over a decade. She doesn't want to get married again. Theresa had a brother who is twenty-nine and still lives at home. They got on. The family all liked her boyfriend, too. It was a pleasant set-up. Average. Middle-of-the-highroad. But none of them has seen or heard from her in over a week.

And Pace turns it all upside down.

'Can I see her?' Sally Palmer composes her tears for a moment.

'We will need you to formally identify her, Ms Palmer, but I need to prepare you for what you are going to see.'

Pace doesn't want to go into too much detail, particularly in front of her younger sibling. He tells her that they are currently unsure of the cause of death, though he knows it was likely to be strangulation, and that her body was tampered with after her passing.

Sally Palmer takes a frightened inhalation but Pace is more concerned with the men in the room. Her stepfather looks sad and shocked, but nothing is manifesting physically. And Theresa's brother looks pissed off.

39

Pace suspects both of them.

No family is that normal.

'I'm going to need to ask you all some questions but, before I do, I just need some information on her friends, boyfriends and girlfriends, and the people she works with, please. I need to question all of them so that we can get to the bottom of who would want to do such a thing.'

For twenty minutes, Pace sits with Theresa's family; they drink tea, he doesn't drink anything. His presence makes the living room darker, he can feel it. There is evil. All around him. All the time. Following him. He will need to solve this case to get away. If only for some temporary relief.

Detective Sergeant Pace is suspicious.

Detective Sergeant Pace weighs three times more than his body.

He asks his stock questions, gathering information on the dead girl's life and links and relationships. The family, at this point of shock, are hard pressed to think of anyone who had a grievance with their daughter. Their relationship with her boyfriend will break down eventually, as he will be blamed. Pace already suspects him.

The investigation has truly started. He has a list of co-workers and friends to follow up on. He has one eye on her stepfather. And another on his own shadow.

Detective Sergeant Pace has one more question. He has been waiting.

'Did Theresa or you, or anyone you know, have any contact with Daisy Pickersgill?'

WEDNESDAY

40

Unrelated.

There are two bodies, now.

Theresa Palmer and Daisy Pickersgill were undoubtedly killed by the same person. Pace knows it. Both strangled, bruises to the neck. Bleached skin and hair and eyes and teeth. Post-mortem will undoubtedly reveal the same internal vaginal abrasions on Theresa Palmer that were found on Daisy Pickersgill. These details were never released. Only the killer, the coroner and Pace know. Tests on the plastic used to wrap both bodies should indicate that they were cut from the same single piece.

Undisputed.

They both lived in London, one in the east and one in the north. Both were in employment. Both were in seemingly stable relationships. Both showed no recent signs of emotional struggle. The only medication prescribed to either woman was Theresa Palmer's contraceptive pill.

And both were somehow made to disappear with only the slightest murmur of concern from their loved ones, only to re-emerge more than one hundred miles away as albino cadavers.

Unfathomable.

And it is still in doubt whether these innocent, young women were killed and then transported to Warwickshire for a lazy, makeshift burial or whether they were somehow lured to that location, only to be murdered on arrival.

Uncertain.

Pace sits at his desk looking through both case files. He's been up all night. There is nobody else around. Just him and his shadow. He is cross-referencing everything he has gathered so far. Socially, they seemed completely separate. Digging further into social media might uncover some mutual acquaintances but that feels like reaching, trying to make something fit. In a familial sense, there is no crossover. Their employers didn't move in the same circles. The detective is still waiting for completed phone records, however.

With pictures and timelines and work schedules and statements laid out in front of him, Detective Sergeant Pace cannot find one scrap of evidence that links these two victims while they were still alive. And Theresa Palmer's stepfather said he could account for his whereabouts since the girl was initially flagged as possibly missing.

Detective Sergeant Pace is fighting against the current.

Detective Sergeant Pace is missing something.

Detective Sergeant Pace is lost.

The girls were so alike, yet, also, they were not. Days of work on Theresa, months on Daisy, and there was nothing. Absolutely nothing to suggest that there is any kind of pattern. That they somehow knew one another or the same person. Nothing to indicate a reason for travelling to Warwickshire.

Nothing.

Unbelieveable.

41

Seth knocked on his boss's office door and walked in before he could be summoned inside. That jumped-up, overpaid fucking child. He was sitting at his desk with his feet crossed on top where the keyboard should be – the keyboard was pushed under his 22-inch monitor.

He was on his phone, looking at Seth as he stepped closer towards the desk. His red glass eyes squinted, his thin lips curling into a half snarl. He continued to talk to whoever was on the other end of the line, Seth was sure it wasn't work-related.

'...I like to punch her between the legs so it swells up and feels a bit tighter.' And he laughed.

He made Seth feel sick. He had a wife he spoke of deploringly. Not in a manner that suggested that their relationship was strained in any way, just that he had less than no respect for her. And she probably had no idea. Because she was at home, diligently taking care of their three children.

Seth put a piece of paper on his desk, upside down. He looked at that stupid, vacant expression for a half-second, then he turned and walked back out. His boss waited two seconds and then Seth heard the paper rustle as it was turned over to reveal a copy of the purchase order he had just received and had already placed on the system.

He had been on the phone for most of the morning, calling in favours and trading on relationships over pricing and product quality. Four thousand monitors to ship that day and three thousand on the last day of the month. At a margin of six percent. High enough that he didn't have to run the order past the boss. Seth hit 108 percent of his target with most of the month left. His boss would be livid. He'd get paid for Seth's success but hate that Seth was having it.

Seth returned to his desk. He didn't smile. He didn't look to the right through the glass wall that kept their boss separate but always there with them, on them. He looked at the clock on his screen. There were three minutes to go until the working day ended but he shut down his computer, picked up his car keys and left without saying goodbye. His month was done. Maybe he could put his feet on the desk for the next twenty days.

It took a lot for him not to throw his boss a look, to rejoice in his victory, but there was a nagging sensation that held him down. He wouldn't be talking with Hadley that night. And it left him feeling lost. Tired and lost.

42

I finished work and started that twenty-minute walk back to my flat. Some days I jump on the bus. It really depends on what I eat for lunch. I listened to music through my earphones, scrolled through a few interesting articles and funny videos that people had shared on my various social media pages and I messaged my friends about our night out.

It was amazing how many people were doing the same thing, lowering their heads as they walked along, eyes fixed on a tiny glowing screen – after spending nine hours staring at a much larger glowing screen. People rarely bumped into one another. Multi-tasking with great dexterity but ignoring the great, wide world they strolled through blindly, instead, cramming life into six inches of glass and aluminium and circuitry.

I hate it and I love it, all at the same. It's not going to change, might as well embrace it.

I barely looked up twice in the time it took me to get from the office to my flat, which is impressive and disconcerting as I have four major roads to cross on that journey.

I guess I'm just excited about my night out. I'm immersed in the lyrics of the song in my ears. Maybe I'm feeling happy. Maybe I'm just feeling not sad. Seth has enabled me to get excited. That sounds like nothing, but when your self-esteem is this low, you dread everything. It's exhausting.

The front-door key needs a wiggle to get it going and the door gets stiffer at this time of year but I push into the flat. Where I live alone with my cat. We roll our eyes at one another and I shut the door behind me with my heel.

43

So, of course she hadn't noticed Ant, standing across on the opposite side of the road.

Ant knew the region Hadley lived in from the area code of her phone number, so he knew he'd have to take the car out. It was around thirty miles away. He had enough information on her to reverse search her address. It was the middle of the week and he wasn't sure what he'd find but he just had to see her.

Partly to make sure that she was still alive, that she was real. Partly something else. Maybe he was always trying to save James again. Maybe he got something from helping these people. A sense of achievement. A rush. Closure.

He was wearing a grey windproof jacket with blue jeans. It wasn't like he stuck out. He wasn't worth remembering. A white man in his thirties, average height, drinking a cup of coffee while stood outside an estate agent's window. He could've been looking for a house in the area, somewhere to rent. He could've been a mature student.

But he wasn't. He was there waiting for Hadley. And he'd seen her now. What he would do next was unknown even to him. He could see that she was pretty, even with a day of work in her hair and on her face. He liked the way she walked and carried her bag over her shoulder. She held herself confidently, not like somebody who had called him a couple of nights before, seemingly suicidal, and hanging up on him, sending him spiralling once more.

There was a coffee shop next door to the estate agent. He threw his jacket over a chair near the window and went to the counter to order himself another flat white. He took the final almond croissant, it looked lonely and leftover from a quiet breakfast period that day. It was hardening at the edges but he didn't mind that. And he took his seat by the window, staring across the road at the home of a woman he didn't know.

The light flicked on upstairs and he watched as Hadley scrutinised herself in the mirror.

She looked, first, at her face, pulling at the skin on her cheeks and stretching smooth around her eyes. She viewed herself, face on, and adjusted her breasts, then in profile, sucking in her stomach. And she looked at the shape of her buttocks, once with flat feet and once on her tiptoes.

Hadley unbuttoned her shirt, pulled a clip out of her hair and exited the room, unaware of the man watching her every well-lit move.

Ant sipped his coffee and let his imagination wander. He pictured her in the kitchen making herself a herbal tea. And in the shower washing her hair. And with her hand between her legs as water trailed down her breasts and onto her stomach, which pulsed and tightened as she came. And in the bath, drinking pills down with a glass of rosé wine and a solitary razor blade to run down the length of her arm, just to make sure.

He was fascinated by her. Enthralled. She had sounded so desperate a few days before; but now her shoulders denied the notion of her instability. He liked her walk, her hair and what he'd seen of her face. Maybe, if circumstances had been different, there may have been another destiny for them.

He just wanted to save her. Now. Maybe he wanted more after.

She appeared at the window, once more, a purple towel wrapped around her breasts and a smaller white one around her head, hiding her hair. She looked out of the window, down onto the street below then pulled her curtains closed.

Ant could still tell that she was in the room. He ordered another coffee and sat back in the same seat. He watched the world pass by but kept one eye on Hadley's flat.

Directly across from his window was a lesser coffee shop. The coffee was bitter and the furniture less comfortable. Outside, two women sat, smoking. The woman on the left had a baby's pushchair next to her. The child was probably two years old and seemed delighted to be where she was. The mother's friend blew smoke towards the child and Ant's top lip turned into a snarl. Still, the child seemed to be smiling.

A man with a pot belly, fisherman's jumper and scraggly white beard was enjoying his coffee alone, a few tables to the right. A friend appeared with a dog, Ant didn't know what breed it was. He poured something from a bottle wrapped in brown paper into his friend's coffee and sat down next to him. They both looked forwards the entire time, talking but not making eye contact.

The coffee was working its magic. Ant felt alert, awake. But he also needed to use the toilet. He didn't want his post unmanned.

The curtains twitched. Ant clocked it immediately. Hadley looked down on the street below, the towel was still wrapped around her hair. She seemed to be waiting for somebody. He had time and took the opportunity. When he got back, the light was still on in her room. He settled back into his seat.

Twenty minutes later, two young women, dressed to party, knocked on Hadley's front door. She let them in. One had a bottle of wine in her left hand. Twenty-five minutes after that, they left, giggling as they walked in their heels towards the nearest pub, unaware that they were being followed.

44

Something in Seth wanted to tell Maeve about the purchase order. About smashing his target for the month. About sticking it to his boss. But she never once asked him about his day.

She stood in the kitchen doorway and told him all about her office politics. She mentioned peoples' names he'd heard a thousand times before, of whom he felt he had an understanding; he had their backstories. And she droned on about something while drinking her usual gallon of wine as Seth stirred the prawns into a too-mild curry sauce. He'd chopped a couple of red chillies to sprinkle onto his bowl when he served up.

The night progressed as usual. They ate. They watched the news – police tape and talking heads and memories of a kind girl and something about being wrapped in plastic and a shallow grave that should have been discovered sooner. Family tears and a sceptical police force.

He didn't want to watch it but could tell that Maeve was mesmerised. He saw her expression change whenever the detective was on screen. She looked almost excited, turned on. He wasn't sure how he felt about that. She changed.

Then Maeve slept. Seth waited. But his evening would drag, time would elongate. He wasn't able to speak with Hadley because she was out with friends. He wasn't jealous but he did begrudge her that when their relationship was still fresh and in those exciting early stages of courtship. What was he going to do?

He couldn't go to bed, have an early night. That never worked. He looked at the phonebook but he couldn't bring himself to call another stranger; it felt unfaithful. To a woman he had been speaking to for three days. Not to his wife, who he had been with for over a decade. He was being ridiculous and he knew it but he couldn't stop the way he felt. It wasn't love, of course, but it was something. And that's all it takes.

Seth knew where it was going.

He knew where it would lead.

45

Maeve was in bed, her light was still on so Seth assumed that she was either reading or lying asleep with a book on her chest. He didn't make a coffee; instead, he turned out the downstairs lights, locked the front door and walked upstairs. She was reading, lying on her side. He didn't have long until she fell asleep.

He brushed his teeth and took a piss. He washed his hands and the end of his dick. He could barely remember the last time that had been necessary.

Maeve's light clicked off. It would look to anyone else that she was telling him not to bother, but he knew that woman better than anyone, she was succumbing to her fate, her duty. Maybe even her need.

Seth undressed and pulled his side of the duvet back before sliding in next to her. He left a small gap and put his hand on her hip beneath the covers.

'What are you doing, Seth?' Her tone was knowing but playful.

'What? A man can't hug his wife at night before they go to sleep?' He stroked his fingers gently against the skin on her thigh.

She turned around to face him and he found his hand on her other hip. He coaxed her T-Shirt up a little and moved his hand around to her back. Then he moved it down and ran his finger beneath the waistband of her underwear. Seth could feel where her pubic hair began as he edged his hand around to the front. And she wasn't rejecting his advances, there was a subtle twitch as she pushed herself into his touch. He could hear her breath.

Their faces were suddenly much closer but they weren't kissing, just breathing into each other. Her left hand moved to his leg and she worked her nails up slowly, stopping and grabbing him, hard, the way she knew Seth liked it. Squeezing as he grew inside her grip.

Seth moved his hand inside her underwear. She gasped. He hadn't touched her this way in a long time. As her mouth opened more, he moved his own forwards to meet hers. They kissed, their hands working each other, matching speeds, stroke for stroke.

He stopped and yanked her underwear down to her thigh. He pushed himself up with the other hand and Maeve twisted over onto her back, still holding him, looking up at him through the dark.

And he climbed between her legs and moved up to kiss her, the pressure from his body weight pushing him down onto her. They kissed again. She wanted him inside her. He could feel her. He pulled her nightshirt up and over her head.

Maeve's breasts were small but they stood up and her nipples were a beautiful dark pink. Seth put his mouth over the right one and licked it delicately, putting it between his teeth. Her back arched and she grabbed hold of him, trying to put him inside of her. But he pinned her wrists down against her pillow and kissed her neck.

He worked down to her breasts again, and then her flat stomach before letting go of her hands and putting his mouth between her legs.

Her reaction was instant. It excited Seth to hear her like that. He was doing that to her. He flicked his tongue lightly against her. Teasing her, she tried to push herself closer to his mouth but he pulled away. He was taking his time. Savouring her. He liked the way she tasted, the way she smelled, the way she moved. He liked it all. And that made him feel bad. He wanted to feel bad.

Seth moved back down and shot his tongue deep inside her. His right hand stroked her legs. He circled his finger close to her anus but never took it further.

She was getting close. He could tell. Her breathing changed. He'd found the spot that worked for her and he kept at it, applying a little more pressure, moving faster.

Her stomach spasmed and tightened, her head dropping to the side and her right hand swiping at Seth's head halfheartedly to stop him from teasing. She was sensitive. Overly sensitive. Curling herself into a ball, the occasional aftershock rippling through her body. And Seth moved around behind her.

She told Seth to give her a moment because she felt too responsive. 'Shh. It's okay, I'll go slowly.'

And he pushed into her from behind. They were both lying on their sides. He grabbed her stomach to pull her closer to him, so there was more of him inside her. And he moved slowly, just as he'd said.

Then he moved his hand up to her hair and twisted it tightly, pulling it back. She made that noise he knew so well. The one that was on the cusp of her asking him to let go and telling him to pull it harder. Maeve was not as innocent as she seemed. He knew what she liked by now. She wanted him to make love to her, look her in the eyes like she was the only person in the world, but she also wanted him to fuck her, pound her like he was just trying to get something out of his system.

They fucked. She made noise. So did he. Their bodies slammed against one another. Slapping. Crashing. Seth's hand never left Maeve's hair.

She pushed herself up to her knees. Seth was behind her. A hand reached between her legs and stroked his balls as he moved in and out, in and out. Then she let go and focused on herself.

They stayed like that. Seth was feeling excited but he controlled himself, moving slower. He wanted her to come again with his dick in her. He told her that and she breathed out her excitement.

'Come on,' he willed her to climax, feeling it building in himself.

Her hand moved furiously between her legs and Seth started to go faster.

'Come in me,' she requested.

And that was all it took. He was so excited at that prospect that it was almost instant.

There was noise and then everything went black for a moment. In that moment, Seth couldn't lie, couldn't hide his feelings. Couldn't deceive.

Then Seth collapsed onto the mattress next to his exhausted, sweating, satisfied wife. He fell into the pillow. Crashing back down into his tired reality. Into the lie. And, in that very next moment, he wondered what Hadley was doing.

46

Hadley was being watched.

Ant didn't stand out. He wasn't striking to look at but he wasn't hideous. He was five feet, eleven inches tall. Not a giant, not a dwarf. He dressed in dark-blue jeans, grey T-shirt with no logo or branding, and a sensible windproof jacket. Well presented, but by no means a slave to fashion.

Three women hopped from bar to bar. Sometimes he stood in a dark corner and viewed from afar, others, he sat alone on the table next to them, picking up on the odd comment or element of conversation. He smiled into his pint of lager as they discussed and laughed at the banalities of life. And he wondered why Hadley had called the Samaritans in such a mess the other night.

And he thought about Australia and that spotless bathroom and how he had no idea that his best friend was in trouble. How could you ever really know another person? Could you even know yourself?

Nobody really knew Ant. He had systematically cut himself off from everybody that was in his life. Choosing, instead, to put his efforts into people he did not know, who didn't know him. Psychologically, that told you what you needed to know about him. But nobody knew. Because nobody was watching Ant.

In the third bar, he deliberately bumped into Hadley as she wobbled her way down the corridor to the toilets.

Hadley registered him in her mind as he apologised, but almost instantly forgot him.

He was already one pint over the legal driving limit at that point but his car was nothing. Not flashy, not a banger. Not worth pulling over. A crude mechanic had referred to it once as a clit car. 'Because every cunt's got one,' he'd laughed.

As Seth and Maeve fucked, Hadley was ordering a bottle of prosecco with three straws. And Ant was playing on a fruit machine along the opposite wall looking at the dirt in the room. He thought about how many strangers had touched the same buttons with unclean hands and it panicked him. He would have to wait until one of the party he was following used the toilet before he could scrub that away.

47

'Oh, Had, you could meet a guy tonight if you wanted.'

Bex was my outwardly confident friend and it was completely justified. Fiery red hair, delicate Irish lilt to her voice, a well-paid job and she was a beautiful, healthy, fit vegetarian – one of those who still ate fish.

'I met up for dinner with someone I found online. We ate. He was a playwright. Very understated. He hadn't been part of any huge hits but he was living off his job, you know? He'd made that decision. He'd chosen art and poverty but he was as content and troubled as anyone you know. And he was very sure of himself, in a positive way.'

'And?' I asked, smiling at the others and taking a sip of my drink.

'And where else am I going to bump into a handsome, self-assured artist? Not in this bar. Not in my office. The world is bigger and more connected than ever. Why not use it? It's not as frowned upon as it used to be.'

She didn't want to sound like she was justifying her actions but she was, slightly.

'Will you see him again?'

'Well, I've already slept with him so what's the point?' She laughed loudly and we all took a swig of the Prosecco, smiling at her openness.

'You're terrible, Bex.'

'I'm kidding. Not about the sex. That happened. It was good. I'll see him again.'

The fruit machine beeped and coughed out a load of one-pound coins. We were drunk and young and happy. The entire bar heard Bex laugh and saw her throw her hair to one side.

I should've felt better, but I started to compare myself. That's what I do. All the time. And it left me feeling like I was in the background. Being me is exhausting.

48

Ant scooped the coins out of the tray and into his trouser pocket. Looking over his shoulder, he could see that there was less than half a bottle left between the three women he was tailing. He had enough time.

Jangling obviously, he strolled to the toilets and hit the hot tap on. The water was scalding hot, just the way he liked it. He rubbed the soap into a lather all over his hands and scrubbed at them beneath the burning water. Then he soaped again. This time using the thumbnail of one hand to clean beneath all his other nails. His hands were turning pink. And he cleaned them one more time after that. Who knows where those coins had been?

When he opened the door back to the bar the three women were pulling their jackets over their shoulders and the bottle was empty. Ant walked past them and out the door. He crossed over the road and stood in a shop doorway so that he could see which way they turned when they left. He assumed they'd continue in the same direction they'd been travelling. There was one more bar before the local club.

He had a pocket full of coins and no idea where his night was heading or what he was going to do next. But he knew it was wherever Hadley would be. He was watching her. Checking in on her. Maybe even protecting her. He was a Good Samaritan. And he wouldn't lose her. Not this one.

49

It didn't help Seth sleep. The connection had been short. Maeve lay on her back for a while, breathing steadily, staring at the ceiling. Her hand was resting gently on his stomach. More a gesture of thanks than simple affection. Then she turned her back and went to sleep, her nightclothes still strewn across the carpet beside the bed.

It hadn't been something he'd planned on doing but once he was in the moment, it had felt incredible. They'd never had any trouble in that department when they'd both been motivated. And it felt a hell of a lot better to be wrapped in Maeve than it did to be gripped by his hand when he came. But pleasure is fleeting.

Seth turned his back to hers as he always did. And his eyes stayed open just as they always had. His vision had adjusted to the light. He could make out the lamp on his bedside table and three books he'd never read stacked neatly beside it. All fiction. Maeve had three books on her side table, too. One contemporary thriller that was already being made into a Hollywood film and two self-help books. One about managing time better and one about headspace and cognitive theory. All dog-eared, but neatly dog-eared.

The room smelled like sex. Good sex. Messy sex. He lay there, cold and naked, wondering how he let himself get carried away so easily. How that switch just flipped from apathy to desire and there was nothing he could do to control it. Was it just as easy to flip it back the other way? Could he flip so drastically to any emotion?

His irritation kept him awake for another three hours. Then the infuriation of not being able to sleep kept him awake for another two. Doing nothing. Seeing books he would never read in close-up, his wife unmoved from her post-coital foetal coma.

He thought about Hadley. He hated that he hadn't spoken to her. And he hated that he had no idea what she was doing or who she was with. And he told himself that she was probably drunk with her friends and making bad decisions just as he had done.

She was damaged, just as he was. She wasn't fully in control of herself. She couldn't be, otherwise she wouldn't get into the position of trying to kill herself. If she was in control, she would have done it by now.

Seth imagined her kissing a faceless man on a dance floor. He pictured his horrible boss punching her between the legs then sticking his ginger cock into her and laughing like a maniac as he pounded his hips into hers. Seth gripped his fists and bit his pillow. Maeve didn't move.

He told himself that he couldn't complain. He had just fucked his wife. Hadley and Seth weren't together, that was stupid. They were phone buddies, pen pals, it was a holiday romance at best. Maybe he needed to step things up. Maybe they could meet. Maybe she was already home in bed and thinking the same thing.

50

I could feel the shape of his dick. The antithesis of eroticism, he rubbed it against me from behind as I danced, his hand reaching around and holding my stomach so that he could pull me into him. It wasn't an attempt at turning me on, he was just letting me know that he was there, that he appreciated the way I looked and that he was pretty secure about his own presence. He was showing off a bit.

I was drunk. So when he moved his hand down between my legs, I carried on dancing. My friends stared at me and laughed, seeing what was happening. They looked over my shoulder, decided that his face was good enough and his hair was neat and dark, and they nodded their approval at the prospective suitor. I'm sure he smiled at how obvious they were being and added a little pressure to me with the tip of his middle finger.

Of course, I did not move away. Even though I knew it was wrong, somebody wanted to be with me. And that was enough. I turned around to face my potential mate. He was a little under six feet but still taller than I was. His hair was so dark it was almost black. The slightest hint of stubble. And I could now feel his dick against the spot his hand had been.

We kissed. I was still dancing, though not as wildly, and his fingers squeezed my behind like he was digging through sand. Both of my friends understood what was happening; it had happened before. They pulled themselves away and danced with each other nearer the centre of the dance floor.

I pulled out of the kiss but kept dancing close to him. Then I reached down between us and grabbed him tightly in my right hand.

And I whispered into his ear, 'Let's get this home'.

51

Ant had watched from the bar. He had a vodka and tonic in his right hand and was now well over the driving limit. But he lived miles away and would still take his car later that night. For ease. He didn't like that guy's hands all over Hadley. It made him angry. He hoped that she would move away. He was worried about her. It was dirty.

When they kissed, he gripped his glass tighter and shook his head.

In a way, he admired the guy for being so brazen. He saw what he wanted and he went out and got it. Ant had been watching her, following her, getting to know her without even speaking. But he hadn't acted on his impulses.

Four minutes later, he was following her again, this time as she made her way back to her flat with a man she didn't know at all, only that his cock was way more than one handful.

They stopped in a shop doorway on the way to the taxi rank and Hadley pushed her hand down his trousers while they kissed. Ant could see everything.

She wrapped her hand around him and made a noise to say that she approved. Ant could hear everything.

They drove off in a cab. And Ant couldn't see or hear anything anymore. And he wondered why he had made such efforts to ensure this woman's safety. If this was who she really was, she was as bad as the crank calls that wasted so much of his time. He started to think that maybe he didn't like this girl, after all. That, maybe, she didn't deserve to be saved.

52

We stepped into a cab a moment later and kissed and groped and stroked each other all the way back to my flat. And I turned the key and we fell through the doorway. And we closed the door behind us. And the man whose name I had not even discovered, pushed me against that door and kissed me. And it was dark. And he was hard.

I didn't know him but I was desperate for him.

That's my way with men.

And I grabbed hold of him again and his hand was between my legs and his finger circled softly. And he pulled my top down over my shoulder and kissed my breasts, putting my nipple in his mouth and playing with it with his tongue and sucking at it. And I pushed my breasts forwards, telling him to suck me even harder.

And I said, 'I want you inside me.'

I craved the closeness. Powerless over it.

And he wasted no time in pulling my underwear down and then his own. And he grabbed me by my other shoulder and flipped me around so that my chest was against the door. And he pushed his full weight against my back and I reached between my legs to grab him and guide him into me but he was big and even though I was excited and wet, he couldn't push straight inside.

'Go slowly,' I told him. But he thrust forwards. 'Wait!' I gripped him hard and held him away. And I told him to wait again, though I was thirsty for it.

And I moved my hips back and forth, slowly. Inch by inch I forced myself towards him until his thighs were slapping at the back of me. And it hurt a little, but in a good way. And I pushed my hands against the door, forcing him backwards, but he didn't stop. And I bent myself right over until my hands were on the floor and spread my feet wide and it made sure that he entered me at an angle that worked for me. And, for him, it felt tighter, I was squeezed around him.

And I bet it hurt him a little.

But in the good way.

And the noises I made just seemed to turn him on even more, so he reached forwards and put his hand in my hair and twisted it around his fingers before pulling me back up, my back arching away from him, my head ending up next to his. I looked to the side and we kissed as he continued to fuck me from behind. And he pushed me back against the door.

And, with his other hand, he reached around to my mouth and put his finger inside against my tongue and I sucked it and bit at it. And he kept fucking. And he grabbed both of my wrists and pinned them to the door but this gave me the opportunity to push him back again so that I had the angle I wanted.

And my hands went back between my legs. And I touched myself, making my own small circles, feeling it build within me. The cock with no name slowed down, seeing what I was doing. He wanted me to get there, to remember fucking him.

'Oh, my God,' I breathed out, getting closer.

'That's it. Go on,' he urged me. 'I want to feel you come around my cock.' And he pumped himself a little harder to punctuate his statement.

And I rubbed myself while he thrust forwards and back, in and out. And I told him I was going to come. And he said, 'Yeah, that's it, baby. Come on.' And he knew he was close, too.

'I'm coming. I'm coming.' And my stomach tightened and spasmed and I pulsed around him. And he followed me a few seconds later, pulling out in time and ejaculating over my back before resting the tip against my anus, wishing he could have fired something in there, I'm sure. And it dribbled downwards but we were both out of breath and standing up before it became something awkward or ugly or self-conscious.

We stood facing each other for a moment, I leant against the door and pushed my knees together to hide anything that had started to trickle down my legs. And we both breathed heavily but he was already pulling up his trousers and tucking himself back inside his pants. And I followed by pulling up my underwear, which would be stained with a mixture of fluids. And he kissed me again when we were both dressed and he smiled and looked sexily ruffled but still manly and beautiful in my drunken eyes. And I felt drunk and stupid and a little numb.

And then we both felt a bit awkward to be stood at the door.

'You want another drink?' I asked, 'Coffee, maybe?'

And he tilted his head to the side, half apologetically and half patronisingly.

'I don't think we need to do that, do we?' But he wasn't asking a question. And he leant past me to grab the door handle and I took the hint to move out of the way. And he opened the door, stepped out onto the street, ran his fingers through his hair and started to walk back towards the club.

And I felt even more stupid and used and dirty and impetuous. And lonely. I yanked my underwear down away from me, pulled them off and wiped at myself before slamming them down on the floor and then closing the door with equal ferocity.

And this is living.

53

And Ant was walking the journey back to his car and he passed Hadley's flat at that point but on the opposite side of the road. And he saw the man from the club strutting in the opposite direction and told himself that there was no wonder this woman was calling him up, hysterical, asking for Seth when there was no Seth there. She was spiralling.

And he wanted to see her and talk to her again.

But he knew that it was not the right time.

And he carried on walking, trying to remember where he'd parked his car. And he told himself that he would see Hadley again and that next time would be different. He would help.

And he sees a newspaper through a shop window and thinks of the dead girl. And he knows that he can't save them all but he could try.

And he told himself that she didn't have to die. But, of course, deep down, he knew that she would. Everybody did.

THURSDAY

54

Seth finally got to sleep when Maeve's alarm clock sounded for the fourth time. He had to nudge her to wake up when it first let out the irritating sound of water trickling down a brook. Apparently, it woke her in a 'nice' way. It didn't. It was too quiet. It would ring and ring and ring until Seth pushed an elbow into her back.

Then she would let it play another three times, hitting snooze and drifting back to sleep while he waited, tense and on edge, for the next digital burp of liquid cruising over rocks and pebbles.

As soon as she peeled herself from the sullied bedsheets, Seth felt the stiffness in his shoulders release. She picked her clothes up off the floor and tiptoed downstairs to make her cup of morning breakfast tea.

Almost instantly, he dropped into the deepest of sleeps. There was absolute nothingness. It was black. There were no thoughts. It was bliss. He couldn't feel guilty about what he had done. He didn't think about Hadley. It was exactly what he needed. It was his routine. And then it was interrupted by the sound of the front door slamming as Maeve left for work.

She glided around the house like a ballerina all morning, warming oats and drying her hair and getting clothes from the wardrobe. No sound. Then, just as she leaves, she punctuates her time with a crashing door. It's as though she does it on purpose.

Seth is functioning on autopilot now. Tipping himself out the side of the bed, scratching his balls, trying not to open his eyes too much because it feels more like he's not really up. He showers and lets the scalding water beat him in the face. He doesn't want to masturbate but he still does. Then he wraps two towels around himself, one around the waist, the other over his shoulders. The house is always so cold at that time. Maeve has probably adjusted the timings of the heating to make him more uncomfortable, he thinks.

He lies down on the bed and falls back to sleep for fifteen minutes. When he wakes up, he's dry. He slips into the same suit he wears every day with a clean shirt on and matching tie. Then he makes a coffee, forgets about breakfast and he gets into his car and heads in for work. Late. Again.

And he hates himself a little more today.

The boss is outside, smoking. As Seth pulls in, his mobile phone vibrates in his trouser pocket. It's a text message from Maeve: *Last night was amazing!*

He reads it and sighs. It's not something he wants to think about.

But he texts her back with three kisses.

And the cycle continues.

Things can't change if you keep allowing yourself to repeat the same mistakes.

Seth collects mistakes.

55

The abrasions are there. The coroner confirms that a toothbrush was used to scrape around the walls of Theresa Palmer's vagina with bleach.

'To cover up forced intercourse?' Pace asks.

'No. There is no sign of sexual activity, forced or otherwise.' The coroner is so pragmatic, it's unnerving. He is desensitised to this on account of the things he has witnessed over the years.

'So, what, this guy just gets off on it? He's thorough? He just wants to make sure these women are clean?'

'Perhaps he sees them as dirty.'

'I've investigated both women, they were hardly whores. You couldn't find two more average women if you tried.'

'Then perhaps he sees himself as dirty. Or the world.'

That thought sits uneasily in Pace's mind. If this killer sees the world as dirty then he is probably building up to something larger, a cleansing of sorts. Maybe something mass. A shooting. A homemade bomb. Another idiot with a copy of *The Anarchist's Cookbook* underneath his pillow.

The coroner continues: 'Maybe he just hates women, you know? How often do we see that? Some guy with mummy issues. Maybe she fed him bleach as a kid or made him clean his room every day.'

His unvarnished tone is unsettling to Pace. These kinds of incidents are becoming too frequent and accepted. Pace is out there every day, blaming himself, being hard on himself, trying to stop these things from happening, trying to locate the perpetrators and take them off the streets. And this guy is talking about a human being like she is a coffee table.

'Is there anything else I need to know? Anything that stands out, that's different to the first victim?'

'I found the same marks around the anus. Also made with a toothbrush. No penetration. She had also been drinking before she died and she'd eaten a lot of rich food. Could have been out for dinner. Cause of death was strangulation, same as the other. Nothing abnormal. I'm sorry I can't give you more to go on.'

Detective Sergeant Pace is stuck.

He understands that people are sick or unhinged, that men and women do despicable and unlawful acts in the name of love or hate or loneliness. The fact that these women were beaten and bleached and scraped out on the inside is disgusting but somehow comprehendible. It's the reasoning behind it that is the issue. Why do it? Why these women? What possible motive could there be? He feels like he knew them, he knew their families and friends. What made these two so special? Or was it that they were not special?

Staring at their corpses isn't going to help.

Detective Sergeant Pace makes a decision.

Somebody has to be lying.

Everybody lies.

He has to come at it from a different angle. Rather than thinking about the killer's motives for taking their lives, he has to come at it from the victims' point of view. What was it that they needed, what was it that they were missing, that made them come into contact with the killer?

He needs those phone records.

56

It was a low day for me. I'd showered, scrubbing my body hard in too-hot water. Scratching at my skin. But I couldn't get to my mind. I couldn't clean out what was so filthy in my mind. And I looked through myself in the mirror as I slapped on enough make-up to disguise who I really was.

You're a fraud, Hadley. A fake.

I straightened my hair and grabbed at the ends, pulling them down tight so it hurt. It was a small release but I thought long and hard about cutting it off. I wanted to change myself, just not be me for a moment.

And I thought about my strange friend I had met on the phone and how he accepted me for who I am. He knew about my darkest times, he would probably be understanding of my indiscretion the night before, I imagined. That's how Seth was. The best friend I never had.

And I wished that I hadn't gone out the previous night, that I had just stayed in with my girlfriends and the wine and made that our night instead. Because I was stuck on a wheel. And maybe I should have sent them home and spoken to Seth because that would have been a perfect night: some foolishness with the people who loved me – despite the fact that I was a complete fuck-up, all I had put them through – and then onto some drunken honesty with my new friend. Maybe more. Maybe taking things further. I don't know why I think like that.

I liked Seth. He was good. He was taking my mind off my mistake.

But part of me thought it wasn't a mistake. It had felt good. The guy had a great dick. It touched parts of me that others never had. It was exciting and naughty and just what I needed at that very moment, but living in the moment was only ever good in the moment. *Oh, fuck. I'm a mess.*

My head was heavy from booze and my heart was heavier with regret, or, at least, the thought that I should regret. And I could still feel him between my legs. Right in the moment, sure, but it would be a constant reminder for the rest of the day every time I sat down. Or stood up. I would feel his beautiful cock inside me. And I would think of the next way that I could try to kill myself.

I unlocked the front door that I had been pressed against in the early hours, when the darkness was ready to turn and the streetlights were becoming redundant. I was a drunken good-time girl, out with friends, where nothing mattered but fun and frivolity and getting my most sensitive area filled by a stranger whose name I never even bothered to enquire about.

And I was trying to make myself feel disgusting. Because I thought that I should. But, actually, I had loved it. Even his come dripping down my arse or his balls beating against my clitoris as he pounded away at me, not caring about my name, either.

So, I looked at the door and smiled to myself, took a deep breath, turned the handle and stepped out into the cold; the bright-grey English sky piercing my eyes and thumping my brain. I deserved that much. And, though I wasn't ashamed of my sexual spontaneity, I was blue. I knew that going in to the office was only going to make me feel worse, but I wanted that a little.

I could wallow in my self-pity. Roll around in that feeling all day. And then deal with it when I got home. More wine. More thoughts of death. More justifying a world that didn't contain a Hadley Serf and how it would not impact anything. I was delicate but felt my significance was less than the beating of a butterfly's wing.

My death wouldn't even cause a ripple, I told myself.

And that's how I started my day.

Spiralling.

It was happening again.

The only difference was that I had Seth to talk to.

57

A van comes around at about eleven. Seth has spent the morning trying to clear his email inbox. It's one thing that gives him a little pleasure in his job. Like he beats the system by getting ahead of himself and being organised.

He's bored and numb and his body is translating that feeling into a hunger he does not truly feel. When the van arrives, he queues up with the rest of the lemmings for a foot-long baguette with brie and bacon. He takes a packet of crisps, too, and a chocolate bar that he wants to eat with his coffee but always finishes before the kettle has boiled.

He feels fat, sick and unhealthy but it's his habit now and he doesn't have the energy to fight it. And he watches as his braindead colleagues line up, even though they have a lunch already made.

Gluttons. Filing outside so they don't miss out. Choosing convenience over effort. Wanting everything right now. A world of abundance and we're all starved of nutrition and focus and appreciation of art and books and the other people around us. And Seth is one of them, to a certain extent, but at least he has the self-awareness to know that. It's what sets him apart from these animals.

He takes his cellophane-wrapped junk into the kitchen. He flips the switch on the kettle and thinks how great his chocolate will taste with a mouthful of black coffee. The mere suggestion is enough to cause him to salivate and light up the pleasure centres of his sugar-addled mind. So he bites the top of the purple wrapper and spits the corner onto the kitchen floor before tearing the rest with his hand and taking a bite. And another gluttonous chunk until nothing is left but the click of a switch and the boiling of water. And he stares at the scuffs on the toes of his work shoes.

The coffee steams away in his right hand. He takes it back to the desk. Just as he hits the comfort of his chair, the boss emerges from his glass cube and calls a meeting in the irritating regional accent Seth has learned to loathe.

'HQ need to shift three thousand laptops.' That's how he greeted them. His underlings. They all just stood there in silence, waiting in a line in front of his desk. They could have been blindfolded and on their knees anticipating that bullet to the head and their day would not have been any worse.

'A schools project in Poland has gone tits up. They've managed to shift a load in Germany but we need to get rid of the rest. Doesn't matter what you are doing, you're all on laptops for now. Make the calls. I'll send over the spec and cost price. Whoever shifts the most can have a laptop. They're good machines, so get on it.'

They didn't ask questions, they nodded and started to walk out. Seth wished all meetings were that succinct. A couple of his colleagues were excited about the possibility of winning a free laptop but they didn't have the accounts to pull something like that off.

'Seth. Can you wait behind?'

Seth rolled his eyes without actually rolling his eyes. He couldn't think about what he had done or hadn't done. He'd hit his targets. Maybe it was his lateness. He needed to find something to pull Seth up on.

'Have you still got your contacts in online retail?'

It wasn't what Seth expected.

'Yeah. Sure. I still talk to a few of them.'

'Look, can you try them with these laptops? A one-off spot deal. You can go in at a two percent margin, if you want. Just get rid of them. You'll be doing me a huge favour.'

'Isn't it going to piss the other resellers off like it did last time?'

'I'll pay you on them. You've already hit your target. You can add this on to your turnover and boost your commission. Fuck the other resellers. You know they're only going to take them in tens and twenties. You could shift them all to one place.'

'Sure, I'll see what I can do. I'm going to go out and make the calls, though. I don't want everybody listening in and getting their fucking knickers in a twist like before.'

'Do what you need. Thanks, Seth.'

Seth wasn't sure he'd ever heard his boss be grateful before. Thanks, Seth? He must really be in a bind. He'd made promises, probably, and he was panicking. He had no reason to think that Seth couldn't sell all of the bloody things but it might be fun to make him sweat a little.

Seth walked back to his desk, everyone was looking at him, wondering why he had stayed behind, some of them hoping he was in trouble, others more cynical. He perched on the edge of his office chair, opened the email with the laptop spec and price, printed it off, shut down his computer, grabbed his belongings, including the baguette he'd just bought and he left, scouring the sheets of paper in his hand, knowing exactly who he was going to call and what he was going to say.

The coffee on his desk was left to go cold. He didn't need it. He was going to sit in a café for the next couple of hours and do absolutely nothing. He was going to pick an object that he could stare at in close-up until his mind drifted to a comfortable nothingness.

58

Ant slept in. He'd had way more to drink the night before than he should have but he still managed to get his car back home without so much as a scratch.

Light was creeping through a gap in the curtains and his gut was cramping but it was cold outside the covers.

Maybe thinking about Hadley would take his mind off things.

He couldn't take it anymore. Ant flung the covers back, grabbed a T-shirt from the floor and pushed his arms and head through as he walked to the toilet, where he sat down and immediately evacuated his bowels of the booze and bad food.

It stank. He wiped. Flushed. Scrubbed his hands. And went to the kitchen cupboard beneath the sink. There, he took out one of the bottles of bleach. He poured himself a pint of water and drank it in one. Then he went back to the bathroom, which smelled worse on return.

He squirted half the bottle of bleach into the toilet bowl and he scrubbed it with the toilet brush for a good couple of minutes. And he flushed. Then he squirted the remaining half-bottle in the same way and left it to soak against the porcelain. It was amazing what bleach could do to a toilet bowl, to clothing, to skin.

Back in his room, he opened the curtains and made the bed. He put the empty bleach bottle in the recycling and washed up the plates he'd used for toast when he'd got in, drunk.

Ant, then, made himself a coffee. It hurt to grip the handle. His hands were red from cleaning and the knuckles on his right hand were tender. He thought about Hadley and her friends and the bottle of Prosecco and the man that he'd watched her kiss, who he'd seen leaving her flat. And whatever feeling it stirred within him helped with his grip on that cup of coffee.

He sat on his lounge sofa and scrolled through his numbers, stopping on the one that said 'Jackie – cousin'. That's what he'd saved Hadley's number as. It was too early to call. He could wait, make sure it was the right time. These things often required a delicate touch. He wasn't sure what he was going to do, but he knew he needed to see her again.

59

This was everyday.

The coffee was so much better, for a start. And, even though it was noisier – people shopping next door, people ordering their drinks, baristas shouting those orders across the room while a colleague repeated it back to them, mothers with babies, kids playing about – it somehow seemed more serene than Seth's office of twelve people, sitting uncomfortably, hoping people weren't listening in to their conversations.

An overweight man in his late forties was on the table next to Seth pontificating to the woman opposite him about fitness and eating well.

He bitched about his wife and the way she stuffed her face. Seth didn't like that. Not one bit. She wasn't there to defend herself and he was hardly in the right shape to be sermonising about such a topic. But he, like everything else, became white noise.

Seth's Americano was too hot. He'd ordered it black but was still asked whether he would like room for milk. These poor automatons. Grilled into staying on script. 'Good morning. How can I help you today? Would you like anything else with that? Would you like to try our Sumatran coffee bean instead, today? Can I take your name?' Two women at the end of the bar giggled as their fake names were called out by the poor student who had foamed their soya milk.

Seth pulled his mobile phone from his trouser pocket and nearly dropped it on the floor. He fumbled it a few times and broke its fall with a well-timed foot-in-the-way. He couldn't believe the screen didn't smash.

He called an old partner at an online retailer he had worked with a couple of years back. If the price was right, Seth knew he'd take all the laptops.

Two percent margin was what he had to work with. He didn't have time to play games and bump up some IT buyer's ego with negotiations he had to win. Seth gave him his rock-bottom price at four percent margin, knowing he would still want a little more off. He dropped it to the two percent he had already confirmed with his irritating boss.

'Any marketing to go with that?' the buyer asked, already knowing Seth's answer.

'They'll fly out at that price and you know it. It's a quick turnaround, Lee.'

'Ha! You're such a dick, Seth. Never give me anything.' He laughed. 'Am I going to have a bunch of disties calling me up all pissed off again?'

'Nope. Total exclusive.' Seth lied, but the ten that had probably been sold back in the office would never register with him. 'They won't even be in the warehouse a week. And I've got them ready to ship to you today.'

'I'll fax the purchase order over now.'

'Mail it to me, if you can. I'm not in the office.'

'No probs.' And he put the phone down.

Seth rested his feet on the chair opposite him. The fat guy complaining about his fat wife looked at Seth like he was a piece of shit. Seth didn't care. He dropped his chin to his chest, shut his eyes and fell asleep as his delicious coffee went cold.

60

Maeve sat in the meeting room and didn't hear a word that anybody said. Jenny's mouth moved up and down like a ventriloquist's dummy.

Wah, wah, wah. Something about current trends.

Blah, blah, blah. Something else about focus groups and testing.

Yawn, boo, hiss. Some old shit about products and branding and nothing that she could care less about while she imagined Seth above her, his skin glistening with sweat, his hips thrusting almost hatefully against her; she had felt every inch he had to offer.

She wasn't thinking about the last time that had happened. And she wasn't imagining the things that he could've been saying on the phone late at night to strange women, though her head told her she wouldn't like it if the information became something more definite. She was thinking of how close she felt to him in that moment.

Luckily, Maeve was respected enough in her field that people were intimidated by her mere presence. She could nod. She could smile. She could ignore everything that was being said and people wouldn't say a thing. Because she was Maeve and she knew. She had a golden touch and a wicked tongue when needed.

She looked out the window, the fingertips of her right hand resting against the side of her jaw. Her mind wandered and her fingers lowered so that she stroked her own neck. She let her hand fall to the table in front of her. She picked up her pen and put it in her mouth. She wasn't really listening to the presentation but had trained her ear over time to soak up the pertinent information.

Carly, her twenty-something assistant, nudged Maeve subtly against the leg and tilted a notepad towards her boss. It said, *'Want me to take notes?'* Then *'Zzzzz.'* Each z was smaller than the one preceding. The gesture made Maeve smile. It was bold for such a junior member of staff. But she was right. Another update meeting to ensure everyone could showcase their involvement in the current project.

Maeve gave Carly a subtle thumbs-up and her assistant diligently scribbled, verbatim, the information she considered of worth. And Maeve switched her attention back to her husband and her marriage and wondering what he'd made of the previous evening, whether it would settle him or aggravate him more.

The meeting finished and everyone left.

'Carly, can you type up those notes for me, please? Email them to me when you're done.'

'Absolutely. I'll do it right away.'

'If anybody needs me, I'm going to work from home this afternoon.'

She shut her laptop, threw it in its case, slung it over her shoulder and paced to the lift without looking at anybody.

She felt on edge. At once, turned on as much as she was angry. As connected as she was isolated. It was an emotional purgatory.

It wasn't where she needed to be. Not on that day.

Maeve needed a plan.

61

I took my laptop away from my desk. I'd had a habit of eating lunch there and flicking through the Internet for recipe ideas, checking my social media and watching the news. My boss had decided that, while he was pleased that I often worked through my lunch, it set a bad precedent to the newer colleagues to see me 'watching TV' instead of working – whether I was on my lunch break or not.

So, now, every day, I upped my belongings fifteen feet and sat on a sofa in the break-out area and did the exact same thing I had always done at my desk before political correctness had invaded the office with its ridiculousness.

I chewed at a triangle of crayfish, rocket and lemon mayonnaise sandwich that I had bought on the way in to work and scrolled through my friends' latest status updates. Both of them had commented on the amazing night they'd had. Pictures had been uploaded of all of us sipping Prosecco through straws. They'd commented on each other's remarks rather than just talking to one another, and other acquaintances had liked what they'd said.

Next, was my personal email account. Some junk from the many online retailers I had used that had confused me with their tick boxes. Click here if you want to receive news. Click here if you do not want to receive news. I selected all. Deleted all. Shut the page.

Then stumbled on a humorous video where a couple broke up midway around a rollercoaster ride. It was awkward but I laughed and finished the first half of my sandwich.

And I drank a carton of coconut water as I rolled my gaze over a local news story concerning the beating of a young man seemingly returning to a club the night before. I read his name – Charlie Sanders – but it didn't trigger anything in my memory. But the article described the mugging as happening opposite the chemist on my road and I wondered whether it had been the man with the beautiful penis that had fucked and left me and never made it back to the club because somebody had punched him repeatedly in the face a couple of minutes after he had left my flat. Fuck. What if he blamed me? What if he came back for me?

The story asked for anyone who may have some information to come forward. I could eliminate myself from enquiries by coming forward, telling the police what had happened, that I had been the last person to see him that night.

But I did not do that. It was probably somebody else, even though the timings seemed to correlate. I shut that page down and went back to my social media profile. And I wrote, '*Feeling it this morning. Prosecco head.*' Then I tagged my friends who undoubtedly felt the same. Each of them had clicked 'like' within two minutes of its posting.

I finished my sandwich and went back to work a little early. Best to keep myself busy. Get through the day. I hadn't beaten the guy up, it was nothing to do with me. I'd only just read his name and was already trying to forget it.

I just wanted to talk to Seth. Seth would help.

First, I drank my coffee and watched a video of 'hilarious' sporting failures.

I just wanted an escape. I knew what it felt like when my mind was beginning to falter. I was telling myself that I needed Seth but it had never mattered before about being with somebody, so I knew it didn't really matter now.

62

Things were different. Maeve was home early. Seth could smell food. She was stood at the cooker where he would usually be standing and he was in the doorway where she often lurked.

'Hey, babe.' She said, like this was normal.

'...Hey...' he hesitated.

She stirred whatever was in the pan. Seth assumed some chicken, vegetable and noodle combination, the height of her culinary expertise.

Cooking relaxed him at the end of the day. It took him away from work anxieties and the impending monotony of home life. He looked at the fridge and wondered whether the roles had reversed so much that he was contemplating pouring himself a huge glass of wine.

It was a change.

'Pour yourself a drink,' she said, as though reading his mind. He was scared to think anything true in case that was what she was doing.

Seth opened the refrigerator. There was half a bottle of Sauvignon

Blanc in the door. Maeve pushed her empty glass towards him without looking but he saw her smile to herself at her apparent coolness.

Seth took a bottle of lager out of the fridge that wasn't there that morning. She had planned this. Was she looking for some kind of repeat performance? It wasn't going to happen. He felt himself closing down. He didn't want this. It was too much. He had to call Hadley later. He couldn't have sex with his wife.

He filled her glass almost to the top. She would be three-quarters of a bottle down by the time that glass was emptied. Seth was feeling more confident of a peaceful evening.

'Go. Sit down. It won't be long. I grabbed a pudding, too.'

'What's the occasion? Big promotion at work?'

'Oh, ha bloody ha. What? I can't cook dinner once in a while?'

'No, no. You carry on. I'll put my feet up. Get the TV on. Not the news, though, eh? I can't see that family crying and pleading again. Something light.'

'Sure, sure. It's up to you.'

He was pleased. The desperation in the eyes of the parents and boyfriend was odd to watch. Not uncomfortable, just strange. Maeve was fascinated by that sort of thing but Seth didn't see the point in looking at it. Ninety percent of the country were watching that and shouting at their screens that the boyfriend or the father were to blame. It's always someone close to the victim. Nobody ever suspects the mother.

Seth does.

You can't underestimate these women.

He sat on his sofa with his cold beer and hit the on button on the remote control. It was already on the news channel. The parents and boyfriend weren't crying and pleading. There was a police detective talking with a field behind him. An area had been cordoned off with police tape. The text at the bottom said, '*Body found in Warwickshire*'. He turned the volume up and the words 'bleached and wrapped in plastic' boomed from the speakers. He heard the wooden spoon drop in the kitchen then Maeve was behind him.

'They found her, then?'

'Looks that way.'

Seth changed the channel to a programme about a middle-aged couple trying to restore an old water tower and convert it into a house.

Maeve went back to stirring noodles and drinking wine.

63

He's so shut down, Maeve thought. She looked across at the other sofa; Seth's back was turned towards her slightly. Not a lot, but enough to convey his apparent disdain.

They'd never been the kind of couple to share a sofa, it had never been like that, but Maeve was left wondering when it had changed to be like this. She wracked her brains to find a definitive time that something had gone wrong. But nothing had. Maybe it was never right. They'd been together so long now it was almost impossible to remember.

And it hurt her brain to go over it by herself for another evening. So she drank a little more to numb herself. And she looked over at Seth again. He just looked uncomfortable. Tight. Hunched. And tired. Always so tired.

But she knew, the more tired he got, the more irritable he became, the more things weren't quite real for him. And the more he didn't sleep, the more he fucked things up – with work, his friends, his remaining family. When he did that, it was the time he needed Maeve the most.

And she loved that.

But he kept his back turned slightly to her that night, not furthering any conversations, not entering into anything with her. She told him how boring her meeting had been but forgot to ask him about his day. She drank some more and watched him fidget in his seat. And she knew he just wanted her to go to bed so he could torture himself with a cup of late-night coffee and whatever it was that tormented his mind so much and he could make those calls to strangers. She knew what he was up to. She knew him. And he wanted her out of the way so that he could get on and focus on his weird, little hobby. His insomnia project.

And she could have made things easier on him, taken a glass of wine upstairs with her, read a little more of her book. But she didn't. She drank on the sofa, her sofa, and she slid down to a lying position once that last drop entered her mouth. She looked over at his back one last time, then shut her eyes and went to sleep.

Why?

Fuck him, that's why.

64

'You want to meet up?'

Seth waited until Maeve hauled her arse up the stairs, he made his coffee and he called Hadley. He was excited. He found that he had missed her.

They talked for a while about nothing. Their days at work, what they had done the night before. Neither of them going into huge amounts of detail. He wanted to hide what he had done. And he didn't want to know if she needed to hide anything.

Then she asked him that.

'You want to meet up?'

'Sorry?'

He wasn't even sure how things progressed so quickly. Sure, they'd started out on a fairly intimate level, she'd divulged her innermost demons and he talked her down from the ledge. He listened. He didn't judge. They'd bonded furiously over her most innocent truth and his terribly selfish lie.

Regardless, something had clicked, sparked, connected.

They were moving fast but he couldn't believe that it had already come to that point.

'You want to meet up?'

'Sorry?'

'Meet up. You know, for coffee, or something?'

It seemed brazen, at first. He was turned on. She was a woman who wanted something and wasn't afraid to go and get it. But what did she mean by coffee? Did she actually mean meeting for a drink and talking face to face or was it something else? All of these questions jumped around his mind and bumped into each other and exploded. Talking to another woman on the phone was one thing, craving her, missing her, thinking about her, was something larger that he needed to address, but meeting her in person seemed too hasty. A step too far. Devious.

He had done it before but it never went the right way. It should have stayed an over-the-phone thing. Faceless and harmless. Maeve and Seth had their difficulties, but he would never cheat on her. Not like that. She didn't deserve that from him.

He couldn't do it again. He couldn't meet Hadley.

'You want to meet up?'

'Sorry?'

'Meet up. You know, for coffee, or something?'

'Coffee?'

'It's a hot, brown caffeinated drink. We can meet somewhere crowded so you know I'm not a psycho.' She laughed.

He'd trapped himself. Painted into a corner. He couldn't back down. And he didn't really want to.

'Sure. Hot, brown caffeine sounds very appealing.'

Her request seemed innocent. Harmless, even. And it probably was. But it always seemed that way to start with.

He took down the details of where to meet. It would be the next day.

He wanted it to be the morning, already.

Seth never wanted to sleep so much in his life.

Of course, he didn't sleep. Not until Maeve left the house with her customary slam of the door.

Fuck her.

FRIDAY

65

It wasn't even a sick day. Seth called his boss and said he needed the day off.

'What's up, Beauman?' he asked, almost sounding genuinely concerned. Of course, he wasn't.

'I just need a day, that's all. I can't put my finger on it, but I'm not quite right.'

'Well, fuck, we all know that.' He laughed.

Seth hated lying and he hated that he was grovelling to his cretin of a boss. He remembered the last time he had taken a day off, and it had been absolutely necessary. It wasn't anything like this.

'Just a day, huh? No longer? No doctor's note?'

'Just a day.' Seth didn't want to give him any more than that. He knew Seth wasn't unwell, he was just prodding him, having a little fun.

'Look, Seth, you've smashed your target already and you managed to shift all of those problem laptops by yourself, so take the rest of the month off for all I care. I've got one of those laptops here for you, too, when you're ready. Just let me know when you're coming back and you can pick it up. Okay?'

'Sure. Thanks.' He hated showing gratitude. 'But it won't be longer than tomorrow. Just a day, as I said.'

His boss left the conversation without saying goodbye. It didn't bother Seth. He was in the house alone and he had a few hours to get himself into a respectable and presentable shape for his lunch with Hadley, the woman he had met over the phone. Who thought he was someone he was not.

Seth was excited and terrified. And turned on.

It wasn't really a lunch date, he'd overplayed that in his mind. It was only a coffee. He probably could've just left the office for a couple of hours, said he had a meeting. Whatever. But he just felt like he needed to ready himself. Steady himself.

He was going to meet up with a woman who was not his wife. Or a female friend. Yes, it was for coffee. Yes, that seemed innocent. But everything was based on a lie. She thought he was someone he was not. They had met in circumstances that were not regular. Seth may not be completely content with Maeve, for whatever reason, but she knows him, she knows who he is. Who he really is.

That counts for something. A lot.

But, still, this other woman, she intrigued him. She excited him in a way that his wife had not excited him for years. A verdant pasture. And maybe that is the damage of time and familiarity but it was something that he needed to feel.

He had to be prepared. He had to embody this personality he had created for Hadley. This laid-back, funny, attentive guy. Seth was sensitive and open. He was willing to be vulnerable. He was confident in himself.

This was some kind of crazy blind date. Except he knew what Hadley looked like. She was the opposite of Maeve. Young and tight and blonde.

He had to be prepared.

But Seth tapped the code into his phone to unlock it and opened Hadley's online profile to take a look at that picture of her with the wet hair. And he pulled his trousers down to his thighs. And he looked at her face and the sunshine in the background. And he tugged and squeezed. It was hard. It was fast.

He had to be ready for her.

They were meeting in three and a half hours.

He grunted as he came over his own stomach. Then he laid back on the sofa he'd slept on the night before, shut his eyes and slept for two dirty hours.

66

Charlie Sanders knew where Hadley lived.

He could go back there any time he wanted, hoping for a repeat performance. Sure, he hadn't left things on the best of terms but he was so full of bravado. That was half the attraction for him. The thrill of the chase. Getting shot down, only to prevail in the end.

He had enjoyed himself. He remembered that.

But he also remembered what it felt like being hit from behind. And he remembered that foot coming down against his face. And part of him was a little pissed off with Hadley about that. And the fact that he had to cancel all of his bank cards because his wallet was taken.

He could return to the scene of the first crime that night, his infidelity with a stranger he had met in a club.

But this was Charlie Sanders, he only did what he really wanted to do, the things that benefitted Charlie Sanders.

And you can read in the newspapers or magazines about cancer and obesity and mosquito bites, but there is never any research carried out on how many deaths are caused by laziness and selfishness.

67

The women in Seth's life went about their days as they usually did, both using caffeine to push themselves over the hump of another laborious week.

Maeve locked herself in her office and barked at anyone who came within ten feet of her laptop. But she thought about her husband. She'd heard the mumbling on the telephone again from what was becoming her bedroom and she didn't like it. Not one bit. She knew he was about to make a mistake before even he did.

And Hadley kept her head low in that open-plan room. Voices

mingled and overlapped around her before turning white. Time was doing its best to stop, that morning. She had taken to writing down every half-hour increment until she was due to leave for her lunch to meet her phone friend. She crossed off 10:00–10:30. She'd been watching the clock in the corner of her computer monitor for two minutes with a pencil poised to scribble out the latest thirty minutes. It was an exercise that was supposed to help time pass quicker. It wasn't working.

She, too, thought of Seth, without knowing what he looked like, his build, his hairline. She didn't care. She hadn't even imagined a face, not one that she could recall in her mind. But she felt like she knew his eyes. Just from his voice and the way he spoke to her, and the way he listened. They were dark and kind. Without ever seeing Seth Beauman, Hadley felt that she knew that.

Maybe he could save her.

Seth managed to hold an affectionate and understanding look with great ease, even through that perpetually tired gaze that had become his trademark. Hadley was right about that. But she had no idea, yet, that, by being so open, she was letting herself become Seth's latest mistake.

At 11:45, both women made themselves another cup of coffee, their last before lunch. Three minutes later, Seth awoke feeling more tired than when he'd shut his kind, affectionate eyes. Before he panicked and lost his breath.

68

Another symptom of Seth's chronic fatigue is the choking, the drowning. That is what it feels like. He wakes up, angrily, and out of breath. It was terrifying at first. He assumes it's his own version of sleep apnoea. But he doesn't snore or talk or laugh in his sleep, he opens his eyes and the air is sucked from his lungs. He fights to drag it back inside himself but panic takes hold.

It still does, even now. And he has learned to calm himself, to regain composure. To breathe. But there's always that moment that he thinks he might die. He calms himself by accepting it.

It took longer this time because he didn't accept it; he didn't want to die. He wanted to go for coffee, sort things out. He panicked. His eyes were wide as he heaved. And he hoped. Hoped it would stop the way it always did. It probably only went on for half a second longer than usual but time can play tricks and that half-second felt like five. He tried to suck air into his lungs but it never got past his throat. His hand went to his chest. Maeve popped into his mind. That said something.

And a little air crept into his lungs. Then more. And more. And more. He sat up on the sofa. His throat felt as though it had been scratched. He blinked his eyes. It had ruined the extra sleep he had sneaked into his day.

After regaining his breath, he wiped his forehead with the back of his arm and checked his phone screen quickly. He still had over an hour before he was due to meet Hadley. There were no missed calls from work. There were no text messages from Maeve. Being here, doing what he was doing, was making no impact on anyone's day.

He was invisible. It was just how he wanted to be.

69

After a while of staring down a list of telephone numbers, everything dissolves into binary or Morse code. It's just lines and dots and brackets. Pace thinks he should just wave his finger over the list and take a punt. But not one of his cases has ever been solved by using mathematics. Not that he can recall.

Detective Sergeant Pace is fading.

Detective Sergeant Pace is being swallowed by his own shadow.

He could do with a break. Or some luck.

Theresa Palmer's mother had tried to contact her every day for a week. She left three voicemail messages per day, spread out evenly across each twenty-four-hour period, morning, noon and night. And then, the day before her estimated death, there was nothing. None. No calls.

Pace's mind jumps to the worst, because that is how he sees people. What if the mother somehow knew that her daughter had died? Perhaps she stopped calling because she no longer needed to, she knew where Theresa was.

Maybe it was an accident and she panicked.

Maybe she was protecting somebody else. Her son. Her lover.

Maybe that's why Pace can find no link to Daisy Pickersgill. The Palmers were alarmed and tried to cover things up by copying a previous murder. They cleaned Theresa up and drove her to a different park in Warwickshire – but still in the vicinity – and dumped her remains to be found and attributed to the same murderer.

Detective Sergeant Pace is reaching.

He can't find a reason that these women are linked so he is trying to find a way that they are not linked. He's forcing it. He wants an answer.

It's all he has. So he arranges to call around and speak with Theresa Palmer's family again.

70

Hadley crossed off that final half-hour. Each one had incrementally lengthened time and only she had noticed. She looked around her office and everything was as it always was. Nobody but her knew that today was something special. Something different. Their days had moved on at that steady, laborious pace that signalled it was a weekday.

She hit the ctrl, alt and delete buttons on her keyboard and logged off. She'd learned not to leave it open, that there was always some prankster around who would change her wallpaper to something inappropriate or email someone from her account admitting her apparent fondness for them. Immature idiots.

As Hadley stood up, Maeve was twirling endless circles in her office chair, turning events over in her mind. The amazing sex they'd had that week. Where had it come from? Even at their lowest, the sex had been great. They had that passion, the connection that you just can't fake – even if the emotion behind it was something much different.

And as Hadley rotated in that swivel chair, Ant was busy cleaning his flat, scrubbing the laminate floor in the lounge by hand rather than using a mop. Getting into every corner. Moving every piece of furniture so that no square centimetre was left unclean. He hated himself for sweating because it meant he had to keep washing himself to avoid contaminating areas he had already cleaned.

His knuckles still hurt from his night out and he needed to sleep before his shift that night, but he kept on wiping and dusting and bleaching, anyway.

As Ant sanitised his home and Maeve rotated in her seat and Hadley paced towards the exit of her office, Seth Beauman was sat in the coffee shop, waiting for a girl he had only spoken to over the phone. And he felt excited. But the coffee cup on the table in front of him was all that he could see. He was more tired than ever and he hoped that wouldn't make him fuck it all up again.

71

He waited. Seth was there early so that he could see her walk in.

He'd told her what he'd be wearing, like some old-fashioned blind date. That had made him feel a little awkward about the meeting. It was the first time he'd really considered how this would make Maeve feel if she found out. But that thought never made it all the way to guilt.

Of course, Seth knew what Hadley looked like, he recognised her the moment she entered. But he had to pretend that he didn't. He held back, though his heart was racing furiously.

She looked as though she had made no effort. Like she was wearing the same old thing she usually wore for work. Her jeans were a dark blue that held on to the skin of her legs for dear life. And she wore a plain black vest that made her look like she might work in GAP. But her movement was fluid and her neck was long as she peered around the café for her unknown new friend, who was also wearing jeans and an ill-fitting burgundy Ramones T-shirt despite only having heard one of their songs.

She trod carefully, scouring the room. Her eyes went past Seth twice before locking in. She stepped closer and closer. Seth tilted his head to one side and screwed his eyes slightly as if to say, 'Is it...?'

'Seth?' she asked. Her voice sounded different to the phone voice.

'Hadley?'

She smiled a great, white, gravestone-teeth smile and lines appeared around the sides of her eyes that Seth was sure she undoubtedly hated and thought aged her but he thought was a beautiful quirk. That thought alone told him that he was heading down a path of no return.

He stood up to greet her. He didn't know whether a hug would be too much and ended up just moving his hands about uncomfortably. Eventually, he held out his right hand and she took it in hers. Like he was greeting her for a job interview.

'Sorry, I've been here a while so I already have a coffee. I'm going to get another one, what would you like?'

'It's fine, I can grab a coffee.'

'No, no, no,' Seth insisted, ushering her to sit down on the seat opposite his. 'Let me get them. Do you want anything to nibble on?' He immediately regretted that phrase, it made me sound like a dick.

'Food?'

'Yeah. Something to eat.'

'Why don't I come with you and pick something? You can pay, if that makes you feel better.' And she smiled again, the smile he was sure he could sense and feel over the phone had become something real that he could see. And it looked exactly as he had imagined it. This girl was something special.

Seth had a black coffee, BLT on wholemeal bread and a bar of milk chocolate. Hadley opted for a cappuccino, grilled vegetable wrap and blueberry muffin. They sat at the table and talked.

And it was so effortless. They rarely encountered a moment of silence and even when they did it felt comfortable. They spoke briefly about the strange way in which they had met and Seth felt the lies roll off his tongue as easily as the truths. But the rest of the time, they were learning about one another.

'I've never done this before,' he lied.

The hour they had breezed past. Seth felt like they had spoken about everything but also covered very little of what he wanted.

And then she looked at her phone and said, 'Well, I've got to get back to the office.' And she pulled a silly face, an overly exaggerated sigh.

'That sucks.'

'Pretty much. This lunch will be the highlight of my day.'

Seth smiled at that. She was feeling what he was feeling, he was sure of it.

'Hey, we can still talk tonight.'

'Ah, yes. End the day with something positive. An excellent proposition.'

Hadley stood up and Seth mirrored her. It felt like he could hug her goodbye and it wouldn't be misconstrued, but he relented, anyway.

'Until we speak again, then, Mr Beauman.' She walked away with a subtle wave of the hand.

'I'll call you.'

Seth sat back down so that he could watch her leave. She was all that he was watching so was all that he could see.

The excitement dissipated. The tiredness remained. The guilt never came.

It never had.

72

The nicest person you know, the one who is always there for you when you need them, the one who is strong and full of support and great advice, they're not strong. And they don't feel nice. They're wondering why they are never asked how they are doing. They are starting to think that people are just a little bit selfish and self-involved. They are wondering who they have to talk to.

You think they are a great friend, and they are wondering where all their friends have gone.

And that mum or dad in the playground – the one who is always immaculately turned out and on time with their kids, who all look happy and clean and matching, and you're wondering just how they do it all and hold down a job, and volunteer at the school fête and take the kids to ballet or gymnastics or cub scouts – they're a wreck. They're just about holding it together.

They shout at their kids and hate themselves for it. They're constantly tired and caffeine has little effect. They drink too much and eat too little and they bribe their kids with unhealthy food and hate themselves for that, too. And they talk to you in the playground but it's not their real voice, it's their pretending-everything-is-okay voice. And they are slowly breaking down.

There's that rich guy who can't buy love. And there's that poor guy, who is so in love but can't afford his rent.

And that happy couple who met in their teens and have been together since – the ones you look up to and aspire to be like; it gives you hope that there is true love in the world; and you like being around them because it makes you feel good – they are both fucking other people. And they're having trouble juggling their secret lives.

Or the successful, together woman with the great job and workers who respect her. She lies in bed awake at night, listening to the murmur of her husband on the phone to strangers. She knows he's a good man, she knows there's nothing going on, she knows it's a project or a weird hobby, but she wants that energy to come in her direction once in a while.

Who do these people talk to, confide in?

We all need that Good Samaritan at times. To take our minds off the simple struggles and the taxing hardships.

Even that girl, who you don't think about that often, because she's kind of average. She's not bitchy, always polite, gets on with her job. She has a boyfriend and it all seems stable. She is close to her mother and her stepfather. And her younger brother is like a friend. You don't really think about her because she's not on the radar but that doesn't mean that she didn't need somebody to talk to. Somebody new.

Theresa Palmer needed somebody.

And somebody came by, saw her, and took pity on her.

73

Maeve came home to the smell of something delicious and was completely unaware that her husband had taken the day off work. He was worried that it would be the first time she would actually ask him how his day had been and he would have to lie.

But, of course, she didn't. She walked into the house, said hello, grabbed some wine from the fridge and told Seth how her last eight hours had been black-and-white monotonous drivel, that she found herself humming a tune she had made up that was definitely in a minor key. And she gulped down Chardonnay.

'What's on the menu tonight, then?' She stood close to him and looked over his shoulder playfully. Her hand touched the small of his back affectionately. Seth didn't flinch.

'Chickpea and aubergine stew – tomatoey but with some lovely spices – and a lemon, parsley and saffron couscous.'

'Sounds bloody lovely. No meat?'

'Not tonight.'

'And those spices go well with Chardonnay, right?' He felt her smiling behind him.

'Does it matter?' And he pushed open the fridge door without looking, to display the wine bottle for her to top up her glass.

They sat at the table for a change because the sauce threatened to stain everything it was dripped on. The TV still went on. Straight to the news.

Police in Warwickshire have been reaching out to anyone who may have information on the body of a young woman found this week by a dog walker. She has recently been identified as Theresa Palmer, a 32-year-old nurse who went missing six weeks ago.

'Maeve, can we eat one meal without watching this trash? Please.'

'It's not trash. It's real life. I want to see what they say.'

Seth rolled his eyes. It was as if she got some kind of excitement out of it. The same as all those books on her nightstand. He forked another spoonful of the couscous into his mouth.

A dark shadow of a man appeared on the screen. The writing at the bottom informed viewers his name was Detective Inspector Pace.

'He's kind of tired and evil-looking for a policeman,' Maeve said.

'His eyes are darker than mine.'

'Evidence, so far, suggests a possible link to a previous case but we urge anyone with any information about the night Theresa went missing to come forward and aid in our investigation.' It was pretty standard stuff. Pleading with the British public to help a poor young girl's surviving family to get some closure while also getting justice. Striking fear into viewers that this could be a run of murders, that they may not be safe themselves.

'That makes things so much more interesting.' Maeve's eyes lit up.

'Drink your wine, detective.'

And she did drink her wine. And she did lie down on the sofa. And they did watch something else on TV that was more light-hearted. And she did fall asleep. And she eventually dragged herself to bed where she lay awake for a while. Just listening.

She heard Seth squeakily stand up from the sofa. She heard the kettle click on and the creak of the lounge door closing. And the mumble of late-night conversation. But she didn't hear the words clearly. She didn't hear what Seth was laughing at. She didn't hear him arrange to meet with his new secret friend again the next day.

She was getting tired of his project. Tired of work. She switched off from it and, that night, went to sleep thinking about poor Theresa Palmer.

SATURDAY

74

It was the lead story on the early-morning weekend news.

'The stepfather of recently murdered Theresa Palmer has been taken in for further questioning in the early hours of this morning. It has not yet been confirmed whether the man was arrested or came freely. The 59-year-old, Martin Creed, a carpenter from Bermondsey, has known the victim since her early teenage years.'

Then the news cuts to footage of Detective Sergeant Pace walking in through the front doors of a police station. The sky is dark but he is darker. His face is stubble and his coat is leather and everything he touches looks to be turning black.

'Police say that they are following up on earlier questions and would still like to speak with her boyfriend, 34-year-old Jacob Flynn, who has not been seen for almost two days.'

And they bring up a moody picture of Jacob next to the smiling face of his dead girlfriend.

And half the country watch and say that he's run because he's guilty.

And the rest say, 'It's always the stepdad.'

Detective Sergeant Pace sits across a desk from Martin Creed and tells him the time that the interview commences and that it is being recorded.

Detective Sergeant Pace is barking.

Detective Sergeant Pace is a hellhound.

75

Maeve slammed the door – no work, just Pilates class. But she wasn't waking Seth up. He was already awake. He'd been awake for most of the night. His sleep was getting worse and worse. She was worried about her husband. His eyes were ruined, like he spent most of his days crying.

They were getting smaller and darker, with crêpe-paper skin. Lost in shadow.

She hoped it was a consequence of the guilt he felt for pursuing another woman. He'd done it a couple of times before. He'd told her about them both. He'd had to. And he swore blind that there was nothing physical involved. And she had informed him that, 'Just because you're not fucking, doesn't mean it isn't unfaithful.' He'd agreed and apologised and she'd stuck by him dutifully, helping him clean up the mess.

Yet, still, he continued. And he may have thought he was being quiet or secretive but it was brazen and disrespectful and right in front of her face. She told herself it was the tiredness. That he gets lost in it. He thinks he is thinking things but is saying them out loud. He acts differently. She sticks up for him in her head, telling herself that he can't help it. That he has an illness. That it's hard for him on such little rest. He doesn't know what is real? He might not even be doing all the things he thinks he is doing.

But even through her justifications and allowances, it still hurt. And this one was worse because there was a familiarity there that hadn't been before. It felt different. Bigger.

And she knew that his lack of sleep had nothing to do with guilt. Because he was incapable of that emotion. So she slammed that door every morning, whether Seth was asleep or not, whether she was working or not. It wasn't to inform him of her anger, it was to play with him, mess with him, just as he seemed to be enjoying messing and playing with her.

76

They met later in the day this time. For drinks. After Hadley finished her exercise class, later in the day, of course, because she was younger and still had that luxury of a lie-in. Seth probably could have worked out, too. But it didn't seem worth it for one day. And he just didn't want to. Hadley was his motivation, not computer monitors or bonuses or paying off his mortgage or doing some cardio or lifting weights. His boss had mistakenly said that Seth could sit with his feet on the desk for the rest of the month if he hit target early, and Seth was going to be using that against him and the gym could continue to take his thirty-five pounds each month despite not seeing him for almost a year.

Hadley's hair was tousled from tying it up after her shower. Her apparent lack of care for her own presentation merely added to her allure. Seth was mesmerised. Again, he'd arrived early and had a couple of pints of lager on his own.

This time, he didn't have to pretend that he didn't know what she looked like, that he hadn't looked up her social media page, that he'd never beaten off to her profile picture. He just waved a hello. And she hugged him when she got to the table. And kissed him politely on each cheek.

'You got the coffees; it's my round,' she spoke with a fake sternness. Seth held his hands up in surrender. 'Same again?'

'Yes, please.'

He watched her walk to the bar. She didn't look back.

Seth's vision was getting worse each day. He couldn't remember a time it had been this bad. It was so frustrating because he knew how tired he was, he knew what was keeping him up but he couldn't do anything about it. Nothing worked. But even without it, he knew that all he'd be seeing that night was her. It was like she was from another time, another place. He didn't notice anyone else in that bar.

They talked and drank. She was flirting with him; her hand kept on touching his legs as she laughed. Seth found himself to be funnier than he had been in years. He wasn't sure where that fun part of him went. It just died somewhere along the line. He became boring, maybe. Bedded in, somehow. Reclusive. He didn't see any of his old friends. All he had was Maeve. And that was great for a long time, because it was all he wanted.

Now he has a new friend. Hadley. And she is telling him that he is sweet and considerate and a great listener. She says, 'Oh, Seth, you crack me up.' And she drinks a lot of wine but not in the same habitual way that Maeve does. He doesn't want to compare them, but that does stand out.

But she is desperate; even in his fugue state, Seth knows that is real.

All the chatter and rabble around their booth drops into a hum, Seth watches Hadley's mouth. All he can see are lips and teeth and the flicker of tongue as she regales him with one of her post-university travelling adventures or misspent evenings with friends fuelled by alcohol and bad decisions. He wonders whether it is really happening or it's all in his head.

Why would she want to be here with me? Is this too quick?

'Think you've had a few too many, Seth?' She giggles, sipping a cocktail through two straws and pursing her lips at the citrus.

'No. I'm just tired. I don't sleep much.' It felt good to say something true.

A man walked past and bumped Hadley's elbow. He apologised and continued walking. Neither Seth nor Hadley saw his face.

'Bit rude,' she said, half serious.

'He apologised, I guess.'

She nodded, drunk.

'So, we've had lunch and a liquid dinner. Fancy making more of a night of it tomorrow?' It was booze-fuelled confidence on Seth's part.

'You do move fast.'

'I'll take that as a yes.'

She nodded again. 'Life's too short to fuck about, eh?'

Seth lifted his glass and Hadley clinked it with her own.

'To long life,' she suggested.

'Long life,' he repeated.

And they drank.

Then they just looked at one another. It was as if nobody else was there. Just the two of them. Invisible. Like they were falling in love but both of them knew it wasn't that at all. Nobody knew the significance of that night. Nobody else could see them.

77

Ant could see them.

He'd been watching them all night.

And he wasn't happy about it.

He had followed her from her workout, thinking that he might try to call her again when she got home, but she hadn't gone straight home. So he'd ended up in a bar, watching Hadley with another man. For the second time that week.

He looked at the knuckles on his right hand.

Still tender.

He stood at the bar, just as he had done the night she had gone out with her friends. He drank beer and watched.

He watched as she flirted with another man, putting her hand on his arm, laughing at all his jokes, smiling, licking her lips. Why had she called the Samaritans that night? Why had her voice gone into his ear? Why could she not have ended up with someone who wouldn't continue to care what was happening with her?

He just couldn't stop himself.

That was his problem.

The man with her had a loud and annoying laugh. But Ant witnessed how close she was getting with him. He wanted to see who the guy was that was so beguiling, who was undoubtedly going to win over her heart and get into her pants just as that tight-T-shirted muscle-head had done earlier in the week.

Ant had to see his face but obscure his own.

He saw that her arm was hanging slightly off the edge of the table as she placed her hand on her would-be suitor's arm for the fiftieth time. And he walked towards her. Quickly, so she didn't see it coming. She wasn't expecting it. He deliberately bumped his waist into her elbow to jolt her.

She was too preoccupied with spilling her drink to look up at his face, but he managed to catch a glimpse of the man she was with. Ant apologised and kept walking, on to the toilet where he rewashed his face, poured away his drink and then left unseen to wait across the road from Hadley's flat until she got home.

She arrived thirty-five minutes later. On her own. Ant smiled. That idiot must have gone in too strong.

He waited another few minutes before calling her on her home phone.

'Couldn't wait until later, huh?'

She had picked the phone up thinking it was Seth. They'd agreed to talk on the phone again that night. It had become their thing. It was quirky and romantic and individual to their relationship.

'Sorry?' Ant asked.

'Seth?'

And it clicked. She had been with Seth. The man he had seen was Seth, the one she had been asking for when she'd called and barged her way into Ant's life and everyday thoughts.

'Sorry, Miss Serf, this is not Seth. This is the Samaritans.'

'Really? You guys go way beyond the call of duty.' She was drunk.

'It is a follow-up call. I assure you, it is policy when a person in distress hangs up the conversation abruptly.'

'Well, there's no need to follow up again. I'm sorry, I was hysterical that night but I'm okay now. I found Seth. I'm happy.'

Ant wasn't convinced. He had to keep an eye on her. And find out more about this Seth. To keep things clean.

SUNDAY

78

Pace is out of suspects.

Martin Creed's alibi checked out. Either the victim's mother was protecting her partner or the poor guy was innocent and had just lost a stepdaughter he had known from a young age and helped raise into a politely average young corpse. Pace was inclined to think that way, too. But his second bout of questioning meant that Martin Creed was tarnished in the eyes of the public. And he wouldn't live that down until the true murderer was found.

And Theresa's boyfriend, Jacob, hadn't run off. He had taken some leave to get away from the situation because he was so upset. He went to stay with some family in Manchester to avoid the media and all the questions being fired at him.

Deep down, Pace knows that neither of them is guilty but he has to follow some line of enquiry. These two murders are linked. Nothing ties Martin or Jacob to the first victim. The questioning merely helped to eliminate them from suspicion.

There are two dead girls. Their deaths are spaced months apart. Nobody is using the term 'serial killer' just yet but Pace feels it. He knows.

Detective Sergeant Pace knows.

At one time, Ted Bundy had only killed two people. And Peter Sutcliffe. And Nilsen. Gacy. Shipman.

The thing is, when fifteen hookers go missing or a bunch of homosexual men from the same town turn up dead or everyone's grandmother on your street has been euthanised, it gives the police somewhere to look, a place to aim their enquiries.

Detective Sergeant Pace is in purgatory.

Where should he focus? On average women? On sweet, well-mannered women? It may not just be women.

Detective Sergeant Pace is starting to hate the city.

He wants to go back home.

But he can't. Not with this thing hanging around his neck.

Not with that thing following him around every day.

He can't take that darkness back to Hinton Hollow.

79

He told Maeve there was a work night out.

'After work drinks yesterday?'

'That was just a couple of us that have done really well against our target. That was a few drinks. This is dinner and drinks. Maybe a club. Who knows? It's like an incentive. As long as I'm not paying.' Seth smiled through his lie. And she bought it. He thought.

That night, he took the car. He said that he would maybe not have that much after drinking the night before, that if he did end up with a few glasses of wine in him, he would leave the car and pick it up the next morning.

The truth was that he just lived too far from Hadley. And he didn't know where the evening would lead; he might need the car.

He'd been thinking about it all day. He was brighter than usual, seemingly enjoying the trip around the supermarket with Maeve to pick up a few extras: salad leaves, hummus – wine, of course – and the Sunday newspaper with all its many supplements. Maeve was only interested in that front-page story. It consumed her attention.

It was the girl, wrapped up and dumped in the earth for anyone to find.

It was the detective, dark and mysterious and somehow alluring.

It was morbid fascination and curiosity and the preoccupation that most living things have with death.

Seth hadn't slept at all last night, so driving was a huge mistake. Place names jumped off the road signs as he powered down the motorway, Beaconsfield, Thame, Didcot. Then he hit the ring road around Oxford. He could see the old buildings that must have belonged to the various colleges but the one-way system seemed to be taking him away from them. It was frustrating him. He was excited about seeing Hadley but anxious about getting there. He was starting to sweat. He threw on the air-conditioning. It didn't make him dry, it just made his sweat cold.

He eventually found a car park. It already seemed to be emptying out. A few spaces had been cordoned off for a tree surgeon's crane. Spaces either side were free. He guessed that people were worried that their cars could be damaged in the process of trimming some branches, or something. Seth carried no such regard for his vehicle. It also felt like it hid the car from view a little. He was paranoid that he'd be seen by somebody that he knew; even though he was miles from home, there was always a chance.

Hadley had asked him to meet for a drink, first, at a place call Beerd. He typed it into his phone and followed the map on the screen. It took four minutes to walk there from his car. He tried not to look at the screen too much because he didn't want to stand out and look like a tourist.

He saw the sign. A picture of an orange beard with the word 'Beerd' beneath. It was small and trendy and they boasted a wide selection of craft beers, which was very *en vogue*.

Hadley was already there. Sitting at the bar, drinking something blonde. She smiled that smile of hers at the man who was talking with her. A huge part of Seth was excited about that night. Another part was trepidatious; this was a first date, wasn't it? And he hadn't had a first date in almost two decades.

And then there was a part that was anger. Who was this guy? And why was he talking to his first date? If he was that archetypal attentive barman, would Seth be needed?

Was he just being used? He was there, he'd do.

'Seth.' She jumped off her stool and flung her arms around him. Seth looked at the man behind her. He looked at Seth. He knew what Seth was thinking.

She let go of Seth's neck and turned to the man she had been speaking with. 'Anyway, have a good night,' he said. Then he nodded at Seth and walked back to his table with his round of four comically named ales.

'I've had a couple already. Oops.' She laughed at herself and put one of her small, delicate hands on Seth's chest.

'What have you had?'

'A pint of Bounders. And a pint of Cubic ... and some popcorn.'

Seth spotted the popcorn machine behind the bar.

'It's the snack of champions.'

'Exactly.' She drained the remainder of her pint and turned back to the bar. There was one barman on duty and he looked exhausted. He had short, dirty-blond hair and was sweating but his face was kind and he was trying his best to accommodate the masses. He seemed also to be the waiter and would disappear into the kitchen – where Seth assumed there was also only one person – before emerging again behind the bar to pour pints of Darkside and Animal.

The barman chose to go to Hadley before the gaggle of men that had been waiting patiently before her.

'Two pints of Punk, please. And one for yourself.'

'Thanks very much,' he responded, not really looking at either of them.

Seth didn't know if Hadley was flirting or ensuring that he always came to her first when there was a queue. It didn't matter. He poured their drinks, chalked one up for himself to have when the bar closed, and they sat at one of the tables jutting from the wall opposite the bar. The music played at a level that was audible enough for you to know that it was on but quiet enough that you couldn't quite make out what the song was.

Seth drank that first pint quickly. He needed it. The talk wasn't as effortless for him. She was already well oiled and raring to go. Seth was looking at her and feeling things that he shouldn't feel. He needed to feel that way but also, he knew he shouldn't. But he didn't know if he could stop it, how to stop, or if stopping it would even help.

Hadley still had three-quarters of her drink left. Seth went to the bar alone. Looking back, she was swiping through her phone, possibly telling her friends that she was out with him. He'd rather it was kept a secret but he couldn't control everything about this. He was being reckless, that's what Maeve would say. That's how he always got when he was this tired.

He caught a glimpse of himself in the mirror behind the spirits shelf. He looked old. He felt it. He wasn't sure what such a young and vivacious woman found so interesting in him. Perhaps they were just friends. Perhaps that was best. Perhaps this wasn't real. Another thing going on in his mind that he was saying out loud to himself.

The mirror showed his shoulders slouch at that thought. And Maeve jumped into his head. He wondered what she was doing that night while he was pretending to be out with work colleagues. Pretending to Hadley that he was someone he was not.

80

Maeve was alone.

Lonely.

They're different things.

She was both.

She knew Seth wasn't out with colleagues. He hated those guys. He always avoided those events if he could.

Her mind tripped to those late-night conversations. She knew he had made friends with men before. Those others who find it hard to switch off at night and enjoyed the companionship until things started to feel less than normal. But this one was definitely a woman. There was an air about the mumbling she heard from the comfort of her bed. It made her uncomfortable. She was starting to spiral, thinking about who this girl was, her name, what she looked like, why she was so alluring. Was she the opposite of Maeve? Was she how Maeve used to be?

And she sat on her sofa; the house was quiet. She had wine, like she always had. And she watched the news, like she always did. Still, the focus of the national press was on that girl found in Warwickshire. The lead detective was on her screen again. He made her feel excited. Obviously drawn to that kind of face. Weathered. Dark eyes. Mystery. Something lurking beneath the surface that rarely came out but was primal and animalistic.

He triggered something in her that made her feel anxious and excited.

She missed that part of Seth. His spontaneity. His natural instincts taking hold of him. She looked over at his sofa but he wasn't there. Still, recently, even when he was sat in the same room as her, he wasn't really there.

Because he was out with Hadley. They were drinking heavily. His drive home was already going to be over the legal limit and he had more drinks to come before he sat behind the wheel.

They decided to stay in the pub and eat. They were having a good time together. They had a table and two seats. The place served great pizza, according to Hadley, and a dessert of *gnochetti* – deep-fried dough balls dipped in sugar before being covered in honey, chocolate or cinnamon. 'They're to die for,' she rejoiced.

The beer was removing Seth's nerves and drowning those fleeting thoughts he was having about his wife. This woman seemed so perfect for him at that point. She'd come along at just the right time. He needed her.

He wasn't sure why she was there, what she saw in him, but he kept going, portraying only his best features. Just as anyone would on a first date.

But Hadley wanted Seth that night. This was a third date for her. With someone she knew well, who knew her darkest side, all those failed attempts, and accepted her for it. Not like that idiot earlier in the week who just wanted to get his dick wet.

No. This was different. He was different.

Hadley wanted Seth that night. And Ant could see it.

He was sat in the corner of Beerd. On the round table next to the door for the toilets. Beneath the painted 'Craft Beer' sign and the neon 'Pizza' lights. He could see them through the glass. He could see Seth's face. And he didn't like it. Not one bit. This girl was fragile. He couldn't have her pushed over the edge by some idiot she had known for five minutes.

He watched them. He scrutinised them. And when they left, he followed them back to the car park. And he watched them there, too. He watched everything.

81

'Shall we get out of here?' she asked, a naughtiness in her expression that Seth couldn't resist.

He was full of pizza and beer and impure thoughts. A walk in the fresh Oxford air could be just what he needed. She made him feel light. They had fun. They let themselves be silly, didn't take themselves too seriously. Jobs and mortgages and car leases and credit-card payments tend to suck that silliness out of you, replacing it with responsibility and obligation. The truth is, it doesn't have to be a replacement; the two can exist concurrently.

Hadley scraped her stool backwards and stood up. She was the same height as when sitting down. Seth found that very sweet. He'd been finding her every mannerism to be the same. Sweet. Cute. Endearing. She was magic.

The barman bid them good night and they stepped out into the street. She turned immediately to the left, down the street Seth had arrived on but couldn't remember because he had been too busy checking his phone. This time, he took all the details in. He wasn't as paranoid about being seen.

He looked at everything ahead of him and nothing behind.

The Odeon cinema was to his right and he thought about the last film he saw with Maeve. They never went out anymore. They never had fun. They rarely did things together. Between there and the Four Candles pub, he spotted three homeless people. One begging with a paper cup, another stroking his dog, the other resting on what looked like a walking frame with a seat.

'What's down here? Another pub? A club?' Seth asked, not knowing where to go. The air was doing something to the alcohol in his body and his already close-up vision was blurred enough for him to try to blink it away.

'This is where your car is, right?'

They stopped on the corner and he saw a sign for Worcester Street.

'Er, yeah. It's in there. You can't see it. Behind those barriers.' he pointed. 'So we're done? You don't want to go on somewhere else?'

'I thought maybe you could drive me home, first.'

Seth wasn't sure what to say, then she started to cross the road.

As they stepped into the virtually empty car park, Hadley grabbed Seth's right hand with her left, interlocking their fingers. It felt odd but not wrong. He told himself, *You're not doing anything wrong.*

This isn't cheating.

I couldn't do that to Maeve.

He looked all around the car park but he didn't look back over his shoulder. There seemed to be nobody around. He felt himself starting to sweat again. But he dutifully went along with her request. It was what he was used to, doing what the woman says.

Seth fished around in his pocket for his car key and pressed the button to unlock the doors. He forgot to walk around the car and open the door for Hadley and unchivalrously allowed her to traipse around and sort herself out. His mind was buzzing. She obviously didn't just want him to drop her off at her place. Things had gone amazingly well, but was this really the next logical step? Maeve had made him wait for weeks before seeing her naked. It was a long time ago but he remembered that much.

Shutting his driver's side door made the interior lights dim.

'Okay, madam, where to?' He put on what he thought was a cab-driver voice. 'I hope it's not too far as I've had quite a lot to drink.'

They both laughed.

Then Hadley leant in and kissed him on the mouth. Her hand that had just been holding his was now resting against his cheek. There was no tongue. Just a few light kisses on his lips. But it was enough for Seth to start getting hard.

And confused.

He shut his eyes as she kissed him again but felt dizzy so he opened them. It didn't help. Her eyes were so close to his and he strained to bring them into focus.

Then they opened their mouths and she pushed her tongue to touch Seth's. Still soft. Still sensitive. He didn't know where to put his hands so kept the left one against her seat and the right on the dashboard. That way, he wasn't deliberately touching her. He was reacting. That was all.

But her hand moved to his trousers and she could tell he was excited. It was over the clothes. That wasn't cheating, surely. But her hand went inside his trousers. It was dangerous ground. Seth was excited but also something else he couldn't quite decipher.

They kissed as she touched him. Then her head moved down and she put the tip of his dick in her mouth.

'Wait, wait, wait.' He pulled her head up.

'What's wrong? You don't like that?'

'Of course I like that. I just … I just need to tell you something.'

Her hand went back to work as she looked at him, attentively.

'You can tell me anything, Seth.' She gave that smile meant just for him.

'I'm married.'

And, without so much as a pause for thought, she said, 'Doesn't bother me if it doesn't bother you.'

She kept hold of him.

'What? That's your response?' It sounded like shock but he knew he was angry with her.

'Look, Seth, you wouldn't be here with me if everything was perfect at home with your wife, would you?'

Seth thought about it for a second and said, 'No. I guess not.'

He didn't want to be unfaithful to Maeve but part of Seth was so glad that Hadley felt that way.

82

He leant across me and pulled the lever that made my seat recline. I was lying down and he moved on top of me. It was happening.

I looked up at him.

'That face. So pure. So smooth.' He stroked it with the back of his finger. I was trying to be sultry in that moment. Far from pure.

I adjusted myself to pull my underwear down and kicked them into the footwell.

My legs opened slightly to tease him in.

I looked at him, knowingly. Sure of what was about to happen, what I had wanted to happen that night. The barriers shadowed his car.

But he wasn't turned on. He was angry. At what I had said about his wife.

He rested his weight on me.

'You okay, baby?' I asked.

He lifted his chest so that he could look me in the eyes. And I searched those dark circles to see if he was feeling the way I was feeling.

Then he pushed his forearm down against my throat. And I liked it, at first. Of course. I'm a dirty fucking whore, right? Men either wanted me to be dirtier or they wanted to clean me up. I think I got Seth wrong.

'I am married,' he said again, deliberately separating each word. He pushed down harder against my throat. 'Don't you ever disrespect my wife like that.'

I was struggling now. Arching my back to force myself upwards but I was too weak. Or he was too strong. I tried to call out. I wheezed. I was grinding my teeth. The noise was getting to him, I could see. I kicked my legs against the glove compartment, in desperation. I wanted to break the windscreen, cause a scene. He knew it. But he also knew that we were covered.

He punched me in the face.

'That's my wife.'

He punched me again to shut me up but I still wriggled. He smashed his fist down onto my nose and the blood went all over his hand. Water filled my eyes.

He kept hitting the same spot over and over, pushing down harder on my neck. He head-butted my face and rubbed his own all over the blood he had made.

'You don't fucking talk about her like that. You're nobody.'

He moved both hands around to my throat, pushing his thumbs so deep he could feel what was inside my neck. My dainty neck.

Through the blood and tears, I could make him out. I could see the light grow in his eyes. Then it felt like I was drowning.

Then the buzzing in my ears.

Then nothing.

83

Seth watched the life drain from her eyes. It was a feeling like no other on this planet. In that moment, he was God. He was in control.

He finished by screaming once more at her then spitting in her face. And rolled back into the driving seat to catch his breath.

'Fuck.' He was talking to himself. He looked at her body. He didn't need to check, she was definitely gone. He felt beneath the steering wheel and pulled a lever that popped the boot open.

Then he went around to the passenger door, opened it, grabbed Hadley Serf by her left ankle and yanked her out onto the concrete. The back of her head cracked against the floor. He twisted her beautiful hair around his hand and dragged her to the boot and stuffed her inside beneath his collection of shopping bags and one of Maeve's coats.

He didn't want to look around the car park. He couldn't look suspicious. He just had to act like everything was normal. So he jumped back into the car and started the engine. Then he drove out of the car park and turned left, where he sat at some traffic lights for thirty seconds.

It gave him time to reach into the passenger footwell where Hadley's knickers were. He picked them up and wiped as much blood off his face with them as he could. There wasn't a lot of material. She obviously thought she was on to a sure thing.

The lights turned green.

Seth drove on. Never faster than the speed limit. Only looking forwards. That's all he had. Everything behind was done. It was a mess. He passed the Playhouse and noticed they were showing *The Jungle Book*. He wondered how that would translate to the stage.

Left at the next set of lights.

Two Asian girls, probably drunk, were hanging about near the edge of the road by the bus stop, trying to thumb down any vehicle that would accept them. Seth imagined himself running them down but just kept going.

He was wired, his vision seemed to recover well and adrenaline suppressed the effects of the alcohol. He drove on autopilot. Not too slow. Not too fast. Nothing to attract attention. He saw lights in his rear-view mirror. There was still blood on his face. He couldn't get pulled over.

Eventually, the sign he wanted.

London. A40. M40.

One long, straight road home.

The excitement soon dwindled. His heart rate slowed and everything was close-up again. His chin dropped a few times and he had to slap his own face to keep alert. He forgot about Hadley in the boot for about twenty minutes.

Seth pulled onto his road. It was late. The streetlights were illuminated but very few houses were showing signs of life. He crept onto the drive, killed the engine, pulled the handbrake up and got out of the car. The blue TV-screen light danced through the window of the front door. Maeve was undoubtedly asleep on the sofa.

The night air did something to him. He felt drunk again. Low. He started to breathe short breaths. When he got to the doorstep he was already crying and he didn't know why.

He felt in his pocket for his keys but he'd left them in the ignition. That caused him undue stress so he knocked on the door. He looked through the window. He could see Maeve's feet at the end of the sofa. They weren't moving.

He knocked louder this time and it startled her.

She stood up and peered towards the window until she made out her husband's face. It made her smile. A deep, glorious, appreciative smile he hadn't seen for months. But Seth was crying still. And blood still smeared his face.

Maeve got closer. And closer. Eventually unlocking the door and opening it wide.

Seth's tears made tracks through Hadley's blood that he had smudged into his cheeks.

Maeve looked right at him.

'Oh, Seth. Again?' she asked, unflinchingly.

'I really liked this one, Maeve. I didn't want to kill her this time.' He was still crying.

'Where is she?'

'In the boot.'

'Get her in. Clean yourself up. I'll get the bleach.'

Seth did exactly as she said.

Maeve shut the door, kissed Seth and smiled.

She couldn't stop smiling.

THAT NIGHT

02:32

I know that I'm smiling. We've been here before. I know what has to be done and how Seth will act and how he will change for a while once we've cleansed the body and disposed of it. He needs me.

I have him.

It was shorter than last time, though. Maybe this time will be shorter, still.

And I think about how grateful he will be towards me, how he will become subservient. And I think a little further ahead to the bottle of red wine we will share while we witness the police fumble their investigations on television. How Seth will get nervous and want to change the channel, like he always does, while I cross my legs a little tighter, watching that dark shadow of a detective tell the rest of the country not to worry, his team wandering behind him, fucking up more than they are discovering.

I always make sure there is nothing left to discover.

I clean. I clip. I cut. I trim.

And Seth cries. He shakes. He moans. He apologises.

So I start to think back. I think about his late nights alone in the lounge and the mumbling that vibrated its way up the dull, neutral grey carpet of the stairs as another midnight conversation was had. I look back to the way he fucked me last week and I question it. I wonder what this one will look like and whether he fucked her like that. Maybe he learned some moves from her.

Then I question whether it was more than that. Maybe he made love to her. Maybe I was his dirty little whore, not the other way round.

02:34

Ant didn't know what to do. He could see the driveway of Seth's house. He sat there, motionless and terrified at what was unfolding in front of him. He didn't really know where he was. London, somewhere. The outskirts. A fairly wealthy borough, if the size of the houses were any kind of clue. The last place he expected to find himself, watching a man pull a dead body from the boot of his car.

He thought about calling the police. But what would he say? That he was stalking a woman he had miscommunicated with over the phone? He had been following her? They'd want to know how long he'd been doing that. And that would surely lead to suspicion surrounding the assault of the man who had left her building late at night earlier in the week. He didn't want that kind of exposure.

Seth emerged from the house.

Ant knew what was happening. He was going to get Hadley Serf. Seth was going to get that sweet, fucked-up young lady from the boot of his car and take her into the house.

Ant knew what he should do. He should call the police, immediately. Maybe he could do it anonymously. Perhaps he could make the call and then never use that phone again. He didn't want any kind of reward or recognition.

He carefully slid his hand into the pocket of his jeans, moving at a pace that wouldn't rock his car. He was slumped down in his seat, so only the top of his head would be visible. Not that Seth was looking. He had more pressing concerns.

I should call the police, Ant thought to himself. He looked at the blank, unlit screen of his phone, then eked himself up slowly as Seth ungracefully kicked the driveway stones on the way to his car.

Then Ant pressed the button on his phone to bring it to life. The light disguised the fingertip marks all over the screen. He was doing everything as quietly as possibly. The phone recognised his fingerprint and illuminated into life.

He should've called the police there and then. Put an end to everything. Eased the suffering of three families. But Ant did not do that. Instead, he swiped up the screen to activate the camera and he photographed everything.

02:35

I watch as he lifts her out of the boot. He is clumsy and indiscreet. I know he is ready to break down again.

He cradles her in his arms, somehow looking strong and pathetic at the same time. A man and a child.

She, whoever this one is, looks heavy in his arms. But lighter than I would look. And I can't look backwards or forwards, or even at this moment, now. I can only see what is inside my mind. Things that may never have happened. The worst things. Happiness that I haven't seen in my husband's eyes for longer than I can pinpoint. The closeness that eludes us.

And I'm no longer smiling.

Seth stands in the doorway with another dead dalliance. I wrap a good clump of her hair around my right hand and drag her from his grasp, yanking her further into the entrance of our home, her stiffening frame slapping against the wooden flooring.

'Get away from the door, Seth.'

He just stands there, staring at her. I see his eyes welling up again. He looks at his hands, then at me, then back at the pretty little dead thing in the hallway.

'Get here now. The whole fucking world can see us.' I pull at his jacket and he steps further inside. I peer through the window at our quaint street. There's a car parked across the road that I don't recognise, but I tell myself it's paranoia. It's just the situation.

'I'm sorry.' Seth speaks so quietly.

'Are you talking to me or her?'

He takes too long to answer and it starts to annoy me.

I want to enjoy this moment but he won't let me. She won't let me.

'Get it upstairs, Seth. Into the bath. Then get yourself clean and into different clothes. We've got a lot to do and I need you to go out. Okay?'

Nothing.

'Seth!' I raise my voice. 'I don't have enough bleach. You need to go out and get more bleach.' I'm direct. Clinical.

He just looks at her.

'Seth.' I try. 'Seth.' This time tugging at the shoulder of his jacket. 'Seth.' I slap him hard around the face and it snaps him back into our reality, his back leaning against the wall, his eyes now fixed on me.

I step closer to my husband and place my hand gently on the area I have just struck in frustration.

'Listen, baby, it's going to be okay. But we have to sort this out.' I move closer to him. He has her blood smeared across his face. 'So get yourself upstairs and dump her in the bathtub. Then wash the blood off you and change your clothes – we'll burn them. Then I need you to go out and buy me a few things. So that I can clean up your fucking mess again.' With that, I grab his face and pull it into mine so that we can kiss. A passionate moment filled with desire and loathing and fear and excitement. Blood and tears and spit.

I can feel it all.

And that cold, beautiful mistake on the floor next to us, lying there, oblivious, is lucky that she will never feel anything again. Because I know what I'm about to do.

02:37

His tiredness heightened everything. His pleasure was amplified as he blocked the flow of oxygen to Hadley Serf's brain in the reclined seat of his car. His panic intensified as he stopped at that first set of traffic lights, blood on his skin and a corpse in his boot; that light took an hour to change from red to green. And his sadness was worsened as his shoes dragged across the gravel driveway to his own front door. And his disappointment deepened at the realisation that he had forgotten his keys. And his fear was inflamed as his wife walked unknowingly towards the window. Seth wasn't sure how much more she could take.

But his relief was boosted at her reaction to his latest mistake. And that made the body feel lighter as he carried it into the house. Then, as Maeve yanked the dead girl from his grasp, pulling at her hair, making her hit that ground with an unnerving crack, he numbed. Like a shocked soldier at war, hearing nothing, or a monotonous ringing sound, as bullets zipped by his head and explosions detonated all around him. Seth was there. But he wasn't.

Not out of control. But not in control.

Maeve was talking, he could see her lips moving, but it wasn't audible. The only thing that made sense was the pale and bloodied face of the girl in his hallway. A crossed wire. Sour serendipity.

Then Maeve slapped him hard around the face.

And he remembered the pleasure of killing, again. And he felt the blood rush to his dick as she pushed her weight into him and kissed him hard, her moist lips grazing the blood of the girl he had killed that lingered on the skin around his mouth.

He knew what he had to do. They'd done this before.

Seth bent down and slid one hand beneath dead Hadley's neck and the other beneath her dead knees. He used the strength in his legs to pick her up. She felt heavy again. And he walked her up the stairs, banging her dead head twice against the banister as he tried to fit them both between the modest gap.

Then he dumped her into the tub in the guest bathroom, rolling her off his arms. She hit the steel with her face and the rest of her twisted body followed. Seth took a final look at the girl that had so enamoured him over the phone and stroked his ego in the café and bar, and his dick in the car. And he shook his head at her. Half in pity. Half in disgust.

He undressed in front of her and left those clothes on the tiles in a pile, to be burned later. Everything in that room had to be cleaned and disposed of. His trousers and underwear could go the next day. The girl in the bath would take a little more time.

Maeve was banging around in the kitchen. Opening cupboards and pulling things out. Seth thought he could hear the kettle boiling. How very British to think of tea during a crisis.

As he walked across the hall landing, naked, he could see Maeve at the bottom of the stairs cleaning the small patches of blood on the hallway floor where Hadley had been dropped. Just a cloth and some kitchen spray for now, but she would bleach that floor eventually. She would bleach everything.

Seth turned the shower up to the hottest temperature he could. The en suite shower was better than the guest bathroom, which only had a handheld attachment. He stood under it; though it hurt, he wanted to kill any remnants of that evening that were left on his skin. He washed his hair twice, digging his nails into his scalp to clean beneath them. He got out of the shower, dried his hair, his torso, his legs, then wrapped the towel around his waist. He cut his fingernails down as close as he could get without drawing his own blood and had a wet shave.

Then he showered again. This time with cold water. He dried off. Dressed and went back downstairs, where Maeve was waiting for him with a fresh mug of coffee and another smile.

03:09

He looked so handsome. That's what I was thinking when he walked into the room. I knew he'd dumped her in the bathtub. She was there waiting for me to clean her. Twisted and bloodied and fully clothed. I knew how Seth had been when he'd turned up on the doorstep, crying again, creased, slumped shoulders. And I knew what we would have to do. What I would have to do.

But when he appeared at the top of the stairs, all I could think was just how handsome my husband looked.

Sure, his eyes were still dark through lack of sleep but his face was smooth and his hair was clean and tidy and he was mine again. In that moment, I looked at him and he looked back at me. Not at the television or into his dinner or his mobile-phone screen. Me. His wife. And, with everything going on around us, with the dead girl in the bathtub and the blood in the boot of his car, I knew he was exactly where he was supposed to be, where he needed to be.

With me.

'I made you a coffee,' I said, as he reached the bottom of the stairs, and handed it to him. 'We're going to be up a while longer.'

'Thanks. I know.'

He took a sip of his coffee but it was too hot.

'You cleaned that up already?' he asked me, pointing at the hallway floor where the blood had been.

'There wasn't much. A light clean, for now. I'll do it properly, later.' By properly, I meant with bleach. That was my weapon of choice. Our weapon.

We walked into the kitchen. I'd made myself a green tea. Seth and I rested against the worktop. We drank our hot drinks and spoke about what was to happen next.

'Seth, I need you to go out. Do you have any cash?'

'Sure, a little left over from earlier. Maybe thirty or forty...'

'Here, take another twenty.'

I pulled a crisp note from my purse and handed it to him, then I explained what I needed him to do.

He needed to take my car and buy my bleach. Six bottles. All from different places. I didn't want him on camera going somewhere and picking that up, it would look suspicious. He had to go to a petrol station and top up, then go inside and pick up a couple of bottles of bleach, some toilet rolls, bread, milk, and pack them in a bag. He could jump on the motorway and park up in the closest service station and do the same. He could then drive around waiting for a supermarket to open or corner shop or Polish convenience store, it didn't matter. I needed a lot of bleach for the girl.

'I have enough in the cupboard under the sink to sort out the house but we'll need more.'

He nodded at me and even smiled a bit. I think he liked how I took control.

Seth finished his coffee and, with his mouth still warm, kissed me, pressing his body against mine. His hand was on the small of my back, pulling me in. He felt strong. And he looked handsome. And I wanted him, in that moment. But he needed to go. I didn't want him to and I could tell he felt the same. But we had to sort out this mess.

Together.

'Where are the keys?'

'In my coat pocket in the hall.'

'Okay. I should go, get this done. Will you be alright here on your own?'

I wanted to say that I wouldn't be on my own because there's a dead fucking girl in the spare bathroom. I wanted to tell him that I've been on my own for months while he gradually faded away from our relationship, choosing the comfort of strangers to his own wife. I wanted to tell him to man up and get what we needed to make this go away again.

But I didn't say that, because his hand was still on my back and his face was close to mine and I also wanted to wrap my legs around him.

'You go. I'll be fine. I've done this before.'

I smiled and he smiled back. And he kissed me again before walking into the hall and taking the keys from my coat.

'Seth,' I called, as he opened the front door to leave. He turned back to me, his hand holding the door ajar. 'I've got you. Okay? I'll take care of everything.'

03:16

Ant was still out there. He didn't know why. His mind was whirring. With images of his friend hooked to the back of that bathroom door, with the thought of that girl hanging up on him, with that guy he had followed and punched and left, with the recent memory of what had occurred in that Oxford car park. He didn't know what he was going to do. He'd been sat there for forty-two minutes. Doing nothing.

So he had just sat there in his car. Thinking. And overthinking.

He was scrolling through some grainy, zoomed-in pictures of the man he believed to be Seth, who did not work with him at the Samaritans, as he pulled that girl's body from the boot of his car and took her into his house. The police could have been there thirty minutes ago but how would he have explained his involvement? Why was he there?

But he was there. And, as confused as he was, adrenaline refusing to release its hold over him, he wasn't going to let this go.

Then the front door opened again. And he saw Seth. A cleaner, tidier version of Seth, but it was him. Ant ducked down again and took another picture of the man getting into his car. A different car. His picture would automatically record the time and location that it was taken. He was building evidence.

The car hardly made a sound as it started – one of those hybrids. It pulled out of the drive and turned left, away from the direction they had arrived. Ant wondered whether he should follow the car but Seth wasn't acting as anxious as he had been before. He was calmer. Ant could see it in the way he moved and carried himself, and Ant wasn't a detective, he wasn't skilled at this game he'd been caught up in.

So he stayed. He waited until Seth's quiet hybrid car had pulled out of sight and he sat up. And he looked at the house; the lights were still on. He was cold and restless and knew that he should just stay in the car and wait for Seth to return. He could be ten minutes or he could be two hours.

Ant knew he had a choice, he could stay in his car, in the cold, with his phone that was losing battery life with every passing second, and stake out the house. Or he could call the police and let them deal with it. Maybe he could do that anonymously. Would they really care that he had been stalking Hadley if they found her murderer?

What he knew, too, was that he should absolutely not, in any circumstance, get out of his car, approach the house and try to look inside.

He should have called the police.

He should have driven away and watched the results of his call on the news the next morning.

He should have stayed in his car.

03:27

Fifteen pounds worth of petrol, two packets of salt and vinegar flavoured crisps that were on offer, a tub of low-fat hummus, two bottles of bleach, some toilet roll, a three-pound scratch card and some peppermint chewing gum. That was Seth's shopping list on his first stop.

The bleach stood out. It was incongruous. He should have picked up some other toiletries or some cloths and scourers.

Seth chose a petrol station that was five miles from the house. He should have gone further. The assistant behind the till was bored but chatty.

'How are you today, sir?' He was professional. He was being friendly. It was somewhere between the middle of the night and the start of the morning.

'Fine. Thanks.' Seth wanted to be as unmemorable as possible. The teller looked confused as he packed Seth's bag. It was a strange array of products to purchase together.

Seth could see him examining every item as he scanned it. He tried to subvert the man's attention.

'Can I grab a number seven scratch card, too, please?'

'Number seven?'

'Yes, please.'

'Just one?'

They always asked that. Like it was programmed into them.

'Just one.'

Seth was nervous. He just wanted to get out of there. He had four more bottles of bleach to buy for Maeve. He needed to erase Hadley and the night they'd had together in his car. And he went to a place in his head where the short, affable, Indian man across the counter from him was being beaten in the face and gouged in the eyes and bitten through the neck. Seth was imagining himself taking out this weakness in his plan, this possible complication. And his nerves were replaced with an excitement.

He was jolted back to reality with the sound of beeping as another late-night driver squeezed the handle of a petrol nozzle into his car.

The teller was holding a handful of change out for Seth. He dropped the coins into the killer's hand and walked across to hit the button that would cause the beeping to cease and release the fuel into another customer's car. He turned around to speak with the bleach buyer again but he was gone. And shortly forgotten.

03:36

I didn't like being alone with her. Seth had only been gone for twenty minutes and the house felt colder, somehow. And human intrigue is a simple, alluring poison.

I hadn't seen her properly when he carried her in. She was small. Petite. Not like me. But he couldn't have known that when he called her. He wasn't looking for somebody who wasn't his wife. I don't really believe he knows what he is looking for when he does what he does. Maybe it's the rush of the unknown. Whatever motivates him, his hunger for that feeling is growing. This girl is too close to the last one.

The green tea really did nothing for me. I flip the switch on the kettle again and spoon eight heaped tablespoons of ground Columbian coffee beans into a cafetière. While the kettle boils, I walk to the front door and look out of the window. I'm not expecting Seth back any time soon but it's something to do. It looks peaceful outside. Everyone is still asleep. Everyone is unaware.

Only the animals are awake now. The ones who have to kill.

I hear the click of the kettle and return to the kitchen. In the downstairs hallway, I hear movement upstairs. It could be the sounds that houses make as air rushes through pipes or water falls through plug holes. And it could be in my head. Because I want it.

I don't want to stand around doing nothing while the coffee brews so I go upstairs. I convince myself that there is something shuffling in the bathroom, the sound of slight banging against the bathtub, the rustling of a shower curtain. I creep steadily up the stairs. The second to last one makes a creak and I stop. Everything is silent. Maybe everything was already silent. I clench my right fist and step up onto the landing. The bathroom is several paces down on my right-hand side.

She can't be alive.

I look back over my shoulder and down the stairs through the window. I think I see a shadow moving outside. My heart rate increases. Not because I'm scared. But because I'm excited, I think. Maybe both. Maybe I want to walk into that room and find a disoriented, petite, scared girl who wanted to fuck my husband, so that I can be the one who chokes the last bit of life out of her. But that's not me. That's not my role. That's the fear.

I stand to the side of the door and push it open enough to see the bottom of the bathtub. I think I still see her in there. Hadley. I didn't know her name but everyone would, soon enough. Maybe she did try to get out. Maybe she's jumped back in after hearing the stairs creak. Maybe she's playing dead, hoping to catch me off-guard.

My left fist is now clenched as I push the door further with my right.

I have to calm myself. I can hear my own breathing, it's so silent in this chaos.

Maybe I'm covering the sound of her breath.

Edging in slowly, I'm cautious. She's there. Lying in the tub. I don't know the position Seth left her in. And he's not here. I am. Cleaning up after him. Again.

Then I'm at the side of the tub. I don't know if I want to look at her or not but I definitely don't want to look away. She doesn't seem to be moving. I take my face closer to hers.

I brush the girl's hair away from her face. The strands are stuck together in clumps and I have to press it down hard against her head to keep it in place. I'll wash the blood out later. I can see that she was pretty. Not a knockout but something interesting and offbeat. I know why Seth liked her.

I don't like her.

But I look at her a while, waiting for my breathing to slow. She is pale and cold and does not smell pleasant. Of course. I can't help but touch the skin on her cheek. It's smooth. No wrinkles. Plump and full. She looks more and more beautiful as each second passes. Her lips are dry but even that dead pout seems kissable. I don't know if I'm tempted.

I look down and see the marks on her neck again. I trace around them gently with my index finger.

'Don't move, dead girl,' I say to myself. 'Please.' And I hold my breath. So that everything is silent. Everything is still.

I wait. Breath held. Looking over the girl.

I wait.

Then I scream.

03:38

It is only the animals that are awake at that time of night and Ant is one of them.

Curiosity gradually ate away at him in the front seat of that car. He felt like he had waited a good twenty minutes to act on it, but time can play tricks on you like that. It hadn't even been five minutes and he was overcome with the urge to look inside the house.

He sat up in his seat and checked his phone. The battery was at thirty-eight percent. Plenty, he thought. He turned down the screen brightness to preserve power. There was nothing on that London street. The street lights were still illuminated but daylight was threatening in the distance.

Ant opened the door as quietly as he could manage and turned in the seat to take both his legs out onto the road. It was cold. The morning cold that England gets at 4:00 a.m., no matter the season. He looked up and down the road several times. There was the occasional sound of traffic several roads down but that London idyll was at peace. Dead.

He didn't close his car door fully. He was only going across the street. Nobody was around. Nobody would want to steal it, or anything inside it.

What did a killer's house look like? Ant asked himself. Was it like his flat? Immaculate. Ordered. Are they all the same? Not all murderers are the same. His mind was buzzing.

The driveway was gravel and made him pause for a second and panic a little. He wanted to get close. There was just enough grass along the side next to Seth's car. Ant crept along the front garden on his tiptoes, trying not to impress his weight into the ground and leave a footprint anywhere. He moved quickly towards the front door and then left to a window, which looked in on a reception area. He could see the stairs that led upstairs – where a dead woman was being scrutinised – and a light was on in the far right corner that seemed to be a kitchen.

Why had Seth left the lights on? Maybe he was expecting to be home soon?

He took three pictures through the glass. But his hands were cold and he started to shake. Or it was nerves. The phone slipped. Then he hit it upwards with his other hand. And it hit the window. And the windowsill. Then dropped. As it fell, Ant swiped at it, caught it, stumbled forwards and kicked a plant pot over.

Within seconds, he was back across the grass and over the road. He didn't want to make any further noise, draw attention to himself, so ran behind his car, ducked down and waited.

03:40

A scared sound as my lungs empty. It isn't a loud scream. I'm just startled.

There is a noise from downstairs. Something breaking. It jolts me back to reality.

I jump away from the bath and out into the hall. I don't know where the noise came from and I wasn't expecting Seth back yet.

'Hello?' I call down, in case it is him. In case he has ignored my instructions and just bought six bottles of bleach from the first place he passed.

'Seth?' I ask again.

Nothing.

So I work warily down the stairs. A shadow that I can't quite make out passes over the driveway. It heads out towards the road. I run down and look out of the window, there's nothing there.

I unlock the front door and jut my head out slightly, looking out across the road. A parked car. I look left and all seems normal. To the right, a plant pot has tipped onto its side. It hasn't smashed but a segment has chipped off the top.

The shadow outside was probably just an animal, I tell myself.

I close the door and plunge the lever on my coffee.

03:41

The door never opened. *He must live alone*, Ant thought.

Of course.

Ant decided there was no reason for him to stay any longer. He had seen what he had seen. He needed to get back to his immaculate, ordered home. And there, he would decide how to play this out.

Hadley was dead; she couldn't get any deader. He couldn't save her.

But Seth had taken her away.

And Ant could make sure that he didn't get away with that.

That he would pay for what he did.

03:50

The scratch card was an eight-pound winner. It was Seth's lucky night, he thought.

He was almost fifteen miles outside of London when he stopped to rub a coin against that silver foil and reveal the three rainbows that would help pay for the next two bottles of bleach.

Heston Service Station had plenty of people around – these places always do. Lorry drivers stopping for a sleep or picking up some suitably beige food items that contain very little nutrition but provide a short-term buzz of energy and feeling of satiety that will push them through the next part of their journey.

There are men and women in suits and blouses, grabbing large coffees and pastries before they drive up north for a meeting at nine. They're discussing how to play it, who will present each part. They talk in numbers and acronyms.

And there's one clean-shaven killer with a winning scratch card, wandering around the all-night supermarket next to the food court, searching for a product that will clean and burn away any evidence of his involvement in the murder of a young, naïve woman who thought she had finally found someone who would listen, who would care. Who would want her to kick her underwear into the footwell of his car. Who would want her soft lips around his hard dick.

Seth saw the truckers and the business people and the travellers because he was looking for them, he was looking out for himself. But they did not see him. Nobody was looking for a killer. They were looking for caffeine and crisps and processed junk. This was the reason Maeve sent him there.

But he couldn't find the bleach. The supermarket was food only. He could've picked up the latest bestselling paperback or a magazine but all the place offered was eight pounds in exchange for his scratch card.

He left the main building and strolled back in the cold to his car. There was an option to drive to the petrol station on the way to the exit but that had not been in Maeve's instructions and he didn't want to stray too far from what she had said. The last time he had used his initiative and gone at it alone, he'd turned up on the doorstep with a third dead girl.

Seth thought about texting Maeve to update her, but it was stupid to create any kind of trail. He stared at his phone and thought about his phonebooks in the lounge. And he wondered whether he could just type in a phone number and hope for connection.

But he collected himself, placed his mobile phone between his legs and pulled out of the car park and back onto the motorway.

And he could drive around running late-night errands. He could buy the bleach. He could clean the house from top to bottom. But he would still have to dispose of a dead body. He would still have to burn a pile of evidence. He was who he was. He was what he was.

He was Seth.

He couldn't sleep.

He wanted to talk.

He needed it.

03:51

I drank the coffee and didn't give a second thought to the broken pot outside.

But I couldn't put it off any longer. I was wasting time.

The caffeine gave me the quick buzz I needed as the adrenaline dissipated and dragged me down. I took a bottle of bleach and some rubber gloves from the cupboard beneath the sink and headed back upstairs to work.

First, I had to undress her. This is more difficult than it sounds. She was an adult. (Technically, she still is an adult but I say 'was' because she is dead.) And she is deadweight heavy, which makes even the most petite frame like hers almost double.

I learned from the first two that the easiest thing to do is cut the clothes off. I keep the scissors in a drawer in that bathroom. First I release her legs, cutting from the waist of her skirt down to the hem. She has no underwear on. I throw the cut garment onto the tiles.

I start from the waist when I cut her top, working the sharp scissors up towards her throat. I'm not even looking at where I'm cutting. I'm staring at her face. I'm looking at her perfectly smooth vagina, all creamy white and tight with youth. I want to jam the scissors up there but I don't. Her time will come.

I snip the centre of her black bra and her breasts sit, predictably, to attention. Her nipples were an obvious plush pink that would've complemented her milky skin. Unlike mine. Older and browner and wider. Small hairs.

Her clothes lay in a pile by the side of the bath and she is completely naked in the tub. I start the tap and mix the cold and hot to a temperature that won't burn my hands. And I hose her down, washing the blood off her skin. It collects between her legs before disappearing down the plug hole. I have to turn up the heat a little and hold the shower head closer to clear the mess Seth made of her face.

Then I turn the temperature back down and climb in with her. I sit her up and move myself in behind her. I pull her wet hair away from her bludgeoned face and run the water over it, combing my fingers through it and straightening it downwards. There's an unused bottle of shampoo on the shelf. I squirt a healthy amount into her hair and rub it gently into a lather, pushing my fingertips into her scalp and massaging deeply.

I wash it out again. My clothes are wet. I don't care.

There's a full bottle of conditioner. I repeat the process. Her hair is blood-free, soft and shining. This part of the process is complete. I lean forwards, turn off the tap and replace the shower head. I move her out of the way and stand up.

I get out of the bath.

She is lying on her back in the tub.

I strip off my wet clothes and add them to her pile. I will burn them all.

A minute later, I am also naked, with the exception of my rubber gloves.

My eyes do not leave her face as I look down on her, my left hand squeezing the lid of the bleach bottle to open it. There's only half a bottle left, that's why I had to send Seth out for more. I pour every last drop over her face and rub it into her cuts and wounds and eyes and mouth.

And I like it. I really like it.

But the feeling doesn't last long. I ditch the gloves with the forgotten clothes and move over to the sink. There's a wooden container on the storage unit to the left. I keep some toiletries and brushes and things in there. And nail clippers.

For all I know, she dug her nails into Seth's back while he pounded away at her in some seedy fucking hotel room. Or she stuck her finger up his arse. Maybe she just clawed at his chest while he beat her to death. Either way, I need to cut her nails down as close to the finger as I possibly can before I scrub away any hint of his adulterous DNA.

I start with the toes. Sure, they're a little tougher, but it's good practice and it doesn't matter too much if I make a mistake. I don't make a mistake. I cut all of her fingernails without so much as a nick. Then I take the shower head once more and wash the fragments down the plughole. I can smell the bleach on her face.

Then I walk out, shutting the door behind me. I slip into some comfortable grey joggers and a black vest. There's no need to shower. I don't feel the need to get her off my skin. I just need Seth to come home.

So that I can get her cleaned up.

And out of my house.

04:35

The adrenaline wore off after four junctions of the motorway. From that point, Ant was just tired. The things he'd witnessed that night and into the early hours of the morning, what he had done, where he had been, it drifted from his mind for long enough to allow him to shut his eyes.

He woke up, suddenly, with the noise of his wheels veering too far left and vibrating over that strip of road that is designed to wake you up in just that situation. He gripped hold of the steering wheel, turning right quickly, but his speed had descended enough that the movement wasn't too sharp and the road was relatively clear so he put nobody else at danger. Ant put his foot down to speed up again but stayed in the left-hand lane.

The battery symbol on the phone screen indicated that he still had nineteen percent of power and he smiled to himself about the pictures he had taken that the police could use as evidence.

Another two junctions passed without incident but Ant felt himself drifting again, his head lolling slowly down towards his chest then jerking back upwards suddenly as he woke up. He turned the radio on and blasted it loud through the speakers but that soon became normal and his eyes started closing. He opened his driver-side window to let the air rush in and hit him in the face. It was cold but he hoped that it would keep him going long enough.

Even that started to wear off. Ant started hanging his head out of the window slightly, to really get that smack of air in his face but it became comfortable. Nothing was working.

Then he came upon the sign for his turn-off. Once he was away from the monotony of a long, straight motorway and onto the winds and lights and turns of regular roads, he found it easier to keep his wits about him.

He'd never been so pleased to be home. It smelled clean and everything was in order. The straightness of the furniture, the plumpness of the sofa cushions, the flatness of his bedspread, all helped to calm Ant. He wanted to take his clothes off and put them away properly. And shower the day off him. But he was just too exhausted, the experience had taken everything out of him.

Ant kicked off his shoes at the door and pushed them neatly against the skirting board. He climbed into his bed with his clothes still on – he was still cold from driving with the window open for so long – and he wrapped the duvet around his shoulders. His face hit the pillow and he smiled, the mobile phone clasped in his right hand. He would remain in that position until the morning.

That is when he would deal with what he had seen.

He would put those photos to good use.

05:17

Seth was home before six in the morning. He didn't notice that Ant's car was no longer parked outside his house because he hadn't noticed it was there when he left. He took three carrier bags from the boot of Maeve's car. Each with a different logo from the shop or petrol station he had visited. He had obtained the six bottles of bleach his wife had requested and the tub of hummus. Along with various other items that were not required but hopefully diluted interest in his early-morning need for biocides.

He noticed straight away that Maeve had changed her clothes.

'You made a start already?'

'I hosed her down and cut her nails back. I washed her hair and bleached her face. She was pretty.' Maeve said the last sentence so matter-of-factly that it somehow gave the sentiment a little added bite.

Seth didn't know how to respond and that's exactly what she wanted.

Of course she was glad that he was back, that he needed her, that they had a connection again. But she was still about to be pissed at him for how this had come about.

Maeve broke the uncomfortable silence.

'You got everything?'

'Exactly as you asked.' He started walking towards her with the bags.

'And the hummus?'

'Yes. Yes, I got the hummus.'

This was the first time that Maeve looked up at Seth since he walked in. She put down her cup of coffee on the kitchen counter and stood up from her stool.

'Great. I'm hungry.' It was as though none of this fazed her.

Maeve took a sharp knife from the magnetic holder and Seth stopped in his tracks. She looked at him. She wanted to smile but held back. Then she turned her back for a moment and pulled two wholemeal pitta breads from one of the cupboards, cut them in half with the knife and placed them in the toaster. She walked over to Seth, kissed him on the lips, lingering for just over a second, and dipped her hand in the bag to retrieve the hummus.

Seth stood there like a little boy who was scared of being told off and a man who got off on feeling like that boy. He watched her body move inside the loose jogging bottoms and could tell she wasn't wearing underwear. He'd forgotten how much he liked the shape of her arms. He stayed still, bags of unwanted groceries cutting dents into his hands with their weight. Standing. Waiting.

Seth had already forgotten about Hadley. He assumed he'd get away with what he did, just like before. He wanted to fuck his wife again. He wanted to hoist her up onto the kitchen work surface. He wanted to take the straps of her vest down and trap her arms so she couldn't move, so she would want to fight back and hit him.

He wanted to feel in control.

The bread popped up in the toaster and the sound jolted Seth back to the reality of his situation. Maeve turned around, tore a piece of warm pitta and dipped it into the hummus.

'Why don't you put the shopping away and leave out what I need over there?' Maeve pointed to a part of the work surface then took a bite of her snack.

'Is there anything else I can do?'

'I don't know, baby. Maybe just stay out of the fucking way until it's a good time to burn her clothes.'

The domination he was experiencing, that usually forced him to disconnect, was now a huge turn-on. But he knew he wasn't going to fuck his wife until she had exorcised her demons.

'Okay. Well, I'm awake, so just let me know.'

Seth went into the living room and sat in his seat. He turned on the television and flicked through some channels without really watching anything. He looked over at his phonebooks and wondered. He even put his hand against the phone in his pocket.

Then he did something he hadn't done in longer than he could remember. He just fell asleep.

05:20

It doesn't get you clean. Not that much bleach. Sure, there are face creams that you can buy that will help with dry skin or dark patches left from overexposure to sunlight and they're clinically proven to help. But it's a trace amount.

And, for those suffering with eczema, a bleach bath may be recommended. Your dermatologist will tell you that the bleach can significantly decrease the infection of Staphylococcus aureus, a bacterium prevalent in those who are plagued by this skin condition. Still, it is recommended to use no more than half a cup of bleach in one half-filled bath of water.

Because it won't make your skin sparkle like it does your toilet basin. It will burn. It will blister. You will bleed. It will hurt like hell.

Unless you're already dead.

Unless you were stupid enough to answer the phone to a complete stranger and strike up some kind of conversation.

Unless you found some kind of common interest with a nobody, you were pleased because somebody was actually listening to you. You were turned on because they told you the exact things that you wanted to hear from the people that you had in your life that you did know, the ones you thought knew you. But weren't giving you what you needed.

Unless you decided to take a risk on a blind date and fell for some charm and attention. And that turned into drinks and food and blow jobs and strangulation and repeated blows to your once-pretty little face.

Those are the things that will hurt. The betrayal. The loss. The thoughts of those loved ones that you didn't get to confide in or say goodbye to. The huge things on your bucket list and the small things on your to-do list. They are the things that will hurt.

And the buzzing in your ears and the sudden sense of vertigo, that you've never experienced before, as you battle to inhale some air. And the terrible weight on your neck and the burning in your lungs, and his knee in between your legs and the thought that his cock's even harder than that moment you put your filthy lips around it. That will hurt.

But not the bleach.

Not the six bottles of bleach that I am now pouring over your body as the bath water runs as hot as I can make it. Not me, Maeve Beauman, with my naked-body-and-yellow-rubber-gloves look. I'm not hurting you, Hadley. I don't hurt anyone. I haven't hurt any of them.

I'm just the wife.

The cleaner.

I've done nothing wrong.

I dip my gloved hand into the bath and move the water around, mixing the bleach into the end where her head lies. The colour will start to fade in her hair and eyebrows.

I will leave her in there for a few hours to soak before I return to scrub the area around her nails that I have already cut. To brush her teeth and scrub her tongue and eyeballs. Before I take a brush to every hole and rid her of bacteria.

I drop the rubber gloves on the to-be-burned pile. I close the door behind me. My tracksuit bottoms and black vest are on the floor outside. I don't want to risk any fibres contaminating my work.

But I don't put them back on. I walk downstairs with nothing on. The television is still murmuring in the living room and Seth is asleep on his chair. He's still sitting up but his head is lolled backwards.

Delicately, I straddle him. He doesn't move. I kiss him on his neck, presented to me like a wolf in submission. I bite at it. Not hard, but enough to force a reaction.

Seth wakes up and looks at me.

He can see only me. I know that. It's what I wanted.

It's the reason I kept him tired, made him reckless.

We have a couple of hours to kill. And, when we're finished, it will be tomorrow.

And we start all over again.

MONDAY

100

Detective Sergeant Pace has no idea what's coming.

There's an emptiness in him that he can't get rid of. He's tired. Sitting up late and working a case alone. He doesn't want anybody else with him. He doesn't want some other officer nearby in case they get infected.

Detective Sergeant Pace is paranoia.

But it's more than that. There's delusion there.

In his darkest moments, when he is alone in that pit of his, trying to find something to help him claw his way out, he sees them. Flames.

Black flames.

At first, they spill out from his own shadow like dark, flowing water. They spread across the room. He feels their heat. Wave after wave. And he feels like he is evil. Or a conduit for evil. Or a host.

Detective Sergeant Pace is a trigger.

And he doesn't want some young, hungry constable to be contaminated by whatever it is that feeds off Pace's fear. This thing, whatever it is, whether it is real or not, it makes him act differently. He isn't himself. It makes people around him act differently to how they would normally act.

Everything he touches turns to shit.

That's how he is starting to think about this case. He is blaming himself. He is dirty. He is fucking it up. People are dying because of him. Because of his incompetence. Because of that sinister presence that he feels, that he knows other people feel when they are around him.

And it is getting worse.

There will be another body.

101

There was only four percent of battery life on the phone when Ant woke up but it was still safely in his hand. He clicked on his photo album to check it hadn't been a dream.

He plugged the phone into the socket to give it some time to charge while he threw his clothes into the washing machine and showered off an unexpected Sunday night of misadventure, running through it chronologically as the hot water pelted him in the face.

He dried and dressed and flicked through all the pictures he had taken. Then he uploaded them to his computer to back them up. He had enough on there to at least implicate this Seth character to the police. If he decided to share the information with them.

'You took her away,' he kept saying in his head.

You took her away.

From me.

It was James all over again. It wasn't Seth's place to decide.

Ant found the cable to his printer and plugged it into the USB socket of his laptop. He changed the setting to the highest possible quality and printed out a copy of every single photo he had taken on that night. He looked through them again. You could see everything: Seth dragging Hadley from his car to the boot; Seth unloading her from his boot at his London home; Seth driving off in a different car from the one he had arrived in; and the inside of the killer's home.

He made three copies of each picture. Each set was carefully taped on the desk along every side so that they lined up perfectly then paper-clipped in opposing corners to hold them together. Ant sealed one envelope with a damp sponge rather than his own tongue. He had licked the first envelope then thought about DNA and thrown it away.

The other two were left open. One on his desk in full view. He could look through them at any time he wanted. And the other was hidden beneath the coffee table rug. An obvious place to look but that was the point. He didn't know where this was going to lead and, if somebody was going to come after him to get his copy of the photos, they would probably leave after finding the envelope on his desk; they wouldn't want to hang around for too long once they had what they came for. And they were in close proximity to the computer should such a person need a reminder to also delete the digital copies.

He was incredibly lucid and well rested for somebody who had witnessed a brutal attack less than twenty-four hours earlier.

He had seen death before, though.

And he dealt with its possibility every night at work.

Each had their own level of anxiety. Each had their own level of pleasure. A different high, each time.

There were eight missed calls on his phone when Ant pressed the button to look at the time. It was late afternoon. He'd missed most of the day at work. It was probably them. He didn't care. The only people that thought his job was important were the people above him and that was only when they needed to blame him for something they'd got wrong. He knew it was meaningless automation. How dare they tell him any different?

The pictures needed to be deleted from the phone. Ant swiped across the screen to do so and nicked his finger on the third swipe. Closer inspection revealed a tiny chip in his screen.

'Fuck.' He spoke out loud to nobody. 'When it hit the windowsill. Shit.'

It was minuscule. A diamond-shaped indentation, barely visible to the naked eye. But Ant knew that the piece of glass need only be a few atoms in length and it tied him to that scene.

He would be implicated.

The photographs under the coffee table would also do that but they were only meant to be discovered upon his death, which he hoped was not on the agenda.

Those were the copies he made for the police.

Not the ones on his desk.

And not the ones he had sealed with a loving swipe of the sponge he had already thrown out.

And, in five hours, Ant will strap on his headset and listen to a bunch of whining babies moan about how difficult their life is.

He was thinking differently. He was different.

Still dirty, though.

So dirty.

102

I don't know when we got so reckless. In the early days, when love was just love and not a cancerous relative or strangled mistress, I used to make Seth wear a condom when we had sex. Even while I was getting fat on the pill.

Now I just let him blow it all inside me. I can still feel it in there when I wake up. Like it's moving around, trying to change my body.

I made Seth come upstairs with me. We fucked on the sofa a little, I was on top of him, I held his hair tightly in my hand. I was in control. The idiot was distracted by those fucking phonebooks, I could tell. Itching to fumble to a clean page and dial out. Already hungry.

'Get upstairs.' I told him. It wasn't a request. And I led him up there by his dick, clamping it tightly in my left hand, my right hand on the banister for balance.

I rode him hard and made all the noises that I knew he liked and I was louder than I needed to be because I wanted the sound to travel through the walls and under the bath water. I wanted her to hear what it was like to be fucked by my husband.

And when he unloaded inside of me and grunted like livestock, I tightened my stomach a few times and thrusted against him and shouted his name as I pretended to climax before falling on his chest and rolling off once his dick had softened a little.

Now, I'm awake. It's light outside and clearly late in the day. She has been soaking for hours and Seth is still resting. Sleeping soundly. Deeply. Untroubled. Like he was the one doing all the work.

All he had to do was beat up someone smaller and weaker than he was and then do some grocery shopping. The hardest part of his day was taking a shower and shaving off his stubble.

I want to shower. I want to wash some of this off. But there doesn't seem to be any point. I need to think about scraping my husband out of another woman's vagina more than I do my own. I have to get in there later. And her anus. And her mouth. I'll clean her teeth, too.

For him.

For us.

I need to clean my teeth. I can still taste his dick. And that hummus.

I get out of bed and he still doesn't move. Calls himself an insomniac. I can see myself in the mirror. I turn to the side and put a hand on my stomach. I look head on, checking the weight of my breasts. I can't see why he would prefer her body over mine. Her skin was a little tighter, maybe. Her tits, firmer. But not better. She was no steak to my burger.

He breathes silently. I haven't seen him so peaceful in a long time. It must be years. I can't decide whether I love him to death or I hate that he's alive, right now. Part of me wants to kiss him and not disturb his sleep. Another part wants me to smash something heavy into his face for fucking with everything so drastically again. I opt for neither.

The shower is perfect. Just what I need. To close me off from life for a while. I lock the door behind me in case Seth wakes up, but I doubt he will.

The water beats warmly against my head and I brush my hair back with my fingertips. The shampoo drips down between my breasts as I wash it out and the glass door is completely steamed up.

I'm not here. I'm not anywhere. I'm just warm and wet and comfortable.

I step back in the shower and the power of the water ripples against my stomach, cascading down between my thighs. I move slightly again and the droplets hit me where I want, pelting against me. I want to lose myself completely.

The middle finger of my right hand. Between my legs. Slow, soft, wet circles, at first. Just grazing. I'm thinking about Seth inside me last night and how I wished it had gone. How he was a little too soft, a little laid back. How I wanted him to hold me tighter, to dig his fingers into my skin with more venom. To fuck me like he was unsure whether he loved or hated me. I wanted him to be where I was. To love me but fuck me like he didn't.

I wanted to ride his face in the same way he was fucking my mouth. I wanted him louder, saying my name so she could hear him. I wanted to feel myself tighten around him at the point he was about to come. I wanted those thrusts to be as real as the ones I felt building in the shower.

Then there was black. I exhaled my orgasm and, when I opened my eyes, my left hand was resting against the shower wall as my right was still gripped by the tops of my thighs.

I am back to reality but thankful for that fleeting moment of nothingness. And pleasure. And escape.

I wrap a small white towel around my hair and a larger, softer one around my body and go back into the bedroom. And the bed is empty. Seth is gone.

103

Across the country, thousands of people had decided to throw their duvets back over their heads when the Monday-morning alarm called. Or they accidentally hit off instead of snooze. It happened. Or their weekend celebrations had bled into Sunday morning and they had decided to relive the adventure over a pub lunch and that had stretched into the evening when Monday had seemed too far into the future to give it any consideration.

Hadley, Ant, Maeve and Seth could all be tied together as four people who failed to call in to work at the start of the week, to inform their employers that they would not be in that day, but they joined a large group of illustrious, carefree shirkers. They lived miles away from each other. The greatest criminal minds would never be able to draw any comparisons that would link the four together.

And, at that moment, it was all the police would have. A heap of nothing. A tepid bath, at best.

The name of the second girl was already out. Seth wasn't even thinking about the law. He'd got away with it once. And then again. He hadn't done anything different this third time. He'd met Hadley over the phone and then in person and eventually put an end to her life, her trust. And he would dispose of her as he had with the other two. With Maeve's help, he fully expected to get away with it again. He wanted to. He didn't want to goad the police or the investigating officers.

It wasn't that he wanted anything more. He didn't want to rape the next one or kill her in a different way, a more creative way. He wasn't that guy chasing the next big sale or searching for a bigger thrill than before. To bite his next victim's neck out. Seth never even thought of them as victims. He wasn't looking for somebody to kill. He was looking for somebody to connect with. That's what he told himself. As only a delusional murderer could.

He didn't want more; he wanted the same thing. He just wanted it sooner.

Seth had slept and slept well. He could see all of her. Things weren't close up anymore. There were tiles and a pile of clothes and the bright-white tub and the girl in the cold water being stripped of colour, her once-pale skin now pinking and burning and blotching.

He stands next to the bath with his arms folded and his dick hanging between his legs. His head is cocked to the side like he is wondering what he ever saw in Hadley Serf.

The sound of the shower dies and he hears the unlocking of the door, then his wife's voice as she calls him from the bedroom, wondering where he has gone.

His mind flits to her holding onto his hair tightly and he feels the blood rushing to his dick. He doesn't want her to walk in and see him looking over the dead girl with an erect penis but now it's all he can think about.

Maeve calls again but all he hears are the noises that she made the night before. But he is fixed to the spot he is standing in. Getting harder. He looks at Hadley and remembers her lips brushing against his dick and he wonders whether he could make himself come before Maeve finds him.

The bottom of the bedroom door scrapes against the carpet and Seth knows he doesn't have any time.

But he tries.

There is nowhere to look but at the dead girl he never fucked. He keeps going. He closes his eyes and thinks of his wife, the muscles in her thighs.

Hadley creeps into his vision. She is joining in.

Whatever it takes.

Seth is breathing heavily, panting.

In the back of his mind, away from the depravity, is the realism that Maeve would soon walk in.

She is already there.

Maeve stands three feet away from the bathroom door her husband left ajar. It's wide enough for her to see him standing there, naked, his back towards her, the woman he killed submersed in bleach a few feet ahead of him, and the quiet but unmistakable sound of male masturbation.

She doesn't want to watch but she does. Out of intrigue. In despair. They're under a lot of pressure, she tells herself. Like the beaten wife or the person turning a blind eye to some other kind of abuse.

She is stuck. In a loop. In the situation she continues to enable. In that hallway. Where one end contains pleasure and the other leads to the antithesis of orgasm.

And it is another thing she will have to forgive.

Maeve shuts her eyes and turns away, deliberately stepping on the stair that creaks as she descends, remaining controlled. She has a role.

Seth hears the sound of his wife's foot hitting the groaning wood of that step and knows that she isn't going to walk in.

Without Maeve, Seth wouldn't know when to stop.

104

This is my shitty day. The thing that has brought Seth and I closer together. That has reignited our passion and want for one another.

It starts with a hot shower and the orgasm I never made it to last night.

Next, we're eating a meal that is neither breakfast, lunch nor dinner, because we slept in to such a strange time. And we're drinking coffee and fresh orange juice as though what happened didn't happen or is *de rigueur* for this household.

And he's cleaning the house to a substandard level that I will have to go over again at some point but at least it's keeping him busy and away from the phonebook while I use a soft toilet brush to scrub the skin of Hadley Serf.

And the three toothbrushes. One for her teeth, of course. One that I push into her vagina. And the last, which scours her perfectly whitened arsehole before plunging a few inches inside to be safe.

I then use that same brush on her teeth again. A little payback from me, though something tells me she probably wasn't one to shy away from some arse to mouth.

She's burning up nicely now.

I pull the plug to release the water, hose her down with cold water from the shower then refill the bath with more cold. She can lie there overnight. It's almost time to wrap her up and dump her.

It's dark when I go downstairs and the oven is on in the kitchen. Something smells great. It's too late for dinner but I need it. I can see Seth through the kitchen window out the back burning the clothes along with some twigs and leaves he has raked together in the garden.

I open the fridge door and take out a bottle of wine and pour myself a large glass. It's familiar. Have we gone back already? I take two gulps and top it up again before placing the bottle back.

And then we are sitting down in the lounge and it's the late-night news and they're telling the country the name of the girl they found in the woods and there's a picture of her on the screen from when she was alive and she wasn't that pretty. And I remember her. She was no Hadley Serf. No firm tits and plump skin. Seth certainly has no type.

Just lonely ones. People who will talk back. Who listen or want to be listened to. That's his type.

We're both tired, even though we haven't been up for most of the day. I don't want to leave him down here alone because I'm already worried that he will start calling out again.

I use what I have to get him to come upstairs with me.

He is kissing me in the hallway and pushing me against the same wall I pushed him against last night. And now he's leading me.

But that's when I see it. Hanging from the letterbox by its corner.

I don't know when it happened because neither of us heard it come through. And it was obviously hand-delivered because it's a plain, manila envelope with the words, '*For Seth*' written on the front.

This is the beginning of my shitty night.

105

He writes, '*When did you realise? Where did that happen / what happened? How did that feel?*' on a pink Post-it note and sticks it to the corner of his monitor. He prefers the yellow ones. Now there are green and blue notes, too. Who ordered them? Did they think it would brighten up the room?

Ant is trying to keep things as normal as possible. And now he has to deal with pink fucking Post-it notes.

Nobody calls that is suicidal. A call from some guy who sounded young – late teens or early twenties – and was experiencing growing feelings of attraction towards other men. He said he'd already told his mother that he wasn't gay when she asked him a few years before and he didn't know who to talk to. He felt bad about lying to his mother. Ant didn't even break into a sweat on that one.

Six calls in and he is still in the same T-shirt he arrived in. Maybe the things he has seen have changed him. He has been hardened. Desensitised. He doesn't know.

He is distracted. By the pink note on his screen. And the manila envelope in his rucksack.

The room is filled with a forced lack of judgement and an insincere tone of understanding. Not everyone answering the phone to these people is here because they care or want to give something back. A lot of the time, it's about balance. People do something they shouldn't: they're mean to someone, they misbehave and deride and fornicate and bitch and bully, and they think that showing some compassion will somehow even out their misdeeds. Like it will forgive the fact that they are crappy human beings.

Altruism is a concept invented by the rich and shallow, who place too much value on their own time. They tell their kids about it like they do Father Christmas or God. They know it's bullshit.

Of course, Ant knows that there are also people there who genuinely care. There are people who feel fortunate and cannot bear that others feel less than they deserve. There are people who hurt when they see or hear others hurting.

And there's Ant. He's something else now. He's tapping his leg nervously beneath the desk as somebody speaks in his ear about loneliness and time away from his children. And he knows this is his last call.

Then he's in his car and he's driving down the motorway to London. He's only been to the Beaumans' house once before but it's like muscle memory, he seems to drive there on autopilot.

And he parks across the street as he did before, takes the envelope from his rucksack and writes, '*For Seth*' on the front in black biro. He scribbles back and forth a few times across the lines of each letter. It's not his handwriting.

The lights are on in the house and he can feel his heart hitting the inside of his chest so hard, it's almost unzipping his jacket as he gets out of the car.

This is it. He can't fuck it up. He can't get caught.

Ant repeats the steps he took the night before, walking on the grass so not to disturb the shingle driveway and make a noise.

Now he is sweating.

Now he needs a new T-shirt.

He opens the front of the letterbox and can hear voices inside. It could be the television. It could be the sound of a real-life murderer. His hand is shaking. Maybe this is a mistake. *Am I in over my head? Is he talking to Hadley? Is this crazy?*

Ant doesn't want the envelope to drop through onto the floor because it could alert them and he would have to clumsily speed off in some way. Right now, terrified and trembling, he feels like the one in control.

He pushes the envelope through, leaving a corner on his side of the door and shuts it behind the heavy letterbox opening. It hangs there safely. Still and unknown. For now.

Then he tiptoes like a cartoon villain across the grass and back to his car. He pulls away. He's confused. He's terrified. And he's more excited than he has ever been in his life.

106

He looks as white as the one I have bleached.

'What? Seth, what is it?'

His mouth is agog like a moron. No colour in his face. He rubs the back of his hand against his forehead.

'Are you going to answer me?'

'Fuck.' He isn't speaking to me, he's talking to whatever just came out of the envelope. I can see the inscription. It was hand delivered for him. Must have been some time this evening because I've already picked up the mail today.

'Seth. Seth.' I raise my voice to click him back to reality. 'Seth, what's going on? You look like shit.'

'Somebody saw us.'

'What do you mean?'

'They know what we did.' With that, he turns around a grainy picture of the front of our house, light poking through the windows in the hallway, a large figure that looks like a dimly lit and pixelated Seth carrying a body from the boot of the car to the front door.

What YOU did, I say in my head. *YOU, Seth.*

'What the fuck, Seth?'

'I didn't see anybody, I swear. There was nobody around. I kept checking.'

That sentence makes me wonder. Had he been checking all night? Had he gone out there with the express intention to kill that girl? A crime of passion is different to premeditation.

I block the thought from my mind.

It doesn't matter now. I've made my choice.

'Is there anything else in there apart from pictures? A note?'

He flicks through each page, turning it front and back.

'There's nothing here. No writing. No note. Nothing. What kind of sicko would do this?'

I look at him for a moment. He has no idea.

Then he's at the front door and opening it. And he's outside on the path before I know it, looking around frantically. I half expect him to shout out at nobody.

'Seth,' I hiss through my teeth. He's looking left and right, left and right. 'Seeeeeth.'

He comes back in. Paler. Paranoid.

'What does he want?'

'Why do you think it's a he?' I ask, screwing my face up.

'Oh, Maeve, it's always a fucking he.'

'Come in. You're getting agitated.' I touch his arm to guide him back into the house. Any potential ardour has evaporated. This is serious. It's not part of the plan.

He pulls his arm away from me, like he can't stand the contact.

It hurts.

We sit in the lounge and I tell him, 'If this person wanted to go to the police, they would have knocked on our door by now.'

He says nothing.

'There's obviously some other agenda. I don't know what it is yet – maybe they want money, to blackmail us.'

Nothing.

'Are you sure there's nothing in there?'

He throws the envelope over to me, sits back in the chair and runs his fingers through his hair. He looks as though he may be thinking of something but I assume he simply despairs at my questions.

Like I'm the irritation.

Still, I open the envelope and rifle through the images. I haven't seen them all. He must have been outside the house for a while because he has a picture of Seth getting home that night and another of him pulling out of the drive in my car. There's no sign of me.

Fuck. Seth has me thinking of this person as a man, now. And that's stupid. It could be anyone.

I tear the envelope and open it out flat, just in case there is something written on the inside. But there isn't. Seth was right. It's just the pictures. No message. No way of contacting whoever delivered them.

'What are you thinking about?' I have to ask because he's giving me nothing.

He shuts his eyes and takes a deep breath. Like this is somehow my fault. Like I fucked up our lives in some way.

'Well, you sit there and have a think to yourself. When you're ready, let me know. Because we have to get rid of this fucking body.'

I walk out of the lounge. Leaving him to wallow with his self-pity and his hands in his hair and his beloved phonebooks.

This was supposed to bring us closer together and, already, it's pulling us further apart.

107

One night, there's a last-minute change of heart and your boyfriend doesn't come over.

This is how Theresa meets Seth.

She made the effort to shower and shave her legs and shape her pubic hair into a neat rectangle. She wore underwear that matched; she didn't always do that, it wasn't something that was particularly important to her. Her hair was washed and dried and straightened. Her skin was made up and perfumed.

She was waiting.

And ready.

And willing.

And he cancelled.

The dinner for two that she had prepared became a dinner for one. She always fell back onto her food for comfort. The bottle of wine she had opened that the shopkeeper had told her would need time to breathe was only poured into one glass and completely finished. Both of these made her feel so guilty that she ended up eating the two desserts she had bought, too.

The phone rang as she was flicking through the channels on her television. She hoped it was her boyfriend calling to apologise and grovel. So she could tell him where to go, and hang up. But it wasn't him, so she immediately felt worse.

It was Seth. And he wanted to talk. So she did.

And she did it again.

He was there. He was listening instead of waiting for his turn to speak. He was attentive. And now she is splashed all over the news for being dumped in a Warwickshire field.

She would hate the picture that her parents provided because she thought she looked overweight in that one. She was right. She didn't know it made the public less sympathetic towards her. They cared more if you died and you were pretty.

Maybe she was better out of this world. Her only crime was loneliness. Her fault was naïvety and optimism. And the usual gluttony and guilt.

108

Detective Sergeant Pace has travelled from London because he knows it is going to be her that they have found. More bleach. More plastic. He's been searching around London, and Theresa has been three counties away. He is losing this one.

Maeve has been watching him on the television and she thinks she can see that in him, that he is losing. But she is wrong about Pace, that's how he always looks. His eyes are dark because of the things he has seen. The things he can't stop seeing. That keep him awake. He has escaped his small-town beginnings but whatever he was running from has followed him to London and he has caught up with it in Warwickshire.

It is pale with red blotches and white hair, this time. It is overweight and sad and wrapped in plastic. But it is the same thing he has seen before.

It is evil.

It is everywhere.

109

Seth Beauman looks worried. But that's all it is. A look.

He knows that's how he should feel. Sullen. Pensive. Frightened. Whatever.

He doesn't feel any of those things.

He doesn't even know if he's asleep or awake.

He watches as Maeve drinks herself to sleep, calming herself in the best way she knows. The only way. She's flicking through the channels. The ones in the higher numbers on the television guide that are variations on the same theme: people cooking dinner for one another and being judged, people singing and being judged, people going on first dates and being judged, people getting tattoos removed or letting their mother-in-law choose their wedding dress or making their own cushion covers from clothes they have found in the attic, people selling things in the attic to pay for other things that they don't really want, people who live in a certain postcode who have money they didn't earn and had fuck-all to do with their days.

There are people and things and judges and materials and panels of experts and tears and a lack of talent and bad grammar. And Seth doesn't understand why Maeve likes it so much but she does. And that makes him not like her as much.

It hasn't even really been a day and he's already waiting for her to fall asleep so he can send her to bed and get on with his little hobby. His escape. Itching to get back to his project.

It's his *Bored Horny Crackhead Housewives of Suburbia.*

His *Don't Tell Bridezilla Her Dad Picked the Disgusting Dress.*

His *Tone-deaf Simpletons Get Laughed at by Three Millionaires.*

It's the same thing. The same reasoning behind it. The same motivation.

But he kills innocent people.

So it's a bit worse.

But not as bad as those illiterate trust-fund babies that live in that postcode.

TUESDAY

110

The wine was pretty cheap. It's all the preservatives they put in there. The impurities.

That's why I feel completely exhausted after sleeping. And why I feel sick. And my head aches. And the flatulence. And natural daylight pierces through my eyes, scorches my retinas and dropkicks my dehydrated brain, causing it to rattle around in my skull as a million thoughts ricochet off one another and explode.

Everything is so dirty.

You can get a hangover from one drink if it's impure enough.

I think I had two bottles.

I can't even remember going to bed. I know that I definitely fell asleep on the sofa, so I either walked up and have forgotten, or Seth carried me.

He's next to me, sleeping like nothing has happened. Just another day in the Beauman household.

And that's how we have to treat it. He's right. But I can't understand how he's doing it so well.

'Seth.' I nudge him with my right elbow. He stirs. I need some water. And some eggs. I read somewhere that they contain cysteine and that helps to ease the suffering. Exercise can help, too, but I can't even imagine beating a sloth in a race to the bathroom at this moment.

I wonder whether sex would be enough exercise to speed things along and could I maybe change my get-up nudge to a come-closer prod.

I know it's too late for that when Seth says, 'What?' like I've completely inconvenienced his day already.

'It's almost half past seven.'

'So?'

'So we can't lie here all day again. I have meetings, stuff to catch up on from yesterday...' More thoughts enter the husk in my skull. It hurts.

Seth rolls over to look at me. I love it when he does that.

'Work? Today? We're awake in time, we can, at least, call in sick.'

'That's not the play, Seth.'

'You're the boss,' he resigns, and sits up.

'Come back. I'm not saying that. I'm not the boss.' I have a little room left in my brain to wonder why the fuck I am putting up with this, why I don't just call the police myself. What am I committing myself to?

He lies down next to me and I stroke his face.

'Look, I'm not telling you what to do, of course, I'm just saying that we have to avoid drawing attention to ourselves. We have to go on like this isn't happening to us.'

'And that woman? And those pictures?'

'They'll be here when we get back. We'll get her out of here tonight – we can't do it in broad daylight.'

'You're right. That makes sense. I don't know how you manage to think so clearly in this situation.' He looks right into me. He seems genuine. I see the love. Or I want to see it.

I feel myself blush. Proud of myself for being able to bleach and dispose of a dead body.

He kisses me.

And I forget that I might hate him.

'It's not half past seven yet, is it? So we don't have to get up right away.' Seth smiles at me. And he kisses me again.

Then his hand is on my breast and working its way down over my stomach and ending between my legs. And I can feel his hard dick against my hip.

I open my legs and invite my husband to fuck the hangover out of me.

By filling me with more impurity.

111

Daisy Pickersgill helped people.

That's what she did.

That's who she was.

That's what got her killed.

In her third year at university, studying English literature, her younger brother, destined to follow in her footsteps, went out with friends for a drink near King's Cross and never came home.

He had drunkenly bumped into somebody, knocking their shoulder. His immediate and genuine apology fell on deaf ears. He was with one friend, walking back towards the Tube station. They wanted to walk away. But the group of three young men wouldn't let them.

Two of the men beat his friend to the ground, stamping on his chest and legs and breaking one of his arms. The other pulled a knife and stabbed Daisy's brother five times in the stomach and slashed across his face before they all ran off.

The entire incident was caught from two angles on CCTV.

Freddie Pickersgill bled to death on the street.

And his sister changed her life.

She became evangelical about the rise in knife crime, particularly in London. She formed groups; she was outspoken, she attended marches. And she decided to work with the troubled youth in her east London borough. Even if she could help one person, stop one person, save one person from resolving their differences through violence. If she could be there as somebody to listen to and work with, then it would go some way to ensuring that what happened to her brother was not another forgotten statistic.

So, when she was called by a stranger, late at night, who could not sleep and needed somebody to talk to, she couldn't help herself. Daisy would be that Good Samaritan.

And three weeks later, her parents would lose their only other child.

And Daisy Pickersgill could follow in her brother's footsteps as just another crime statistic.

112

Seth waved Maeve out of the driveway. He was in his work suit and tie and his shoes were shining but he had no intention of going into the office. He had smashed his monthly target. Maeve didn't remember that because she had never asked him about it.

He phoned his boss, apologised for not calling him yesterday, 'I've listened to the voicemails, sorry,' he lied. 'I'm still nursing this sickness so I'm going to work from home today. I don't want to spread it around the office.' He was confident. It wasn't a question, he was telling his employer that he was going to stay at home that day. And that was that.

Upstairs, Hadley was submerged. Her water needed changing again. This was normally Maeve's job but Seth took it upon himself to be useful.

He started in the kitchen, scraping the egg from their breakfast plates, rinsing them under a tap and placing them in the dishwasher with the two coffee cups they had also used. He wiped down the kitchen worktops and took the rubbish from under the sink out the back door and placed it into a larger bin.

While he was out there, he checked on the ash that was once Hadley's jeans and Maeve's underwear. It was all gone. No evidence. He loved the smell.

In the garage was a large roll of plastic. It had been used on his first two victims and would last another three, easily. The police could search for recent corresponding purchases, but Seth had bought several of them a few years back to use as dust sheets when he was going to repaint some rooms in the house. Maeve had decided that the carpets needed replacing, too. So Seth had rolled the paint onto the walls freely, without care for any residual splatter hitting the old carpets.

Upstairs, Seth took all his clothes off and placed them in a pile next to the bathtub. Just as Maeve would do. He hated that suit, anyway. And Maeve's mother had bought him the tie, that's why he'd been specific in wearing it, that day. Everything would have to burn.

With the rubber gloves on and nothing else, Seth unplugged the cold bath, watched as it drained, then showered Hadley Serf with cold water before replacing the plug and refilling the tub.

He pushed his victim's hair away from her face. Those bulbous eyes were not as he remembered her. She was damaged all over. He remembered how he'd hit her and the force that had come from him. He remembered not feeling as in control as when his full weight was pressing down against her neck.

Seth smiled as he sensitively ran a rubber forefinger down Hadley's cheek.

'Why did you have to say those things, eh? You don't say those things about my Maeve.'

He waits.

The bath fills.

He turns off the tap, throws the gloves on his pile of clothes then goes back to his bedroom to take another shower.

Thirty minutes later he is in the lounge on the phone.

'Hi. It's Seth. Want to talk?'

'Who is this?'

'Seth. I can't sleep.'

'It's the middle of the day.'

'Want to talk?'

'Fuck off, you weirdo.' She hangs up.

Everything is back to normal.

About to dial another number, Seth hears a noise at the front of the house. Somebody is trying to post a letter.

113

The world of archiving did not grind to a crashing halt because Ant missed an eight-hour shift on a Monday. His supervisor had to pretend he'd even noticed that Ant hadn't been there when he called in to say he'd be off today, too.

'It's clearing up from yesterday, I'm sure I'll be back tomorrow.'

'Take your time. Rest up.'

And that was that.

Ant got in his car and drove the journey he already knew by heart to the Beauman's detached home.

He waited a while, parking in his usual spot, and ran through that fateful night he followed a girl he didn't really know. And then how he followed her murderer back to the house he now sat outside. The place he was just yesterday, delivering the photos.

And now he was on the doorstep with Seth in front of him.

'You took those photos.' Seth told him. 'You want to come inside and talk, Mr...'

'I don't think you need to know my name, right now. And I don't need to come inside, either.'

'So, what do you want?' Seth was calm. Measured. His insides betrayed that cool exterior. He was wondering whether the easiest thing to do would be to kill this guy. Maybe it would even be fun. More of a challenge.

He didn't want to be one of those guys who only kill women. He wasn't a misogynist.

He thought it seemed like the right thing to do.

But he held his nerve.

'Well, first, I just want to let you know that I'm not here to black-mail you.'

'That's good to know. There's not a huge amount of money flying around.'

'It's not about that.'

'So, what is it about?'

Ant stuttered a little. He hadn't wanted this confrontation so soon. He had planned to drop off another envelope with instructions for Seth – where and when to meet him. He'd even practised what he was going to say. Ant was trying to remember all the information but the conversation wasn't going exactly as he had planned.

'I haven't gone to the police and I'm not planning to.' He exhaled, relieved to have delivered one of his rehearsed lines.

'The police aren't going to be involved and you don't want to extort money from me. But I'm guessing those pictures aren't the only copies of what you think you saw.'

Ant was getting frustrated with how cool Seth was.

'I know what I saw. Of course there are other copies. My insurance. They'll get to the right people if anything happens to me.'

'How did you find me? What were you doing in that car park?'

'I was following her. I had been for almost a week. She called me. She was distraught. Looking for you.' Ant could see that he had Seth's interest. 'I was looking out for her. Making sure that she was coping. I didn't want to see her wasting her life. I didn't realise she only had a few days left.'

Seth was trying to figure him out. What could he possibly want?

Then Ant said, 'You took her from me, Seth.'

And the sound of his own name jolted Seth's composure.

'Took her from you? She didn't even know you.'

'But the next one will.'

'The next one? What are you talking about, friend? What do you want from me?'

This is the part where Ant knew exactly what he was going to say.

'I've seen a dead body before and nothing has ever felt like that. But that's because I've never seen anybody die before. Until two nights ago. That was a different feeling altogether.' Ant waits for Seth to respond, but he doesn't. He just lets Ant talk, gives him his full attention.

Ant continues.

'I want it again. But this time I want to be right there.'

'You want to come and kill somebody with me?'

'I don't think I, actually, want to do it. Not yet. I just want to be there when you do it.'

Seth didn't like the 'not yet' part of that sentence. It implied that it was something he was contemplating. This wasn't going to be a one-time thing. This guy was chasing a high, and Seth knew how that felt. He knew what hunger was. But he had to keep this psycho calm and in his pocket until he knew where all the copies of the photos were.

He didn't seem like the brightest of social outcasts, they were in his home somewhere. Seth looked at the way he was dressed. Clean but plain. Simple. He was awkward. Just the way he was standing told Seth that he was probably alone.

And that's how he wanted to come across, too. He didn't want Maeve involved in this. This guy did not need to know about Maeve.

Not yet.

'You want to be there when I kill someone?'

'That's exactly it. Or I could just submit the pictures to the police. I could do it anonymously. I'm sure they'd find it interesting. I know that girl that's all over the news is you, too, isn't it? Theresa Palmer.'

Seth just looked at him. He'd always been so careful. Killing Hadley in the car park had been riskier than the others. Maybe that was intentional. Maybe he wanted to be seen. Maybe that was the next level for him.

'Do we have a deal or not?' Ant asked, knowing the answer.

'We have a deal. But you need to know some things before this happens. Firstly, you do not come back to this house. You do not contact me. I will contact you. I will call you. I will keep you informed and tell you where to be and when to be there. Okay?'

'Okay.'

Ant was smiling. Seth could see the excitement in his eyes. He did everything but rub his hands together in glee.

'I want it to happen soon.' Ant chimed in.

'You need to stop with that shit. People who run out and jump into this because they're excited or needy make mistakes. And mistakes get you caught.'

Ant nodded. He understood. He agreed.

He had no idea he had acted impulsively about this. That he had put less than a day's thought into what he was doing. That he was the one making a mistake. That his sense of control was completely misplaced.

'You don't live near here, right?'

'That's right.'

'Tomorrow. Eleven o'clock. You meet me where you saw it happen. I'll show you how this works.' Seth was so cold, but he knew that he was the one in control.

'What about Hadley?'

'You don't talk about her. You don't mention her name. To me or anyone. You have nothing to do with that. I will sort her. I will do that alone. Like I always do.' Seth was pushing any thought of an accomplice away from Ant's mind. All that Maeve did for him, you would think that he would feel naturally protective towards her.

It wasn't that, though.

'Eleven o' clock tomorrow night. In that car park. Don't try anything funny.'

'We are both aware of what is at stake here, let's not pretend otherwise.' Seth managed to hit just the right level of threat to make Ant understand his sentiment. But also scare him enough to know that he, too, should not try anything funny.

He wanted to warn Ant further. He wanted to tell him to be careful, that killing was addictive. That it would change him. Just watching it had changed him, probably.

'Do you need anything else, Mr...?'

'No. No. I've got everything I need.' Ant took a step forwards as though he was going to shake Seth's hand but Seth subtly moved himself back inside his home. 'You can call me Mr A.'

'I'm not going to call you that. You know my name. I'm guessing yours begins with an A. Shall I call you Alex? Angus? Arthur?'

'Ant. You can call me Ant.' He looked like a child. So naïve. Out of his depth.

'Thank you, Ant. There has to be a level of trust here. I shall see you tomorrow night at eleven. I don't want to hear from you until then.'

Ant nods. And walks backwards four steps. He doesn't want to turn his back on Seth until there is a safe enough distance. He turns and walks calmly to his car though his heart is beating fast and his face is beaming with joy at the prospect of watching another person breathe their last breath in front of him. But, this time, so much closer.

Seth shuts the door. He curses out loud. 'Fuck'. Just a whisper.

He takes his suit and least favourite tie and throws them into the incinerator with the envelope of photographs that he has no use for. He would explain to Maeve when she returns home.

They had to get rid of Hadley that night.

Then he could worry about the idiotic Mr A.

114

I should have changed her water one more time. That's what I'm thinking as my office underlings feign concern about my health because I missed one lousy day.

They're filling me in and updating me as though I care.

Like I give a fuck about some snappy copy or market research when there's a dead girl in my bath and there's still a little bleach in the water. She needs to be hosed down now and prepared for disposal.

These people talk to me like I matter and I think of Hadley as though she doesn't.

I want to look her up on social media, find some pictures of her before she was bloated and blotchy and bruised around the neck and bleeding from her ears. I want her to be as beautiful as I imagine. I want her pictures to show that she grabbed hold of life and lived as much as she could for as long as she could.

I want holiday photos in a bikini and snorkel with friends and laughter and a different local man every night.

I want her to glow. I want to see that her friends loved her and that she had a family.

Because the last girl Seth killed was a bit pathetic. She wasn't a strong woman. She wasn't ambitious or vivacious. It was difficult to feel bad for her.

I want Hadley Serf to have been an amazing light in the lives of everyone she knew or touched in some way. I want her to be unapologetically mourned and missed. So that I can feel as horrendous as possible that she is gone and my husband took her.

I need to feel like that.

I need to try, at least.

But I can't look her up. That would be stupid. I wonder how many crimes are solved these days by looking through a person's browsing history. I'm sure that all of these social media companies can and do log who looks at who's profile and what time they do it. And I'm sure these records are available to the authorities at their request when it is pertinent to a possible murder or other criminal activity.

Surely Seth wouldn't be stupid enough to have done that.

I thank everyone for the information I never really listened to and dismiss them from my office. And I swivel on my chair for a while, staring at the wall and tapping a pen against my teeth.

Seth was so strong this morning. I think of the shape of his arms as he held his weight up over me, thrusting himself between my legs. It's the third or fourth time we've had sex in the last week and every time has been different. And every time I have let him come inside me. And I don't know why. He likes it, I know that much. He doesn't want to ejaculate inside a piece of latex. He doesn't always want to pull it out at the last minute; it loses the sensation, he tells me. But he also hasn't wanted to fuck me for months. Maybe I'm just letting him have what he wants.

Maybe it's the situation. What we are doing is so wrong that perhaps everything we do needs to feel that way, too.

I'm dirty. Make me dirtier.

You ruined her, now ruin me.

I don't know.

What I do know is that I can't concentrate. I'm hungover and hungry and horny. And I need to get that girl out of my house tonight.

115

He lifts up slightly onto his tiptoes at the end and grunts as he ejaculates into his bathroom sink. Four pictures of Hadley rest against the tiles behind the taps.

Then Ant needs to clean the entire flat.

It's a compulsion, of course, but also a distraction. Tomorrow night seems so far away.

He scrubs the floor and thinks about his interaction with Seth. So cold. Like he wasn't interested, he wasn't frightened by the prospect that Ant could go to the police. Then Ant wonders how many people Seth could have killed. Was it so many that he was bored of it, but he just couldn't stop? Was it like his own compulsions? Ant didn't always enjoy being on his knees with a sponge, scouring the grouting between floor tiles, but he had to do it.

Perhaps Seth and I are similar, he told himself.

He hadn't thought it through. What was he going to do after seeing another person die at Seth's hands? That wouldn't be enough. Would he want to do it himself? Could he choke the life out of somebody? He wasn't as big as Seth, it would have to be a woman. Or maybe he could start bulking up so as not to narrow his options.

He didn't even know how Seth chose his victims. How did he find them when they lived so far from him? What was he doing in Oxford?

There were questions in his mind that needed answering. He would plan to ask them tomorrow night. He wouldn't bumble this time. He'd get it right. He would practise in front of his now spotless mirror.

The floor in the bathroom was also sparkling, as was the sink he had dirtied with his useless, unwanted seed.

He thinks and he cleans and he eats and he gets dressed and he leaves to distract his mind with other people's problems.

He sticks his stupid Post-it notes to his screen with the reminders he no longer needs but can't live without, and he places the headset over his head and logs into his computer. For the first time since he started volunteering, since seeing his best friend dead behind that door, since his life changed forever, he doesn't really care about helping anyone, about saving anyone. He just wants tomorrow. He wants more death. To feel more alive.

116

Social-media statuses tend to put me in a bad mood. When a parent says happy birthday to a child who is not old enough to read, let alone have their own profile to acknowledge, that aggravates me. And it's worse when fifty-eight people then comment on that status, congratulating the illiterate toddler personally.

Or when somebody sends a message to a deceased loved one. What ever happened to people just having thoughts and keeping them to themselves? Your dead uncle is not scrolling through his feed as he decomposes underground.

And those people who write things like, 'Don't even ask', hoping that everybody will ask. Or, 'Some people really need to blah, blah, blah.' They hit return and wait for anybody at all to ask who the 'some people' are and what the 'blah, blah, blah' is all about. Or they write, 'Are you okay, hun?' But they're rolling their eyes as they type it, just as I am.

Don't forget, 'To the guy in the white van who clipped my wing mirror then drove off...' He is never going to see that. We get it, you're annoyed but what do you hope to achieve from this?

And the braggers and ones who only take pictures of themselves and the ones who are fishing for compliments. And those pictures of a beautiful and unfeasibly happy and devoted family that are on the brink of separation.

And the ones who write a huge paragraph about everything that has happened to them in one particular situation, they start with 'When...' and end with, 'That'. Like it's an everyday occurrence but clearly isn't. And fifty people hit a like button and perpetuate this kind of behaviour.

I step through the front door after a completely unproductive day in the office, and these are the things I am thinking of.

Hadley, you were taken too soon. I think of you every day. RIP.

Seven likes. Fifteen sad faces. Eight crying eyes.

To the guy who posted photographs of my husband carrying a dead body from the boot of his car to our house, you should mind your own damn business.

'Everything okay, hun?'

When you arrive home from work and your husband is already at the house but was supposed to be in the office until later and he's obviously taken the day off or only went in until lunch. And he's cooked you dinner and rinsed down the dead body you have been anxious about with more cold water and wrapped her in plastic ready to dispose of after you've eaten your salad and black bean *taquitos*. That.

117

Seth and Maeve Beauman wear gloves to handle the body. She smells of bleach and death and plastic and she fits easily into the boot of Seth's car. Straight. Lengthways. Diagonally. A spare tyre under her arse and a reflective breakdown triangle by her swaddled right arm.

She is wrapped tightly so that no fibres from the car can get past the plastic and onto her skin.

Maeve is overly cautious about all the details. She is the reason that they haven't been caught. She thinks of everything. She drives the car because she is less likely to be pulled over by the police. Not that she speeds, or forgets to signal when she changes lanes.

They listen to a modern song that neither of them knows, and Seth changes the station and says, 'Ah, that's better. Who doesn't like Elton John?'

Maeve concentrates on the road ahead and signals left to exit the roundabout and pull onto the motorway. She feels the body roll a little and shudders quietly to herself. She hates that Hadley is in there.

Seth starts singing under his breath.

'Really, Seth?'

'What?'

It was irritating her that he was suddenly so calm and cool. He was unflustered because she had planned everything out. His job was making the calls and going for drinks and murdering the people who formed a connection with him. Everything else was Maeve. What a team.

Trees were tied together with police tape where the second girl, Theresa Palmer, had been found. Forensic testing was going on as the Beaumans made their way up the M40. Nothing would be found that could connect them to the victim. Detective Pace was back in London, waiting on results. Once again, he was three counties away from the action.

But Hadley wasn't going to that field. Too risky. The Beaumans just wanted to get into Warwickshire, find somewhere quiet, and drop the package off. This time, they didn't care when it was found. The sooner the better.

If the police thought it was some kind of killing spree, like a pattern might even exist, they would want to close it down as quickly as possible. They would want the public's faith intact. They would step up their efforts, maybe increase their resources.

And that is exactly what Maeve wanted.

118

Detective Sergeant Pace is going nowhere.

Detective Sergeant Pace is a ghost.

He has discovered from the phone records that several late-night calls were made to both Daisy and Theresa in the days leading up to their deaths, each from completely different mobile phone numbers that he has investigated and found to be on pay-as-you-go contracts that were no longer in use.

They had been burned.

These women had been deliberately groomed and the killer was covering their tracks.

If he worked backwards even further, he would notice the correlation between the phone numbers that started both relationships. He would have the Beaumans' home phone number. He would have an address. But he was focused on the days that led up to the murders.

Detective Sergeant Pace is closer than he thinks.

The smog and degradation of the city is starting to weigh down upon him. At first he loved it. He absorbed it. He hid in it. And he shone in it. Success in cases meant that he put his old life behind him. He had escaped that small-town existence he had always felt too big for.

But now, that small Berkshire village of Hinton Hollow seems to be pulling him back. The quaint train station and independent bookshop, the corrupt local councillors and the matriarchal figure of Mrs Beaufort. The voice in the woods and the black flames. His old home could now be his escape. The pressure of London is making him feel smaller and smaller.

He lays face down on his bed, his stubble growing into the start of a beard, his long leather jacket draped over him like a blanket, like furled wings. Around the bed he imagines a vortex of dark clouds, waiting to swallow him whole.

He thinks about Daisy, wrapped in plastic.

And Theresa, wrapped in plastic.

If he could just empty his mind for a few hours, get some sleep, the morning would bring him something else to think about.

119

'Samaritans. How can I help?'

He doesn't mean it. Not tonight.

Ant does not care that his first caller feels alone. That he has nobody to talk to. His wife never asks him about his day anymore, she seems uninterested. She's always on her phone. He is suspicious of her. She could be talking to anyone. She's started exercising more. She's on a diet. He talks to his kids a lot but he craves some adult interaction. He loves them, of course, but conversation is limited.

Ant wants to hang up. He wants to tell this guy to grow a pair of balls and talk to his wife. She's the one he should be saying this shit to. If you're worried she's sleeping around, confront her. If you don't care, find a way to live with it. Have a go yourself. Just stop complaining. Act.

Ant feels stronger. Like he is gaining more control.

The next woman was burnt out. Contracted to work thirty-five hours per week, she often went above and beyond those numbers. Sometimes doubling it for very little reward. It was expected in her company. That's how she justified it. If you just did your contracted hours then you weren't really doing your job. If you left the office at five, that wasn't seen as good time management, it was seen as shirking your responsibilities. Typical corporate bullshit. Zero regard for physical or mental health if it got in the way of turning a profit.

And here's the rub, anytime she was successful, her immediate boss and her CEO took the credit. Anytime something went wrong, she took the blame. And they loved to blame.

Her morale was low. They had drained her. They had eked every ounce of effort from her body and mind and reaped the benefits for themselves. And now she was scared that they had chewed her up and would spit her out but she didn't want to continue in the cycle that had become habit for her.

Ant wants to hang up again. He wants to tell this woman to check the company handbook, to get some legal advice. He wants to tell her to stand up for herself, to treat it like a job and not like a career. Go in, do your work, remain focused but prioritise yourself over the company. Otherwise they will break you. And they won't care about putting you back together. Because it will all be your fault.

Then a young caller. Petrified about upcoming exams and late-night cramming. And two more with the same concerns. Worried that failure will harm their futures.

Losing weight. Putting on weight. Not eating enough. Eating too much. Unable to sleep. Drinking to get to sleep.

Every caller, every lonely, isolated individual, who has a legitimate concern or anxiety, finds the courage they need to speak to a complete stranger. To offload. To ease some pressure – whether self-inflicted or not. Tonight, a couple of handfuls of these people in need are greeted by Ant and his apathy.

They don't know that. They don't realise. They think he is quiet because he is listening to them without judgement. He is their sounding board. He doesn't necessarily need to speak or offer advice or another point of view. They just want to share.

So, somehow, despite his absence from the conversations and wayward thoughts of killing another human being, his restlessness at the slow passing of time and his impatience for today to be tomorrow, Ant provides a great service. He helps more people than he hurts.

120

'Here. This is the spot.'

Maeve pulled the car over on Seth's command.

'You think?' She thought it was a good spot, too, but wanted him to justify it for her own peace of mind.

'Look,' he pointed into the distance, 'the farmhouse is miles away from this gate and there are no lights on. They get up early, they're probably as asleep as our friend in the boot.'

She's no friend of mine, Maeve tells herself. She kills the engine and switches off the lights.

'I haven't seen a car for fifteen minutes,' Seth adds. His wife nods.

They speak for another minute in the almost pitch-black about the best place to leave her.

Right there by the gate means that she can be discovered by the farmer or anyone who works on that farm, but can also be seen from the road in the daylight. Or they could lift her over the wall, but there was always the danger that the farmer was monitoring their property with cameras, and there was the added possibility that she wouldn't be found for a while. There were acres of land to cover. She needed to be found, not left to decompose next to a dry-stone wall for another week.

'Get her out. The grass is long by the wall next to the gate. I'll back up a bit and you can drag her straight in.'

'Don't worry, you're close enough.'

Seth opens his door and steps out. He looks down the road and then up the other way. No lights. No sound. There's nobody around. The only people who come along that road are the family that live and work on that farm. And they're all asleep. He looks over at the house again. The only thing moving is the long blades of grass in the night-time breeze. He can't even hear noise from livestock.

He clicks the lock to the boot open as slowly and softly as he possibly can. Maeve waits at the wheel, looking in the rear-view mirror at her husband. He disappears for a moment as he ducks inside the back of the car and pulls out Hadley Serf's legs. It wobbles the vehicle from side to side. Every small movement is exaggerated in this situation.

Now Maeve is the one seeing things in close-up. She sees her reflection in the mirror. Her large brown eyes, every individual eyelash, she blinks and it seems it's in slow motion. *Just get her out, Seth. Let's get going.*

With one hand under her neck and one beneath the small of her back, Seth heaves her out, takes two steps backwards and drops her behind the long grass, next to the wall. Part of the plastic catches a sharp stone and rips. He checks the floor to make sure that the ground is not soft and leaving a footprint.

The body will be visible in the morning, but, for now, she is safe.

She's dumped.

She is gone.

Seth tells himself that it's over. And he shuts the boot down until each side of the lock touches the other. Then he rests his weight against it until it clicks shut.

Five minutes later, they're a couple of miles away, heading back along the winding road. There are still no other cars. The car feels lighter, as does Seth's conscience.

Maeve isn't as naïve. Neither is she hungry for this to happen again.

There is a lot left to do. Possible storms to weather. She wants to get home as fast as she can and drink a cold glass of wine and be close to her husband.

He wants to pick up the phone and start again.

Seth flicks the radio back on once they are well out of range of the dead girl. He doesn't know the lyrics to this one but he hums along to the tune.

Maeve looks at the speedometer; she won't go over the limit, even though she just wants to floor it all the way back to London. She glances in the rear-view mirror. Nothing behind them. Her eyelashes are no longer in close-up.

It's all back to normal.

121

They would need a flash on the camera, it was so dark on those roads. There are streetlights here outside the house but I don't see a car parked across the street or any figures lurking in the bushes. I'm just being paranoid, I know that.

'You don't think he was watching us again tonight?' I ask Seth as we pull into the driveway.

He tells me not to worry and that we don't need to talk about him. He shuts it down. Then he shuts the door behind us and locks it. And I'm shutting the fridge after pouring a huge glass of Chardonnay.

I'm tired.

Seth is wired.

It's been exhausting. Being careful is hard work. Frivolity and recklessness is surprisingly invigorating. The rough, unprotected sex we've been having has energised me. But going over every detail, covering every track as we dispose of another body, has wiped me out. And this wine will knock me out within minutes.

I have to go in to work again tomorrow. I don't know about Seth. I don't want to ask him. I'm scared of his reaction. He leans against the worktop, sipping a glass of water, opening the top drawer and pulling out two breadsticks at a time. I gulp my wine.

We don't talk. But it's not uncomfortable.

We're handling it. This is what we do.

Dysfunction to function.

'I should clean out that bath,' I say, eventually.

'Leave it. That's not important right now. She's gone.'

Then I'm shutting my eyes in bed.

And I'm alone. And isolated. With nobody to talk to.

122

'Fuck off, freak.'

Nathan Miller. Twelve miles north of the Beauman's home.

'You know what time it is?'

Mrs Taft. Sixty-one. Widow.

'I can't sleep. Want to talk?'

Seth Beauman. Hungry. Desperate for connection. Searching for number four.

He falls straight back into the role he has cultivated for himself. The perpetually tired insomniac with the buzzing late-night mind and the close-up vision. His innocent phone voice perfected in its tone to encourage sympathy from the listener.

Tonight is about quantity. Getting in as many calls as possible and hoping something sticks. There's no time for his usual solo debrief after each call. He can't sit back and examine his mistakes or dwell on the words of a stranger. He just has to call, ask the question, cross off the name, move on to the next.

Mr A will be expecting a potential victim tomorrow night, or at least something in the pipeline. Hadley will probably be found in the next day or so, too. He needs to get a move on. It's not over yet.

'Hi. It's Seth. I can't sleep. Want to talk?'

Suzannah Hyde. Single mother of two. Health and safety officer. Food blogger.

'No. I do not. I want to be left alone. I don't want my kids woken up, either. Why don't you call the Samaritans or something, eh?' She hangs up.

Seth laughs to himself at that.

He turns everything off and walks upstairs. He can smell the bleach as he reaches the top landing. The bath does need to be cleaned. Maeve was right. She always is.

WEDNESDAY

123

I was mesmerised. The detective emerged from the side of the screen, looking like Death. Dark hair and stubble, a long, black leather coat hanging like a cloak. A reporter stood in the foreground talking about another body being found in Warwickshire. But I couldn't keep my eyes off the figure in the background. He moved like fire. Black flames dancing around the crime scene.

The farmhouse could be seen in the background and a blue tractor was parked behind the gate. Whoever was driving it that morning must have spotted Hadley. There were cows peering over the wall. Maybe fifteen or twenty of them. Had they been there last night with us?

The public will start to forget about Palmer as soon as the tabloids can exploit Hadley's pretty little face over their front pages.

And they've disregarded the first victim, Daisy Pickersgill. It was so long ago. Seth had only just started out. He wasn't as eager back then. There was a long silence between the first and the second. Police would undoubtedly be looking for someone who may have been in prison for a while. Perhaps they had killed the first woman then been picked up on a less serious crime and served some time. Then re-emerged to kill again.

I watch Detective Pace move in the background and instruct and delegate. And he seems in control. He seems focused. But he's so far away from the truth. And the bureaucracy over police jurisdiction is undoubtedly thwarting his investigation.

What is a London cop doing there? What is he running away from?

Seth is still in bed. I doubt he'll go in to work today. I'm not going to push him. Maybe he'll make himself useful around the house again. Clean the bath out. Mop the tiled floors. Dispose of the ashes.

I make myself a coffee and pour it into my flask to take with me on my journey to the office. Before I leave, I go upstairs and nudge my alleged insomniac husband who appears to be in a coma.

'Seth.' I prod him. 'Seth,' I repeat.

'What? I'm getting ready. I'll just be late. Don't worry about it.'

'It's not that; I don't care if you're late.'

'What is it, then?' He rolls over, his eyes opening into a narrow slit.

'They've found her.'

'Already?' He tries to open his eyes wider but they seem stuck together.

'Yes. It's all over the news.'

'Shit. Well, that's what we wanted, isn't it?'

I like that he said we. We're together. It's something we are doing as a couple, a team.

'It's exactly what we want.' And I kiss him goodbye.

124

He had already lied to his boss about the marks on his face. To some of his co-workers, Charlie Sanders had said he was drunk and dropped his kebab on the floor. As he went to catch it, he scraped his face against a wall.

'I'm always ravenous after sex, you know?' He had laughed.

To others he had said that he was running away from the girl he had just fucked because she was 'batshit crazy' and wanted him to spend the night. But he was drunk and ended up tripping and smashing his face into the pavement.

In whichever overly-embellished-with-bravado story he opted for, Charlie mentioned that he'd had sexual intercourse that evening he had left the club with a hot-looking woman.

But now that woman was on the news. And she was fucking dead. And she looked like those other women he had heard about. Bleached and wrapped in plastic. But he didn't care about them. He had never met them. He had never fucked them. He wasn't possibly the last person to see them alive.

He was panicking now. The bruising on his face had almost

disappeared. He had to undo the top button of his shirt and loosen his tie because his breathing felt constricted. And the girlfriend he had lived with for four years looked worried about him over breakfast. Charlie had told her a different story, a half-truth: that he was hit from behind and the guy took his wallet. He left out the part about his postcoital gluttony.

The right thing to do would be to go to the police and tell the truth: he met Hadley Serf in a club, went home with her, fucked her against the door and then left. On his way back to meet his friends, he was jumped from behind and beaten. He was told to leave her alone.

There would be a time and location. There may be some footage of the incident from the cameras of a nearby shop. The police may be able to pick out Ant's face from the video. Ant would lead to Seth. The case could be blown wide open.

But Charlie Sanders wasn't concerned with justice and he clearly cared very little for Hadley Serf. Charlie Sanders was the most important person to Charlie Sanders.

And he hardly ever did the right thing.

125

And then she's home.

And things look the way they did a week or so ago.

The smell of bleach and disinfectant that has overrun the house recently has been replaced with a pungent array of spices and oil.

Seth's back is towards the kitchen doorway but he hears Maeve come through the front door. He is stirring something on the stovetop.

'That smells amazing.'

Seth turns around and smiles. He woke up this morning and masturbated in their bed. He showered, got dressed, stripped the bed, threw everything in the washing machine with double the amount of softener the bottle suggested, and replaced it with fresh linen. Then he cleaned out the bath three times and rinsed it thoroughly. Next, he disposed of the ashes from the burner in the garden down the drain at the bottom of the outside pipe and washed it down with a hose. He drank coffee. He ate. He masturbated a second time; it took much longer than the first to get where he wanted. He answered some work emails and checked the status of his orders to ensure that they would all ship on time so he would receive his sizeable bonus at the end of the month. He found a recipe for dinner and walked to the shop to pick up a bottle of wine for Maeve that would accompany it perfectly.

'I grabbed you a Viognier. Apparently it goes well with spice.' Seth opened the fridge door and pulled a bottle from the rack – he had ended up buying three – and started pushing the corkscrew into the top.

'What are you making?'

'Well, it's almost done, just bubbling away while the rice cooks. It's a red Thai curry. Vegetable, though. Asparagus, spinach and pak choi. Figured we could try something a little different.'

Maeve liked different.

The meal may have been something different but that didn't mean that everything wasn't suddenly the same.

He pops the cork on the wine, pours a large glass and hands it to Maeve. She takes a sip.

'That is different. It's nice. Can't wait to taste it with the food. You need me to help with anything?'

'No. No. It's fine, almost done here. Go through. I've set the table.'

'The table? Is it my birthday? Did somebody die?' She smiles, unapologetically.

Maeve kicks off her heels and you can see the release in pressure as her feet hit the floor.

'Go, go, go,' Seth shoos her into the lounge.

The table is set for two. Maeve sits down and swigs her wine. She is desperate to turn the television on.

'Don't do it, Maeve. I'm dishing up soon.'

'What?' She peers around the door to see if he is watching her.

'You know what. We don't need the news on right now. I know you want to see it. I don't. Let's just eat and sit and talk and have some wine.'

Seth is only going to have one glass because he has to drive to Oxford later.

'Bring the bottle in. I'm almost done with this glass. It's delicious.'

Seth brings the food through first then goes back to retrieve more wine.

They do exactly as he wanted. They connect. They discuss each other's days, deciding that everything is almost clear but perhaps they should dispose of the roll of plastic in their garage. Maeve even asks him about work and he finally tells her about exceeding his quarterly target. They talk about going away for a week with the money, maybe doing something to the house, upgrading Seth's car.

And, when they're finished, and Maeve has devoured a bottle of wine while Seth sipped his single glass, Seth goes upstairs to change his clothes while Maeve flicks on the television and sits by herself with another glass of cold wine and a tingle of warmth at the back of her throat.

She knows he is going out.

She doesn't ask him where he is going.

She doesn't question what time he will return.

126

Hadley Serf was troubled, that's for sure.

A history of mental health issues. That's what they're saying.

Everybody knows that means she had tried to kill herself before. Attempted suicide is not something that evokes great sympathy in the masses. People don't understand that level of low. They don't think things can ever get so bad that you would want to end it. They don't really believe that people often don't have a choice in the way that they feel. That it can be medical and chemical, not just psychological or environmental.

It does help me understand a little more why she would enter into a conversation with a stranger on the phone.

Loneliness is a powerful catalyst for foolishness.

I don't understand why they have led with that information on the news but I keep watching. Hoping to catch a glimpse of Detective Pace.

But it's a male newsreader that I see. His inflections are spot on for the tone of the piece. His expressions well rehearsed.

They cut to the farmer's son. He has one of those naturally strong physiques; like he has always had to pick up heavy things. His face is friendly and honest. He says he was taking the tractor out that morning and, when he went to open the gate, he saw something behind the wall. Wrapped in white plastic. His first thought was that somebody had been fly-tipping and that he would walk out further and find boxes or a sofa or something.

'But what I found was much worse than that. I knew it was a body from the way it was wrapped and I could see something where the plastic had ripped. It was horrible.' The audience would feel sorry for this guy. He was sweet and stupid and shaken. He goes on, 'I mean, we have to slaughter the cows after a certain amount of time. I've seen it. But that's different. That's so different.'

Somewhere on the demented social-media sphere, a handful of evangelical vegetarians and vegans are up in arms. Outraged that we would distinguish between the life of a person and an animal. In turn, this is infuriating the majority of people who would always value human life over any other species. And, somehow, the real message is being distorted and diluted and forgotten.

An innocent girl in her twenties was strangled to death, bleached to albinism and dumped without care, miles from anywhere for another innocent person to discover.

And some blogger is comparing her to a pig. And a hundred commentators are abusing the blogger in return.

And, somewhere else, a handful of rational thinkers are trying to look at the real issue. They are remembering the name of Daisy Pickersgill and Theresa Palmer and urging people not to forget that.

But, in another dark corner, a pledge to highlight the seriousness of mental-health issues was bubbling. Hadley Serf is creating a legacy. She is doing something good after her death. It was not in vain.

The message is as mixed as any political campaign. And that is just fine with me. It is better for things to get lost.

Those black flames never appear. Detective Pace is not there.

The newsreader moves on to sports.

I pour myself another drink. The house feels warmer today and I feel thirstier. My fascination for this case is dwindling. I just want it to be over.

Seth is out and I am stuck in the house. Things haven't gone back to how they were before. Dinner was delicious. We were connected. I felt it and I know he did, too. It's a case of building on that now. Not taking another step backwards.

And not waiting for the next round of cancers and miscarriages and redundancies and bloodied corpses in the car.

It's almost midnight and he still isn't home. I don't want to be asleep in bed when he gets in so I run myself a bath – Seth has cleaned it out – and I take my wine upstairs with me to drink while I soak.

I have an old Roberts radio in the en suite. Not one of the new retro ones, a proper vintage radio. I like that it looks broken and worn and that it sounds fuzzy and warm.

I undress in the bedroom and walk across the upstairs landing with the radio in my left hand and the glass of wine in my right. The empty house feels safer and I feel freer. I swing the radio as I swig my drink. Something modern plays with a sweet melody.

In the guest bathroom, I place the radio on the floor where the clothes we burned were once piled up. I don't let go of the wine.

Beneath the sink is a cupboard full of products that haven't been used; the Beaumans have not had many guests over the last year. There is a fragrant bubble bath but I opt for the salts. I like the way they effervesce across my skin and how soft it feels afterwards.

With the hot tap running, I tip in half the packet. I place it back in the cupboard beneath the sink and stand over the bath, watching it run. Sipping my new favourite Viognier and staring into the space where Hadley Serf lay a day or so ago.

It doesn't bother me.

This is my house.

He is my husband.

And this is my drink. And it is running dangerously low.

I add some cold to the flow and move the water around with my left hand. It's too hot. I have another few minutes before it gets deep enough for me to dip a toe in. So I tiptoe down the stairs and into the kitchen. The tiles are cold and so is the unopened bottle of wine. I grab the corkscrew from the side and take it all back to the bathroom upstairs. I don't worry about the window. There is nobody watching me tonight.

I turn off the hot tap and leave the cold running while I open the wine. I pour. I stop the tap. I turn up the radio and I get in the water. I lie down and it rises above my breasts.

I drink down more wine, an ice-cold path cutting through the warmth all around me. I could sleep, but I won't. Another song I don't know jumps out of the radio speaker and I swallow more alcohol. It has no taste, now. It is just a refreshing temperature.

My head drops back against the tub; I feel my hair get wet. I lie still. It's great to not move for a moment. I will make the moment last as long as I can. As long as it takes for Seth's key to turn in that front door. For him to walk up those stairs and push that door open. For him to stand over the bath and look at me. To see me.

He'd better not have blood on his face this time.

I don't want tears.

127

There were plenty of spaces in that car park but Seth managed to find the exact one where he had strangled Hadley Serf to death the week before.

That should have unsettled Ant. But he is too excited.

He taps on the passenger window. He is smiling. Seth is not.

Ant gestures the question of whether he could come into the car by waving a finger back and forth between himself and the door handle. Seth nods and beckons him in with his right hand.

Ant sits. He brushes his jacket down flat but fidgets. He can't stop moving, adjusting himself, tapping his foot, bouncing his legs.

'Okay. So, what's the plan? What are we doing? Where are we going?'

'Firstly, you need to calm down. You are a weakness in your agitated state. I don't like that. I don't like the risk. Some people get off on that. Those people get caught. So calm down. We don't get caught.' Seth is looking forwards the entire time he speaks. Ant is an unnecessary aggravation and Seth is worried he could do something stupid to the childish idiot. He has to calm himself, too. He keeps Maeve in his ear.

He doesn't want to arrive on his doorstep with another body in the boot this soon. He wouldn't be able to explain that to her.

'Sure. Sure. Sorry. I'm just a bit nervous, you know?'

'That's understandable.' It is quiet. Menacing. Short. 'Breathe.'

They sit in silence for a while. Ant doesn't know what to say and is doing as he is being instructed. Seth is focused.

Ant finally speaks. 'So are we going somewhere?'

'No.'

'So we're waiting for somebody?'

'No.'

'Then, I'm sorry, what are we doing here?'

'We are talking, Ant. We are getting to know each other. Don't you want to get to know each other?'

'Well ... I ... we should...' He doesn't know what to say to that. Ant was expecting to see Seth kill somebody at the very least. He thought he might even be in the car when he did it. Now he is confused. 'Who is the victim?'

'I don't use that word.'

'Are you being serious? It's just that ... well, I don't understand.' Now they are looking at each other. Ant has turned his body around so that his back is resting against the passenger door. 'What are we doing here? I thought we'd be doing something real, tonight. You know?'

Ant scratches at the back of his hand. It doesn't itch. It's nervousness. It's digging away at the dirt.

'Look,' Seth sits forwards and Ant flinches. 'I can't just pluck somebody off the street. That's not how it works.'

'How, exactly, does it work, then?' It's the adrenaline doing most of Ant's talking.

'I call people. Random people. Phone numbers in a list. I engage with them. Then we meet. We do things like you and I are doing now. We talk. I listen to them. There's a lot of power in listening to somebody, Ant. You should know that.'

'I'm listening now. I know how to listen,' he interjects.

Seth realises just how young Ant is.

'I have to develop it. Cultivate it. We meet for lunch. We go for drinks.'

'I saw that,' Ant jumps in again.

It is here that Seth learns that Ant was watching him even before that night, and he doesn't like the fact that he had been followed.

'Listen. I don't set out to kill. Here is what you need to know about relationships. They go bad. They all do. Somebody fucks up. Sometimes you can find a way to save it and sometimes you can't. And sometimes they do something unforgivable. And before you know it, that person is in the boot of your car and your face is covered in blood again and you have to find a way to get rid of them.' The lies come easy. It's not about connection any more. It's not even about enjoyment. It's necessity. It's addiction.

Ant is completely attentive.

He sees a traditional yellow Post-it note in his mind.

When did you realise?'

Where did that happen/what happened?

How did that feel?

But he keeps his mouth shut.

'So, that is what we need to do. We can't just take that girl off the street.' Seth points ahead at a twenty-something woman, holding a pile of books. 'Because we know nothing about her.'

'She looks like a student.'

'Yes. She appears that way. But we do not know that. And we have to deal in certainties.'

'Okay. So when do we do this?'

'It is happening now. I am grooming someone as we speak,' he lies again.

'Well, I don't want to wait around forever.'

'It has come to my attention that this relationship is not equal. You will give me a number that I can contact you on. When the person is in place, I will call you. The next time we meet, you will give me any other copies of the photos that you took. Do you understand?'

'And that will make the relationship equal?'

'You will need to start trusting me and I will show you what I know. We will do this one together. And then you can do what you want with that knowledge and we can go back to not being friends.'

'This has been a bit of a buzzkill.'

'I am serious about what I do.'

Ant exhales in resignation and gives Seth his mobile phone number.

'You need a lift home?' Seth smiles.

'No, thank you. I don't want you to know where I live.'

'You're smarter than I thought.'

Ant gets out the car, half slamming it before walking back across the car park the same way he had entered.

It crosses Seth's mind to follow him home. To end this. But Maeve's voice is in his ear. He listens to her.

She is the reason he has not been caught.

She is the person that will stop that little prick from ruining everything.

128

Ant looks back fifteen times before disappearing behind a building, where he stops for a moment and rests his back against the wall. He's out of breath. Partly from walking so fast, but also frustration, exhilaration.

It was a disappointing meeting, it wasn't the event he had built it up to be but he still managed to obtain that rush he desired.

And it was fear.

Something in him admires Seth; he likes the way he operates. He is professional and serious about what he does. About killing. But that also translates into something intimidating. And sexual.

Ant isn't gay. He's never even experimented while in college or travelling. He isn't attracted to Seth. But, leaning back against that limestone shop front, he feels turned on. He can understand how these women could be lured into meeting Seth and taking things further. He was intense and nonchalant at the same time.

Ant looks back to the car park. Seth's car is still sitting there.

Ant shuts his eyes and takes a few deep breaths. He is confused. He wants to run but feels rooted to the spot. He is angry and dissatisfied but wired. He hates the feeling and he loves it completely.

One strong exhalation and he looks back to the car park again.

Seth's car has gone.

Ant panics. He flies down that street, pressing the button on his keys to unlock his car before he arrives at the door. But it doesn't work. It never works. Frantically, he looks around as he fumbles the key in the door lock and turns it.

'He's coming', Ant tells himself.

He gets into the car and puts it into gear as he turns the key, then puts his foot down and pulls out onto the road. He doesn't look for traffic. He doesn't put his seatbelt on. He is burning body fat through anxiety.

Negotiating the Oxford one-way system heightens his hysteria, his eyes flit from the road ahead to the rear-view mirror. He sweats and he sweats and he sweats. And he runs into his spotlessly tidy flat and locks the door behind him, places the ineffectual door chain on the door. He showers and throws on an identical black T-shirt.

And he stands by the front window looking out at the road. Terrified. He is blackmailing a known murderer. What is he thinking?

He doesn't sleep all night. He goes through their conversation in the car and forgets the one thing that would have helped him get some rest. If Seth wanted him dead, he would already be dead.

129

The lights are on. His face is clean.

Seth knows that Maeve is still awake. She always turns off the lights. If he was home late, there would be a blue light pushing through the windows from the glow of the television. But tonight it is bright and white and clean and he can feel the warmth as he steps across the threshold. And he can smell the bath.

The journey home was sedate. He didn't even turn on the radio. Seth wanted silence. He wanted to not connect. To be alone.

He's pleased to be home but worries that Maeve is preening herself for more action. It has been a sex-fuelled week or two. He has pounded his wife from behind like he hates her. He has watched her control things, pinning his hands down while easing herself back and forth on top of him. They have tasted each other. They have kissed passionately in bed, against the wall, on the floor. They have kept their bodies close and looked into one another's eyes while making love.

Seth isn't sure he can take any more.

He walks into the kitchen. Plates are still on the side from dinner; she hasn't even got round to clearing up, yet. He throws his keys on the work surface and opens the fridge door. Only one bottle left. Seth picks up an empty glass and takes it upstairs to the bathroom.

He knocks lightly with the middle knuckle of his right hand.

'Who is it?' Maeve asks.

And Seth laughs softly at her humour. He pushes the door open slowly and continues to smile at her.

'Very funny,' he says, stepping in.

She looks relaxed. Pure. The water covers her nipples but he can still see enough of her breasts to arouse his senses. A cleavage that is dark and invites his glare down into the water beneath. 'How long have you been in there?'

'I don't know. Not quite one ... bottle.' She lifts up her glass and nods towards the bottle of wine on the floor.

'Mind if I...?' Seth walks towards the wine.

'By all means.'

He pours a half glass, drinks it in one go, then refills even higher. It's the Maeve way.

'Everything okay?' she asks, not really concerned. There's no blood to be seen.

'Yes. No issues.'

Neither of them freely acknowledges that Seth has been out this evening. And it works for them.

'Cheers.' Seth offers.

'Cheers to you, too.'

Clink. Swig. Breathe.

'You can jump in, if you like. I've been topping it up with hot water.'

The idea of tangling his limbs with Maeve's is somewhat appealing but Seth politely declines.

'I'd rather look at you from here.' He says it in a way that implies he has a better view from where he is, he can see more.

'Well, top me up at least.' Maeve runs her tongue along the inside of her top teeth as her husband pours her another glass of wine. She was drinking when he left and she hasn't stopped. He can see it in her eyes but her openness is incredibly alluring. Maeve has let her guard down and he really does see her beauty.

'It's getting late, maybe we should get you dried.' Seth picks up the towel and opens it fully, inviting Maeve to stand up. She does. A glass of wine in her right hand, her left stretched out to the side. Seth wraps the towel around her and tucks the corner inside to hold it up. And he kisses her once before taking a swig of his own drink.

'What was that for?'

'What? A man can't kiss his wife when he feels the urge?'

'The urge for what?' She tries to be sultry but her words are a little slurred. She runs her forefinger down Seth's chest. Her eyes are half shut.

'Come on. Let's get you to the bedroom. I'll empty the water in here and sort out those plates in the kitchen while you get ready for bed.' He starts to guide her out of the door.

'I can walk by myself, don't you worry.' Maeve pushes Seth's hand off her arm. 'Just don't be long, okay?'

'As quick as I can, I swear. I just don't want to get up in the morning to that mess.'

Maeve walks herself wearily into the bedroom. Seth unplugs the water in the bath. She was right, she's kept it at the perfect temperature. He heads downstairs. There's no noise coming from the bedroom at all. He throws the crockery and cutlery and pans into the dishwasher and wipes the surfaces with a dishcloth.

It's been three or four minutes, maximum, but when Seth pushes the door open, he sees Maeve asleep. Her wet hair is on the pillow. Her glass of wine is resting on the bedside table; she has nearly got to the bottom, too. Her towel is still wrapped around her body. She looks peaceful.

Seth looks at her for a moment, drinking in her image. He always likes her with wet hair. Something about that look, it sits perfectly between purity and filth. And he knows Maeve has a handle on both of those things.

He is a little relieved, though. He knows he could go through with things if she presented them to him. Instead, he turns the light off and pulls the door until it is almost shut.

Then he's back downstairs. He never turned the lights off.

And back in the lounge. He turns the television on. Not to watch anything, just as some background thrum.

He flicks open the phonebook and scans a few of the pages.

Ant is expecting Seth to find another connection. And he will.

He's Seth.

He can't sleep.

He wants to talk.

He needs to.

Seth is not in control.

THURSDAY

130

If you're ever in a cinema and you hear an usher say that 'Mr Sand is in screen seven', run. Get the hell out. The place just might burn down.

If you're worried about a loved one – you haven't seen them for a few days, they haven't phoned you for a week, they're not seeing your text messages – and you decide it is prudent to speak to the police, file a missing person's report, and they tell you that Detective Sergeant Pace will look into your claim, you should look into the cost of flowers. You should start to make a list of your loved one's favourite songs. You should be thinking about whether you prefer a traditional hardwood coffin or a more modern wicker version that is biodegradable.

Pace is losing. And he is sick of it.

But he blames himself.

Not in the way that he feels a responsibility for solving a case in time to prevent the loss of life, but in the way that he feels that it could have been avoided if he were not involved at all.

But, then, it doesn't matter. Because, wherever he goes, this kind of thing seems to happen. That's what he has been telling himself. And the psychiatrist his inspector insisted he speak to.

Pace is from a small, unknown, Berkshire village. Hinton Hollow. You don't know it. He escaped it in his early twenties and headed for the promise of the city but, as he has confided to his shrink, he feels as though he was followed. Not by a person, but by something. And that it stays with him. It makes bad things happen around him. Like he has become a trigger of some kind.

Like he is a catalyst for evil.

Of course, Dr Artaud diplomatically tells Pace that this is utter nonsense. That he is projecting. That he has never dealt with his loss, with her disappearance. That running away from your problems is not the answer. That you will always feel like you are being followed. Because your issues won't let go of you.

And Pace knows that makes sense.

But he also knows what he knows and he knows what he has seen. And he feels like he walks around, casting a dark shadow that infects anyone who is unfortunate enough to stand in the wrong light.

Pace looks into the dead, white eyes of Hadley Serf and asks himself, 'What have I done?' And, before her head is covered back over with a sheet, he tells her that he is sorry.

131

The reckless side of me wishes that we hadn't been so thorough. That maybe if I'd overlooked something, Detective Pace would have a reason to knock on my door and ask me some questions.

He has no reason.

It's all covered. Apart from the plastic. We still need to get rid of that.

I can smell last night's food. Seth didn't clean the kitchen that well. I make a coffee to take with me to the office but the smell is making me feel sick. That was too much wine for midweek. I'm in a fog. I only need water. Lots of water.

The second drawer down, the one beneath the cutlery, is full of stuff. Anything from candles and paperclips to felt-tip pens and a cigarette lighter that says 'I Heart Cuba' in large black letters. Neither of us has ever been to Cuba, I have no idea where it came from. I take some old sticky notes from that drawer and write *Get rid of the plastic*, then stick it on the fridge door.

I can't handle food just yet. I can't handle Seth, either. I feel embarrassed. I remember getting out of the bath, wrinkled and drunk. I remember walking into the bedroom, putting my glass on the bedside table, sitting on the mattress, and then I remember waking up this morning. I was naked in bed and the towel was on the carpet. My hair was everywhere.

I rarely sleep naked unless we've had sex, and I don't remember us having sex. I would remember that. I know I've been reckless there, too. I don't know why. I'm not invincible. We stopped talking about kids years ago. It's just another thing for me to worry about.

We definitely didn't have sex, I feel different in the morning after Seth has come inside me. I don't know what it is but that feeling isn't there. I can't quite recall whether I woke up on the bed in my towel and then crawled under the covers or Seth took off the towel he had so carefully wrapped around me and tucked me in. Either way, I feel silly. Like a drunk little girl.

So I tiptoe around all morning and straighten my hair downstairs and leave a note about the plastic we've wrapped the dead girls in.

I watch the news with the sound muted. Middle-aged men are miming. The dead girl looks so alive in all the pictures. And the dark figure at the crime scenes leaves me mesmerised. The way he moves. Slow. Deliberate. Coiled. Ready. I forget that I'm hungover, for a moment. I forget that I feel silly.

If only I'd overlooked something.

If only there was a way for him to show up on my doorstep and ask me some questions.

I took care of everything. She was cleaned and her hair and nails were cut and she was bleached of identity. It's only the plastic left.

I switch off the television with the remote. I pick up my coffee, even though I don't want it, and I rip the note away from the fridge, screw it into a ball and place it in the bin beneath the sink.

The plastic can wait.

132

If your surname is Taylor, you are intolerant. And rude. You have a foul mouth.

Why can't you be more like the Carrols or the Levinsons? They don't want to talk but they're not mean about it. They're not abusive.

The Taylor page is a rainbow of highlighted text. And Seth remembers them all in the same way. Not one of them entered into conversation with him. Not in the slightest.

Go fuck yourself.

Get a life.

No thanks, freak.

The Taylors were also sarcastic.

Seth gets up later than Maeve. He heard her creeping around a little but fell into his usual deep morning sleep. It's his strongest hour.

He had expected to find her in the same position he had left her in when he finally retired last night but she must have woken up because her damp towel was on the floor and she was under the covers and her hair was tangled and knotted and splayed in every direction. She hadn't moved when he had undressed and crawled under the duvet, feeling the warmth from her naked body.

This morning, he is not thinking about Maeve; she has no need to be embarrassed, he can't get the Taylors out of his head. He had crossed another one off in the night. They had called him a psycho cunt and then hung up. And it has stayed with him.

He runs his finger up and down the ink-drenched Taylor page and wonders whether he should just leave them alone. Maybe he should phone them all in one night, get them out of the way.

Seth shuts the book and puts it back. He can't think about that now, he has to get ready for work. He will be late, of course, but he is pushing his luck as far as it will go due to the success of exceeding his targets. But he needs to show his face today. To show that things are back to normal.

Of course, they're far from normal. There is outstanding business to take care of apart from phoning all the Taylors in the county. Seth irons his shirt in the kitchen. Maeve put the dishwasher on before she left; he knew he'd forgotten something last night. He doesn't eat breakfast or make himself a coffee; he can do that when he gets to the office. He brushes his hair and his teeth, he grabs his keys and his work mobile phone and puts them in his pocket.

Then he grabs another mobile phone. It's empty. No numbers are saved. There are no apps or emails, it's a very simple phone.

He texts Ant.

When he is finished, he resets the phone to its original factory settings, takes out the battery, throws it in a container to be recycled and drops the rest of the phone in the bin with the scrapings of leftover vegetable curry.

133

Tonight. 20:00. Same place.

Ant reads the text over and over. His heart starts to race. He knows it's from Seth even though it doesn't say that. It wouldn't, he thinks, the guy is so careful.

Ant sits on the floor by his living-room window and reads it again, his back rests against the radiator. He has hardly slept. He spent most of the night sitting on his windowsill, staring out at the road, half expecting Seth's car to turn up. He drifted off a couple of times but now he feels as though he can finally relax.

Seth isn't coming to murder him in his sleep. He is living up to his end of the bargain. He must have made some calls already. He must be grooming somebody new.

He's exhausted and exhilarated and doesn't know what to do with himself. His heart rate won't slow down and his mind joins in. He starts to imagine what tomorrow night will bring. Seth might have found somebody to kill that night. Friday night, that makes sense. Some party girl, out for a good time, a few drinks, a fumble with somebody new. It could be that.

He could be stalking somebody. Perhaps he wants to show Ant how he gets to know a girl. Or he is going for drinks with somebody, making that connection with them so that he can take things further on the next date. Maybe he wants Ant to watch. Maybe he likes that Ant was watching him with Hadley. Seth hadn't known about that. Ant spotted the realisation on his face when he'd told him.

He might just want to talk again, assert his authority, keep control of the situation. Ant finds himself getting angry at that thought. *Who does he think he is? I have his pictures. He's fucking with the wrong guy if he thinks that he's going to keep bossing me around.*

But he calms himself. Of course Seth needs to feel like he is control, Ant is the student. He is learning.

Then Ant does something dangerous. He thinks for himself.

What does he know already? That Seth wraps these girls in plastic and dumps them in any old, quiet field fifty miles from where he lives. He doesn't need a lesson in how to dispose of a body. The guy is too lazy to even dig a hole most of the time.

How he kills them, how you go through with something like that, how you make sure they're dead, that's what Ant needed Seth for. And that's what he had him for. Ant only knew how to watch somebody die.

The other part was the grooming – he needs a new term for that, it sounds too sinister. Baiting, perhaps. Courting. Calling a million numbers, waiting to get lucky and find somebody lonely or suffering or feeling isolated enough to enter into a conversation with a stranger, that part had been explained, too. It sounds lengthy. Ant isn't sure how Seth had come back to him so quickly unless he had a procession of people in line.

Does he kill men, too?

Then it strikes him, Ant wouldn't have to get lucky. Everybody he speaks to on the telephone is a stranger. They are lonely or suffering or isolated. And they are all willing to talk. All of them. He has an endless pool of hardship to fish from. He won't have to wait around for months or even weeks if he chooses to go through with this.

Victims on tap.

Vulnerability by the gallon.

So, all he needs is his first kill. He has heard it is the hardest. Then he doesn't need Seth anymore. He could sever the ties or he could still inform the police and get him out of the way.

The idea of being there when somebody's light goes out is too exciting an opportunity to miss. To experience that up close. That's what
Ant needs. That's when he will know if he could take things further.

That is the next high.

He thinks about calling in to work again and having another day off
but figures that he can sleep at his desk if needed and nobody would
even notice. Instead, he texts Seth back. Just a simple message saying
See you there.

But Seth never reads that because he has already burned that line
of connection.

Ant has forgotten that he is the amateur. The exuberance that comes
with youth is his flaw. The need that his generation has been conditioned to feel is clear, that everything you want can be had right now,
and that you deserve it, you are entitled to it for no real reason, that is
his mistake.

It used to be that curiosity was the killer. Now it is enthusiasm and
impatience.

134

'I'll only be a couple of hours,' Seth tells Maeve. And he kisses her on
the cheek.

'That's fine, I've got some work to catch up with on my laptop.'

'You don't have to wait up for me, you know?'

'I know. But I'm not drinking tonight; I have stuff that I need to get on
with. I'm sure I'll be awake when you get back.' She goes red as she speaks,
still a little coy about her state the night before. Seth hasn't mentioned it
to her; it didn't bother him at all. It was what he wanted, anyway.

'Okay, well, I was just saying.'

'It's fine. You go. Do what you have to do.' She punctuates her sentence by opening her laptop where the full stop should be. And Seth
grabs his keys from the hallway and leaves.

He is slightly put out to find that the space he wants is occupied by a blue Ford Fiesta. He parks behind it and spends a couple of minutes repeating the registration on the number plate in case he needs to remember it for the future.

Seth watches as Ant arrives. He, too, is put out by the Fiesta. He looks at the car, then his watch. Then fishes his phone from his pocket to double-check he has the right details. Seth despairs. The guy is an idiot. Seth flashes his lights a few times to put the dumb kid out of his misery.

Ant turns around to see his murderous mentor sat at the wheel of a car that is pointing straight at him. Instinctively, he waves at his new friend. His new friend does not wave back.

They go through the same routine as before: Ant approaches the car; he bends down to look in the window at Seth; he gestures towards the handles; Seth hits the button for the central locking even though the door is already unlocked but he knows that Ant just needs to hear that click, and Ant jumps into the passenger seat.

He is fidgeting. Again. Edgy.

'You have to control this, man. If you're getting this excited about seeing me then you could explode when we get around to what we're really here for.'

'I know. Sorry.' Ant shuts his eyes for a moment and takes a deep breath.

Seth stares at him and waits. And wonders what it would be like to cut his throat. A long swipe across the front with something sharp. He pictures Ant grabbing at the crimson smile across his neck, helpless. Hopeless. He wonders how many times he could stab into it before Ants head would come away from the rest of his body.

'I wasn't expecting to hear from you so soon.' Ant's voice jolts Seth from his daydream.

'Sorry?'

'So soon. I wasn't expecting to hear from you so soon. I thought it would take you longer. You must have people lined up.'

'Sometimes you get lucky.'

Ant doesn't believe that. Sure, he is a little out of his depth and he doesn't really understand the implications on your character once you commit to taking the life of another human being, but he understands about hunger. He understands about pleasure. And he knows how that feeling can grow and how you are only satiated for a while. And that time gets shorter and shorter.

He thinks that they are similar. Feeding an addiction. Chasing new forms of gratification. He hears Seth's words but doesn't believe them. He's got them lined up for months.

'So, what's the plan? It's not tonight, is it?' Ant asks the question in a tone that suggests he already knows the answer.

'Sunday night.'

'Is that a thing with you? You want to be the Sunday-night killer?'

'I don't want to be known at all. You need to stop saying stupid things.'

It hangs in the air for a moment. Uncomfortable. Tense. Both men are angry but for different reasons.

'Look, it has just worked out that way. That's when I can get her out. Sunday night. Dinner and drinks. Then back to yours.'

'Mine? My house? Are you joking? I don't want somebody to be killed where I live.'

'If you don't want to do this…'

'I wouldn't be here if I didn't want to do this. I just don't understand why it has to be there, that's all.' Ant has been caught off-guard with the suggestion. He fidgets again until his back is against the passenger door and he can rest comfortably.

Seth explains it. He tells him that there is no way he is going to do it at his own house because he never does that. He tells Ant that he lives alone and he doesn't bring this home with him. 'I'm not going to change the habit of a lifetime for you, it's not how I operate.' He goes on to placate Ant, telling him that he wants to do this, he wants to demonstrate to Ant what this means when you commit. He wants to help Ant understand it.

But he is nervous. He is nervous of Ant's nervousness. Because he doesn't want any mistakes. And he thinks that Ant is less likely to be like that if he is in an environment that he knows and feels comfortable in.

Ant nods. It makes sense.

'Now, you can either stay and wait there, or you can watch me all night and take notes if you want, come in after us and take it from there. You can either watch what I do or you can get involved and do it yourself. This is your night. But it is a one-time deal, remember that. When we are done, you give me the pictures, including the digital copies – I know you have some – and then you're on your own. Got that?'

'Yeah. Yeah. I've got that.'

'I don't want to hear from you again after that. And you definitely don't want to hear from me.' He was so straight. So level. So menacing. Polite and evil.

'I need to know now what you want to do. So that I can go through the details with you. The next time you see me will be Sunday. No backing out.'

Ant was caught somewhere between joy and terror. This was happening. This was really happening. He was going to block the oxygen from getting to someone's brain. Was he even strong enough to do that? The anticipation alone could be enough to make him piss his pants. He was out of his depth. Could he truly trust Seth? It all made sense, everything he was saying. He didn't want mistakes. All of these things and more swirled around inside Ant for what seemed like five silent minutes.

It wasn't that long. It was almost instant.

'Okay. I'll do it. I'll do it all.'

'Final answer?' Seth probed.

'I will watch you. I'll follow you. I'll come after and finish what you start. I'll kill her.' Ant exhaled like he had just told a girlfriend that he wants to break up, like he'd just told his parents he wants to move out.

A relief.

An adventure.

'Very well,' Seth says, calmly, 'this is what we do.'

135

The toilet seat is urine-free and the roll is folded into a neat point. Ant checks the brilliant white bed linen for hairs – straight and curled. There are none. There's a flat-screen television, a bath with shower attachment, the carpet feels soft under foot.

Ant's hotel room was less than £20 and he wouldn't have to clean it.

But the most important thing is that he was going to sleep.

He'd been running on adrenaline in the car with Seth. When he saw the sign on the motorway for cheap rooms, it just made sense. Seth now knew where Ant lived and, while the plan seemed foolproof and Ant believed that Seth would follow through with it, that fact alone was unsettling. If he went back home tonight, he would sit on that windowsill again, drifting in and out of consciousness.

Ant stands in the bathroom, looking at himself in the mirror. He checked in with no bags, not even a toothbrush. He washes his hands in almost scalding hot water. Then he squeezes some of the complimentary toothpaste onto his forefinger and scrubs it into his teeth.

Squeak. Slurp. Spit.

He doesn't want to wash his face in case it wakes him up. He doesn't want to be awake.

And he undresses in front of the mirror. He looks at his naked body, pinching at his arms and prodding his chest, Ant wonders whether he has the strength to even hold down a smaller woman. Seth was hardly a gym addict or body builder but he looked like a man. Ant was boyish, somewhere between slim and skinny. He is worried.

He doesn't want to worry, either. Anxiety will just keep him awake.

Ant switches all the lights off until it is pitch-black in that hotel room. He lays under the covers and tries not to think about what is coming on Sunday. He thinks about the work he missed and the shopping he had to do. Seth's car pops into his mind. He thinks of all the things he could clean at the flat. Then Hadley being pulled from the boot of a car and his friend hanging from an Australian bathroom hook. It is too much.

Lying on his back in the total darkness of a room hundreds of people have slept in and fucked in before him, Ant decides he should go to a better place. A time when he was most happy. He starts at his childhood. He's three, then he's six, then he's twelve. Nothing has jumped out at him.

He eases through the years of his life, peeking around corners for some kind of contentment. By the time he gets to seventeen, not even the university years, he is deep in sleep. Crashed. The tiredness washes over him completely while his mind is distracted by his life less lived.

136

The skin on his eyelids is black and thin. And his ordinarily grey face is pale white against the blackness of the beard that is coming through. And that coat, which resembles a cape, means that a scythe in Pace's hand would not seem out of place.

He looks like a ghoul. A tired relic. He has tipped over the line from dark and brooding to menacing and frightening. It has happened before and it will certainly happen again. Pace is an island, the other officers know that, but when he gets this way, it is best to stay clear.

There's an element of threat there that wasn't there before. When Pace was sticking to procedure. When he was searching for a killer. This is different. He's pissed off. And he's tired. If he returned home to Hinton Hollow, nobody would recognise him.

Detective Sergeant Pace is sickness.

Hadley Serf was no ordinary girl. She wasn't average. She wasn't sweet and caring like Daisy. She wasn't in a loving relationship like Theresa. She didn't even live in London.

She just didn't fit.

Hadley Serf was troubled. Pace has spoken to her friends about her breakdowns and suicide attempts over the years. At first they could only find good things to say about their dead friend. But the truth has a way of presenting itself. And, once one friend commented on her promiscuity, another mentioned the drinking and another brought up the razor blades and the pills.

She was dirty. Used.

But she didn't deserve this.

The treatment of her body was worse than the other two. She'd been left for longer in the bleach and the inside of her mouth and vagina had been scrubbed and scraped at with more violence. This was more aggressive. Pace wonders whether things are escalating. Maybe this killer is chasing a bigger high. Perhaps he needs something dirtier to clean.

He sits in the driver's seat of his car and wrings the neck of the steering wheel. He bares his teeth. And he breathes heavily. Angrily. Thinking of the bodies of those three women that didn't make sense as a group. He feels frustrated and tormented and galled. He wants to do something but isn't sure what it should be. But it isn't anything helpful or legal.

And he tells himself that if he came face to face with this monster, he isn't sure that he would be able to allow them to await their punishment through the proper legal channels. He isn't sure that he could take that chance. He doesn't want to. And he has felt this way before.

Pace is spiralling deeper into the pit. With every passing case, he is eroding. Another part of him is dying. And the man that is left is more mistrusting and irrationally anxious and overly suspicious. A state of constant torment and paranoia that does not resemble the once promising detective. The wide-eyed excitement and naïvety were the first things to go. Now it is his tolerance.

He wants to find this killer by any means. And he wants to personally ensure that they cannot do anything like this again.

He wants to take the memory of what they did, bleach it, wrap it in plastic and dump it where nobody will ever find it.

FRIDAY

137

Detective Sergeant Pace is darkness.

Detective Sergeant Pace is damaged.

Detective Sergeant Pace is black fire.

I watch him and I don't feel like myself. Everything I am doing for Seth, for us, to keep us going forwards, it evaporates. I'm thinking about seeing Pace. Hearing his voice in front of me. Feeling his breath against my skin.

It's not a psychotic serial-killer thing. Like you'd see in a movie where they want to taunt the investigator with notes or get off on getting close to them, being right underneath their nose.

I don't know what it is.

Detective Sergeant Pace is a puppet.

Detective Sergeant Pace is a television character.

Detective Sergeant Pace is not real.

Watching him makes me want to fuck. Not necessarily him, but certainly not Seth. In fact, anyone but my husband. I start to think about younger guys in the office putting their mouths between my legs while I lie on top of my desk. I wonder whether I could say that I'm working late and take myself to a bar to pick up the first guy that shows me some attention.

I'm not quite myself.

I watch the news in the morning as the anchor describes the death of another young, innocent girl, who I helped to disinfect and dispose of, and all I want to do is push both hands down into my underwear until I'm a shuddering wreck.

Detective Sergeant Pace is making me do this.

Detective Sergeant Pace is a trigger.

Detective Sergeant Pace is disease.

I know it is him. He is the only thing that is different in my life. I only feel these things when I see him. Who is he, really? Why am I so obsessed with this case? I know more than anybody about what happened.

Seth walks into the lounge while I am watching the television, I hear his feet scuffing against the hallway floor and I take my hands out of my underwear.

'Thank God it's Friday.' He looks smart, suit and jacket, clean shaven. I can smell his aftershave. 'What a week, eh?'

He's so casual, talking about the experience like he's been slogging it away in the office, pulling in deals, not crushing the face of some twenty-something lonely heart and dumping her body next to an out-of-the-way dry-stone wall.

I see it in him. He finds it so easy to act normally. He's unaffected. He thinks he can't be caught and that he's invincible. And maybe I feel like that, too, a little. But Seth thinks that this makes him something special.

He's not.

He's one half of a TV show on a late channel, at a late hour, early in the week, called *Killer Couples* or *Couples Who Kill*. He's part of somebody's curiosity. He's half an hour of intrigue. He's part of sensationalism. But he is not sensational.

And that's where we differ.

I know what we do, what we have done. I know what's coming. I know we will do it again.

But it doesn't make us different.

We are just like everyone else.

138

Everything about her is a sigh or a roll of the eyes.

It doesn't seem genuine.

Seth looks at Maeve, slouched on the sofa like it is the end of the day, not the start, and he can see she is distracted. She isn't even looking at him.

'What a week, eh?' He doesn't know what else to say. It feels like small talk.

'Yeah.' Maeve breathes out her answer, trying desperately not to sigh.

Seth continues. He's trying. He sees that she is thinking about something.

'Let's get work over with and we can order in some food for tonight. Keep it simple. Not do anything. Grab some drink, some shit snacks and watch a film or something.'

She seems mesmerised by the television.

'Maeve!' Seth raises his voice.

'What?' She sits up in her seat and mutes the screen.

'Did you hear what I said?'

'Yes. Sorry. That'll be great. Can you grab the takeaway? Not Chinese, though, it just makes me feel awful the next day.'

'Sure. No problem.'

'I'll probably be a couple of hours late tonight. Not too late, just some work to get finished.' She speaks without looking.

It doesn't feel right to Seth, there's no reason but he doesn't trust it completely. He tells himself it's paranoia about Sunday.

'Really? On a Friday?' He questions her but makes it sound more like disappointment than interrogation.

'I'm just behind from missing a day and I've been playing catch-up all week. I don't want to worry about it over the weekend, you know?'

She's so convincing.

Maeve smiles at Seth and, suddenly, he feels like she is back in the room with him. His shoulders relax.

'Sure. Of course. I get that.'

Maeve switches off the television and takes a sip of her coffee.

'Are you leaving now?' she asks.

'Yeah, just need my laptop.'

'Well, I'll walk out with you. Let's go.'

Seth grabs his laptop from the hall and opens the front door to let Maeve outside. They kiss before getting in their separate cars. They're a normal couple. No different from anyone else on that street. They live together, eat together, share a toilet. They kiss each other goodbye in the morning and eat with one another in the evening. They sleep in the same bed and occasionally have sex there, too.

They're the Beaumans, and they're just as unhappy as you are.

'I don't think I'll be any later than eight, okay?' Maeve reiterates.

'I'll make sure the drink is cold and the food is hot.' Seth smiles.

He reverses out of the drive first; Maeve follows him until the first set of traffic lights.

That same Elton John song plays on the radio as Seth pulls into the industrial estate where his office is located. His boss is standing outside the front door, talking on his mobile phone and smoking a cigarette. He looks at his watch and taps it with the hand that holds the cigarette, the mobile phone wedged between his ear and his shoulder.

It infuriates Seth. He pulls into his space gripping the steering wheel as hard as he can. Elton continues to sing as Seth imagines going into the boot and taking out the car jack he has only ever used twice to change a flat tyre. And he thinks about walking up to his boss and smashing the heavy piece of metal into his face a few times before taking the cigarette and making him swallow it.

He daydreams about stamping on his neck and crushing his windpipe so that he cannot scream, meanwhile everybody else is in the office trying to find something important to do when he comes back in.

Then he thinks about taking his phone and texting his boss's wife and his girlfriend so that they know about each other, before wrapping that pile of human excrement in plastic and dropping him off a bridge in some other county.

But he gets out of his car with his laptop bag, locks it and nods a good morning as he enters the building. He can hear that his boss is talking to a woman but he doesn't know which one it is.

And he sits at his desk while everyone else tries to look busy and he opens up his Internet browser to search for a restaurant for Sunday night.

139

The first three times she knocks, Ant doesn't even move. He hasn't moved all night. It has been the best sleep he's had in years. A comfortable, firm, hair-free mattress in a pitch-black room that nobody knows about. It is exactly what he needed.

He wakes up on the fourth knock, just catching the end of a sentence he assumes is 'Roooooom serviiiice'. Before he can answer, the latch on the door clicks and a woman in her fifties with olive-leather skin is standing in his room with a trolley covered in fresh linen.

'Sorry, sir. Sorry, sir. I knocked and knocked and there was no answer.'

'Well, I'm not ready, so if you could kindly leave...'

Ant is cold. His first thought when that door clicked open was that it was Seth and he was going to die.

'Of course. It is late, sir, and we need to get the rooms ready and cleaned.'

'I haven't even eaten yet. Please, can you just leave me to get ready?'

The old maid is flustered. She understands Ant's embarrassment, he is naked underneath those covers, but she is worried for herself. It is a strict schedule to get the rooms turned around and he is preventing her from performing her job correctly and efficiently. Besides, he has already missed breakfast by some time. She wants to tell him that but backs out of the room and shut the door behind her.

Ant drops back down to the mattress, his head being hugged on all sides by the pillow. He feels his heart throbbing, pumping oxygenated blood to his muscles in case his instinct was to flee from that situation rather than stay and stand his ground. And he laughs to himself at how ridiculous it all is.

He leans across to the bedside table where his mobile phone rests.

'Oh, fuck,' he speaks out loud, looking at the time. It's past eleven o'clock.

Luckily, he has nothing to pack up. Ideally, he'd have showered and changed into clean clothes but he was bang out of luck. It was impulse to stay there, and the correct one.

He takes his clothes from the floor and places them back on. The T-shirt smells like yesterday. He hates that. In the bathroom, Ant, squeezes the remainder of the miniature, complimentary toothpaste into his mouth, bends down to the tap, takes a mouthful of water in and swills it around until it burns. He spits it into the plug hole and runs his hand around the sink to clean it.

When he leaves, the maid is dusting the leaves of a fake ficus in the corridor. Her trolley is outside his room. It's obvious that he is the last on her list. Ant wants to apologise but he remembers what Seth told him; he needs to be forgettable. Don't draw attention to yourself.

So he walks past the older woman with his head down and that makes her remember him more, because he was rude. People find it so much easier to remember the negative things.

Ant checks out but, before he leaves on his journey home, he remembers the other things that Seth told him, the things he instructed him to do in order to be fully prepared for Sunday evening.

He walks over to the petrol station. He buys himself a sausage roll and a packet of crisps for breakfast, then he moves to the cleaning section.

And picks up a bottle of bleach.

You will need to buy each bottle from a different location.

Pay in cash.

You will require six bottles.

140

When you work from home, one of two things happens: You either get distracted by everything – because it's a home, it doesn't feel like work, it doesn't feel like an office, it feels like your house, it is your house – you open your laptop and play music or have the television on in the background, you can surf the Internet without fear of your boss sneaking by and leaning over your shoulder. You can update your social media. You can watch pornography. You can do anything but work.

Or, you do the opposite. There is nobody around. You don't have to engage in inane conversations about the football last night or what is going on in the plethora of soap operas. You don't have to listen to stories about kids that only the parent finds cute. You don't even have to talk about work. In fact, you know that if you don't switch the television on or play music or masturbate to interracial bukkake, you can actually get a day of office work done in half a day at home.

Then there's secret option number three. That's where you do half a day of no work in the office because you are distracted, then tell your boss that you are going out after lunch to meet with a distributor but you, actually, intend to do even less work than you did in the morning. And, though your boss knows it's probably a lie, he also realises that he shot himself in the foot by saying that you could sit back after exceeding your target.

Seth chooses number three.

He has spent the morning finding restaurants and bars and checking their distances from Ant's house.

And now he is back in his car with a tuna and sweetcorn baguette, driving to view these places in person and walk the route back to Ant's so that he knows exactly what to expect on Sunday. He needs to make sure that Ant can follow him and go undetected. This is not something he would usually do. He tells himself he's not that cold-blooded. But this is out of the ordinary. It has to go right. No mistakes.

He looks through windows and has a couple of pints of lager in two different pubs. He walks to Ant's house. It doesn't look like there is anybody home. Seth doesn't get too close, though. He doesn't want to spook the kid; he still has the photographs.

Reservations are made for Sunday night, not in his name, of course. His route is planned. All that is left to do is confirm the details with the woman he plans to take out and then share that information with Ant.

It is done.

No turning back.

Seth drives home and arrives at six. He puts the three bottles of Prosecco he has bought into the fridge and leaves the bottle of red on the kitchen worktop.

This is when Maeve would usually walk through the door.

He has two hours left to kill.

141

That feeling I had this morning has gone. I'd like to think that it dissipated gradually throughout the day but it didn't. I kissed Seth goodbye this morning, and any desire I had felt while watching the news shrivelled and died in that moment.

Nothing to do with Seth.

I love him.

I want him.

It just changed. And I'd committed to staying at work late even though I don't have to because I was full of verve and a lust for something strange. I thought I could go to a bar and pick up a man I don't know and do who-knows-what with.

And now I'm sitting in this place with a glass of Shiraz and not one guy has come up to talk to me yet. And not one guy has offered to buy me a drink. The only one who has said anything is the guy behind the bar. He just asked me what I wanted to drink. I told him. He served me. He didn't ask me to share my troubles or offer to light me a cigarette.

So I'm alone. I look around and there are couples laughing together. It feels like they are laughing at me. Their working weeks have ended and they will now drink until they fall into bed later. And there are groups of men in suits, in fours and fives. They laugh louder and lift their drinks higher than any couple. And there are other people sitting alone but they are waiting for company.

And I wonder what the fuck I'm doing. I feel like an idiot. I'm not a desperate woman. I have what I need.

As I lose a little face, a man too young for me approaches and we talk for ten minutes. But I don't want him. I just used him.

I gulp down the last two mouthfuls of wine until there is nothing but a crimson halo left in the bottom of the glass and I leave. I get into my car and drive even though I am over the driving limit. But so are sixty percent of drivers in London on a Friday after five-thirty.

I text Seth to let him know that I have finished my imaginary work early. He messages me straight back to say that the drinks are cold and he's ordering pizza. I don't want it but I tell him that it's perfect.

And when I walk into the house, it is warm and there's just one guy there and he offers me a drink. He doesn't offer a cigarette but he knows that I haven't smoked for nearly five years. But he does ask me about my day and I tell him. And he questions me genuinely about my work this evening and I have to lie a little and avert his attention.

We drink two bottles of Prosecco and eat the pizza I don't want. It helps to cut through the alcohol. Seth asks me if I want to watch the news and I tell him no.

I don't want to see it.

I don't want to change.

142

'Charlie Sanders, I'm arresting you on suspicion of the murder of Hadley Serf.'

That's when Charlie's girlfriend started hitting him, slapping at his face and punching his chest.

'You bastard. You fucking bastard. You've been at it again.'

Pace has two constables with him and they restrain her while Sanders is cuffed in the hallway of his house. He comes quietly. There is no fight in him. His shock has evaporated and all that is left is sadness and disappointment.

As he is led to the car, he tells Pace, 'I didn't kill her. I swear. I didn't kill her.' It is a dejected plea for innocence that the detective is in no mood to entertain. He pushes Charlie Sanders' head down forcefully and nudges him into the car with a prod to the ribs.

As they drive, Pace is silent. Raging.

Charlie is talking at him.

'I didn't even know her name. We just met. We fucked. How is that a crime?' He is talking to himself but making it loud enough that Pace can hear him.

Over and over and over, saying that he didn't kill her, that he hardly knew her. Each word ebbing away at Pace's patience like a drop of water to the forehead.

Tap. Tap. Tap.

Then the cocky sales guy came out.

'You know, I'm pretty sure that dig you gave me could be construed as police brutality...'

'You do remember me telling you that anything you say can be taken as evidence?'

'I heard you. I was just saying that there was no need for that dig, I was cooperating.'

'If I prove that you have killed those girls, a nudge to the ribs will seem like a kiss on the cheek. Now settle down.' Pace hardly looks at the road. Charlie Sanders can see Pace's dead eyes glaring at him in the rear-view mirror. It is like he never looks away.

'Girls?' Charlie Sanders emphasises the plural. 'What the fuck are you talking about? Girls? I thought this was about that one from last week. What are you trying to pin on me?'

'I would advise you to shut your mouth until we get to the station. Then you can tell me everything you know.' Slow. Deliberate. Menacing. It is the truth in Pace's tone that makes it even more frightening for his suspect.

Pace is going to let Sanders stew in a cell for a while and sweat before interviewing him.

He looks at the dishevelled fool on the back seat and he smiles.

Pace thinks he has his man.

143

It takes Ant longer than he thinks to collect the bleach. He has a backseat filled with extraneous items he has no use for. There are bags of salad and deodorants sprays and plasters and biscuits and ripen-at-home avocados. He even panic-bought a box of heavy-flow tampons.

Now he is home.

And feels exhausted.

He unpacks straight away, putting everything in its respective place, apart from the tampons, which he throws out. And he makes himself a coffee.

The flat is cold. He will have to remember to set a timer for the heating on Sunday so that they feel comfortable when they arrive at his flat. Comfortable enough to get naked.

That's the plan.

He runs through it in his mind while sipping at his coffee in the kitchen.

Clean the house, make it presentable for a lady to come back to.

Dinner is at eight. Drinks first. Feel free to be inside the bar but not too close.

Do not come into the restaurant. View only through the window, if needed.

Drinks afterwards. Go home during this time and wait. Lights are off and remain off.

Door should be left on the latch.

Unscrew the bulb in the bedroom.

Stay in there.

Stay quiet.

Wait.

Wait in the shadows then pick your moment to wrap your hands around a girl's throat and wring it out

That's it. That is the plan that Seth set out for Ant. Now that he thinks about it, it all seems so simple. Maybe too simple. But maybe the killing is the easiest part. It's the location and connection and grooming that takes the effort.

For Seth, anyway.

Ant has his own ideas.

He has his own plan.

144

A burner. That's what they call it.

When you grab yourself a pay-as-you-go mobile phone, use it once, rip the SIM card and battery out and dump it all. Keeps you untraceable.

Everything we do is recorded.

Apps are waking us up and saying good morning to us. You drive past a cinema or a bank and something flashes up on your phone because it knows you are near. Or you look at something on a website and five minutes later you receive an email about that very product with some alternatives in different price bands.

Seth always used them. The initial call was made on the house phone, sometimes he'd make twenty in an evening. It would become a very expensive hobby. But if he made a connection and called a person a second time, that phone would be used once. Then destroyed.

He needed to let Ant know the details for Sunday night – the times and locations – but he didn't want to text him and create any kind of trail. On his way home he had bought another three phones and he'd unpackaged one to call Ant. To give him the information he had gathered and to ensure that he was living up to his side of the deal – preparing the place, buying the bleach, removing the light bulb.

He had called Ant but the phone rang and rang and eventually went to voicemail.

Why wasn't the idiot picking up? What did he have to do that was any better than this? Why was he making Seth waste a phone?

Seth was worried. Ant made him anxious. He was the weakness. He was unpredictable.

He didn't have to burn the phone just because it had gone to voice-mail but he did it, anyway. Because he was cautious. He'd learned from Maeve. But he had spent a little on credit. So, before he tore the thing apart and binned it, he called the pizza-delivery place.

145

The Post-it notes stay on the desk tonight.

Ant doesn't write down his usual three-sentence cheat sheet. He is not here to stay on script. He is here to take notes on potential victims. Future connections.

He doesn't need to sift through a phonebook and hope that luck plays a part; he is creating his own luck. He has a rich cross-section of people and personalities to choose from. And he doesn't have to wait for that one special person to not hang up or call him a freak; he doesn't have to wait for someone to feel as alone as he does to want to talk to him. Everybody on the other end of the phone wants to talk to him.

He is their Samaritan.

Ant is so excited by his apparent entrepreneurial spirit that he is not choosy.

Quantity over quality.

He uses the sticky notes to write down the details of everybody that calls in that night. Their names, numbers, problems and confidential secrets they have entrusted to him.

Who would have ever thought that he would have so much in common with a single mother or a closet homosexual or a suicidal pre-school helper?

In truth, Ant is not doing his job any differently. He is still there, being present and attentive and comforting, he's just taking notes as he goes.

He's still helping a tonne of isolated individuals, he just plans on skimming the odd kilogram off the top for himself sometimes.

If he likes what happens on Sunday night, if he gets a taste for it, he has a fountain of despair at his disposal.

He is young and impetuous.

A mistake waiting to happen.

146

The interview commenced and Charlie Sanders spilled everything.

He told Pace how he always loved that club because the girls there were so desperate, he was guaranteed to get laid. He explained how he had met Hadley Serf, that she was with a few of her friends and they had obviously been drinking.

'They were all pretty decent but you could tell which were up for it.'

Pace clenched his fist beneath the desk; his expression did not change, though.

'Look, we left, I don't really know what time it was, probably about midnight-ish. We walked for a couple of minutes, looking for a cab. She dragged me into a side street and started kissing me and grabbing me. We went back to her house and had sex.' He stopped and took a breath at this point, realising that his girlfriend was aware of that part, at least, and that she had probably already moved her things out or thrown his into the street.

'Then what happened, Mr Sanders?'

'Then nothing. We came, we got dressed and I left. I didn't even go as far as the front room because we did it in the hallway. It was just like she needed to get something out her system.'

'That was it? You had sex, rolled up your socks and walked out? No talking? No coffee? No disagreement?' Pace didn't believe him.

'No. Nothing like that. Not every woman wants you to stay around and hug afterwards. Look, I left and went back to the club to see if my friends were still there. She was very much alive when I walked out of the door. I started making my way back to the club and got jumped from behind. Some fucking guy, I didn't even see him. Told me to leave her alone. That she was his, or something?'

'She was his? Were those his words?'

'I can't remember. He knocked me to the floor. Punched me in the face a few times and kicked me in the ribs. I had a black eye for days. You can ask anyone about that.'

It all seemed too convenient to Pace but if this guy was telling the truth, it was new information that could blow the case wide open.

'And you didn't think to report this assault to the police?'

'I didn't want my girlfriend to find out about what I had been doing. I told her I fell over when I was drunk.'

'Quite the convincing liar, Mr Sanders.'

'I'm telling you the truth. What have I got to lose, now? I swear, I didn't even know her name until I saw her face come up on the news the other day.'

Pace suspended the interview and turned off the recording.

Sanders sat back in his chair.

And the second detective in the room, who had remained quiet throughout the interview, remained quite still as Pace grabbed the suspect by the throat, pinned him to the floor and started shouting at him.

'You sat on potentially pertinent evidence because you were worried your girlfriend would find out that you are a two-timing sack of shit? God help me if another body turns up and we could have stopped it had we been given this information sooner.'

Charlie Sanders' face had turned pink and there were tears running from his eyes.

Pace let go.

'Get this idiot back into a cell while I look into his claims.'

Detective Sergeant Pace was so close to finding out the truth.

He didn't have his man, but he had enough information to move forward. He could take footage from the club. He could locate the cab that was used that night. He could see whether any cameras picked up the alleged assault.

It would lead him to the Samaritan.

SATURDAY

147

The day before the kill. Seth hasn't slept. He's adding anxiety to insomnia.

It's a nothing day.

Everything is set up; it's just a case of waiting.

When you have insomnia, all you are doing is waiting. Waiting for night. Waiting for complete quiet, for peace. Waiting for that everyday tiredness that you feel, that never-ending weight – heavy limbs, heavy eyelids, heavy heart – to wash over you and leave you with no choice but to sleep.

And you hear people at work or in cafés saying that they are exhausted. Maybe their kid was up in the night, they wet the bed or they jumped on their parents at five-thirty. Or maybe they have been travelling a lot over the last week. You listen and they say things like, 'I don't have the time,' and you know that time isn't real, because what they consider to be a day is only two-thirds of your day. Because they have already been asleep for four hours when you are just getting to that point where you are so frustrated that you can't drop off, you know you have another hour of irritation left.

There's always time.

You can make time.

Adding waiting on top of waiting elongates time for Seth. Like it would for anyone, but more for him. His days are already twenty hours long. Every hour on this Saturday morning feels longer to Seth than it does to anybody else. And he knows he has so many more to endure.

Later tonight, when Maeve is resting peacefully in their bed, he will be in the lounge seeing that flat screen in extreme close-up. Or he'll be lying next to his wife staring at the ceiling.

Seth lies down on the sofa with his laptop resting on his thighs and clicks on one link that will take him on to another and another until he cannot remember where he started.

He fumbles around and scrolls through words and pictures and stumbles upon an article about sleep conditions and how to overcome them.

Apparently, sleeping on your side gives you shoulder pain. You can overcome this by lying on your back and cuddling a pillow.

Lying on your front with your head on the pillow can cause an unnatural curvature of the spine and cause back pain. Easily solved. Lie on your back with a pillow underneath your knees to force your lower back into the mattress and a more neutral position.

Too many pillows. Lying on your side. You've probably got neck pain. Best if you lie on your back with your elbows on a pillow either side of you.

It seems to Seth that most of these cures involve you changing position to lie on your back.

He reads on.

If you have trouble with snoring or perhaps you sleep next to somebody that snores, it's because they are lying on their back. They should switch to their side.

Until they experience the inevitable shoulder pain.

To cap it all off, there was advice for people who can't get to sleep. Don't drink coffee or energy drinks before bed. Exercise in the morning and afternoon. Swap the laptop or phone for a book.

That was a waste of time, Seth thinks to himself.

But, when he looks at the clock in the corner of his laptop screen, only three minutes have passed. It felt like twelve.

And that's how the rest of his day will go.

148

It's in the newspapers this morning about both the recent women, and Daisy, who they now openly decree have a correlation.

One of the tabloids has obviously paid someone a lot of money to give up a picture of each of the girls in their crime-scene photo shoots.

It's nothing too gratuitous but it's still two dead people. The headline says: 'WRAPPED IN PLASTIC'.

Another sensationalist paper cites immigrants as an issue and reason for the rise in this kind of story.

The broadsheets handle it with a little more sensitivity. One has investigated so thoroughly that they can reveal both women were strangled. Another doesn't even have the story on the front page because thirty-six people were killed in a suicide bombing the day before and they believe that is something worth hearing about, too.

In America they have already dubbed them as the SBW killings. (Strangled, Bleached and Wrapped in plastic.) Exactly the kind of notoriety some killers crave.

Not Seth, he just wants to fade into the background.

And certainly not Maeve, who just wants things back to normal. Not the normal they had, because that was unbearable, but a new normal that sees the connection they have forged over these circumstances to stick around for a lot longer than they did before.

But Ant smiles at the news because he is going to continue the legacy. At first, he will do it the way that Seth tells him. He wants to find his feet, get good. Then he can carve his own way into the history books, get his own name.

He hasn't slept as well as he did in the motel but he did manage to toss and turn in his own bed rather than playing neck-breakers all night on the lounge windowsill. He believed that Seth wasn't going to turn up in the night to strangle him, bleach him and wrap him in plastic.

One day left.

So much to do.

Ant throws a spoonful of butter into a hot pan then cracks three eggs and seasons with coarse black pepper and pink Himalayan salt. As the eggs start to solidify around the edges, he pours in a dash of milk and a tablespoon of cream cheese, and mixes it all together before pouring onto wholegrain toast. The last thing he needs is to feel hungry with all the work he has to do.

He makes a coffee and adds a couple of squirts of caramel syrup.

The sugar is a short-term fix but it's what his body is telling him that it needs.

Beneath the sink, Ant has nine bottles of bleach. Six that Seth told him to buy for Sunday night and three that he already had for cleaning. He hates that the labels don't match.

He takes the kitchen spray and covers the hob in a lemon-scented abrasive foam. He disinfects the worktops and cupboard doors then throws that sponge away. He uses a new sponge for the bathroom. Scouring the inside of the sink and glass on the shower door until the fumes from the spray are too toxic for him to be in there any longer.

The rooms are gleaming. He takes some of his spare bleach and works it into the toilet basin and both the kitchen and bathroom sink.

And he changes the bed covers and puts the old ones straight into the washing machine and vacuums every fibre of every carpet, using the smallest attachment to get into the crevice between the carpet and skirting boards. And he dusts every surface. And he touches up any grubby paintwork where he has inadvertently grabbed a doorframe every time he has entered the room.

And when he finally sits down, it is lunchtime and he is hungry again. He makes a cheese sandwich. Crumbs drop on the kitchen worktop and grated cheese spills onto the floor tiles. He will reclean the kitchen once he has eaten.

He is doing exactly as he has been told.

All that is left is to take the light bulb out of the bedroom.

Ant sits at his desk, eating his sandwich and looking at some of the newspaper websites. The first link has a strap line of 'News, Sport, Celebrities and Gossip'. Ant clicks the blue text, knowing full well that the publication has those things in order from least important to most.

When he sees a plastic-wrapped, pale Hadley Serf, it angers him. He remembers why he is in this situation.

Seth took Hadley from him.

And that still makes Ant want to kill Seth.

149

I read somewhere that thinking about running can help you to lose weight. Not as much as physically running, but enough to raise your heart rate and burn some calories. It's another one of those urban myths that flies around, making people lazier. Like the one about eating celery and how you use more energy by chewing it than the food actually contains.

These mistruths penetrate our rational thoughts because we want them to be true, we want a quick fix or an easy way out. Because the real truth is, if you want to lose weight, stop eating all that cake. You want to be fitter and healthier, stop thinking about exercise and get out there doing it.

And maybe you'd like to earn more money. Do your job. Do it well. Hit your numbers then exceed them. Quit the one you are in and start up your own company. Do the job you want to do. Nothing motivates people to do something extraordinary as much as fear.

And when your relationship changes with the person you once loved, the individual you promised yourself to, the one you told you would be with forever, you don't go cold. You don't push them away because it's easier if they get rid of you or think it's their decision. You don't fool around with some other woman. Somebody you met on a work trip. Some girl you connected with over the phone.

You work at it. You work hard. Go to counselling. Support them when their father is taken by cancer. Help them clean and dispose of a mistake they have made.

I know what I want. I want this ordeal to be over with. I want the worry to disappear. I want to move on. I'm not going to get that by thinking positively about it. It won't happen because I let myself day-dream about a brighter future.

Success only comes from action.

So, while Seth lies on the sofa scrolling through online quizzes and avoiding any news developments, while he worries and stresses and does not sleep, while he thinks about things, I know that I am the do-er in this partnership.

I have certainty.

I know this has to end.

And it will, very soon.

150

Pace discovers that Sanders is telling the truth. He sees a video of him dancing with Hadley at the club. He has spoken to the doormen. He has the camera from the black cab they took home that night. This was a one-night thing; they didn't know each other, there had been no grooming. It didn't fit the killer's profile.

Hadley had gone to work the day after their encounter but there was nothing saying that Sanders hadn't returned a couple of days later to finish the job, so he was still being held. He had a lawyer, now. He never mentioned the nudge to the ribs or the choking.

More importantly, that cheating fuck had been assaulted and Pace is thankful he is living in a nation under constant surveillance because his attacker could be seen clearly from the CCTV camera outside the chemist.

And that means that Pace could scour the footage from the club. And that man could be seen watching Hadley Serf all night. Prowling. Preying.

And Pace could see that he left shortly after the amorous couple.

And his face, Ant's face, would be all over the television on Sunday night along with a dramatic reconstruction of the evening.

There would be hundreds of phone calls leading to Ant and, eventually Seth.

Detective Sergeant Pace is closing in.

SUNDAY

151

Seth waves a hand in the air to beckon a waiter over. He points at a menu. Two minutes later, a bottle of red wine arrives with two glasses. Ant sees it all through the window of the restaurant.

Before that, Seth was drinking a pint of lager and his date had a glass of white wine, complete with those sexy beads of condensation on the glass.

Ant was watching that, too. But he was inside the pub with them.

Just as the plan said.

It was one of those gastro pubs. The ones where the beers have entertaining names. They're pale or blonde or craft, too. And you pay five pounds for a portion of chips because they are double or triple cooked, like that's something new, but you forget that every time you buy a packet of frozen oven chips from the supermarket for 99p, that's exactly what you're getting.

And a pie comes with a foam instead of a gravy and your fish arrives with a *velouté* rather than a sauce.

They could've stayed in there and eaten.

But that wasn't the plan.

Ant sees Seth lift his large glass of red wine up and clink it against his date's glass. He says something and smiles. Ant can't read his lips. He sees the back of the woman's head. Lustrous, blonde hair. She is wearing a black dress. Fitted. He can see the shape of her shoulders and imagines her pretty face. She does not look like Hadley Serf.

Before that, Seth was in the gastro pub doing the same thing, lifting a pint glass up and showing his teeth, tapping it against the woman's wine glass. She was mixing her drinks. Ant didn't know whether that was her idea or Seth's.

It didn't really matter, Ant told himself; they both knew where it was heading.

Her idea was Seth's idea.

Ant couldn't see her face in there, either. He wondered whether

Seth knew it would be that way. Would he have drilled down to that level of detail? Perhaps it would be easier for Ant if he didn't see her face until the last moment. The way that farmers shouldn't name their animals because it makes them harder to kill if there is that familiarity, that attachment.

Maybe, Ant thinks, it's because he wants to keep an eye on him. The way an assassin will never sit in a room with their back to the door, because they have to be facing anybody that comes in.

He sits at the bus stop. Travellers come and go. All ages and races. It's too early for the drunks to be rolling around the paths, asking him questions. Most people have their eyes aimed at a mobile phone screen. Nobody talks to him.

He sits.

He waits.

He watches.

Ant's concentration never wavers. He is focused firmly on Seth. And even more so on the woman he is with.

It's true, when somebody knows that you are going to die, they give you their undivided attention.

152

The first step is admitting that you have a problem. That you are powerless.

That your life has become unmanageable.

I drink down a rather expensive glass of red wine and it makes me smile. I don't feel out of control. Quite the opposite. It's a great night for me that is going exactly to plan.

The second step is to believe that there is a power greater than myself that can restore me to sanity.

We all go a little mad sometimes.

I don't drink every single day. I never drink in the day. That would be somebody with an addiction, surely. Yes, I have a glass or two when I get home from a busy day at the office. And sometimes that can turn into a bottle. Or two. But it's not like I'm some kind of New York ad man, drinking an Old-Fashioned at breakfast and walking into boardroom meetings with a vodka on the rocks at nine-thirty in the morning. (Please see step one.)

What is this power that is supposed to be greater than myself? My only thought is willpower. After a day in that office, I often have none.

Next, I am supposed to make a decision to turn my will and my life over to the power of God.

Skip step three. That cannot happen. I know what I have done and He has no room for the likes of me.

Make a fearless moral inventory of myself. That's step four.

Resentment, fear and sex. Three of my favourite things. This one should be easy.

Obviously I have to resent my own parents. For not believing in me enough and then telling me that they didn't want me to be with Seth because he would be the thing that held me back. I resent my sister for moving halfway across the world with her family.

I resent Seth for drifting away from us, for shutting down and changing. I resent his silly, little late-night game on the phone. I resent his whispering and muffled laughter. His phonebooks. I resent those three girls he brought home in the boot of his shitty car.

I resent social media and the lives that all my friends present that I know are not a true representation of themselves, but it still irks me. I resent even their fake happiness. And the pictures of their cute kids. I can't share any pictures of my kids. I guess I resent Seth a little for that, too.

My fear comes from the idea that I could lose everything.

I'm scared we'll get caught. So scared. Scared enough to overthink every detail.

I'm scared he'll do it again.

And I'm scared that when he does, I will be there to help him again. Hoping it will bring us even closer together.

This wine is fresh, light on its feet, spicy and charming. At the centre there are sweet red fruits. I had the same wine from an earlier vintage and the alcohol level was too high for my tastes.

Is that something that someone with an addiction to alcohol would say? I'm not powerless against it.

Step five: Admit to God, myself and one other person the exact nature of my wrongs.

Dear God, I have covered up and conspired in the murder of three seemingly random women. I have placed each of them in a bath of bleach. I have scrubbed their bodies and nails and teeth and eyes. I have washed their hair. I have disposed of them in fields and woods and by the side of the road.

I have also had a lot to drink. Tonight and many other nights. I find that it numbs me. It helps me to sleep. Sometimes forget. Recently, I have used it to help me relax in the bedroom and on three separate occasions have allowed my husband to empty his poison inside of me with no regard to the consequences.

Amen.

I finish my glass of wine. I want another. I get another.

By admitting to God, I have admitted to myself. But I already knew all of that. And I don't need to tell Seth because he already knows, too. There's nobody else that I trust enough to tell.

I only told God because I know He's not listening.

So, I guess that means I can skip the next couple of steps. I don't think God will remove these defects in my character; I won't humbly request that he also remove any other shortcomings. I'm not sure I view them in that way.

Next, I am supposed to make a list of the people I have harmed.

Most recently was Hadley Serf. Before that was Theresa Palmer. It seems so long since the first girl. I have forgotten her name. But I have had quite a lot to drink.

It was around step four that I realised my addiction was nothing to do with the alcohol. It's Seth. It's this relationship.

I am powerless against it.

I'm back at the beginning.

I try again but I can't seem to get past step two. The thing is, I don't believe there is any power greater than us, what we have. When we have it.

Now I know it's not the alcohol that I'm addicted to, that it's not the thing that controls me, it seems perfectly fine to finish the rest of this bottle.

153

That feeling you get when you sense that somebody might be watching you, it's unnerving, you go cold. It's worse when you know they are watching you. It's worse when they're sat behind your date in the corner. He can't see her face but he can sure see yours.

Seth tries to block Ant out. It's easier in the restaurant than it was in the pub. He was there, looming. Dark. For such a slight frame, he was suddenly imposing. To Seth, he was obvious. He could feel Ant's eyes, scrutinising his every move. Learning. For his own future. For when he would be the one sitting in Seth's chair.

It was too unpredictable before the restaurant. Ant could have done something risky like he did when he had followed Seth and Hadley. That moment where he impulsively brushed past their table. Something within Seth told him that wouldn't happen. That Ant would more than likely not be able to finish the job that night. That he would piss his pants with the fear and reality of what was going to happen.

Seth refills the two wine glasses. He knows that Ant is across the road, outside the window to his right. And he wants to look out there to check but he doesn't. He drinks and he eats and he smiles, showing his teeth in order for his emotion to be deduced from long range.

Through every story that he shares or joke that he tells, Ant is there. For every bite of steak and sip of wine. For every itch that is scratched. For every hand that's been washed. Seth is edgy. Sweating.

But conveying a natural charm and way with the opposite sex that Ant is not sure he really possesses.

'Well, this bottle went down very well.' Seth exaggerates his smile. You could see his teeth from space. 'Shall we get another or would you like to try something different?'

He already knows what she will say. They're only halfway through the main course, there's plenty of time. Probably best to stick with the same wine as they have mixed already.

And that is what she says.

Seth orders another bottle. He and his date drink a glass of water with their food while they wait for it to arrive. It makes him feel French. Sophisticated. He can be somebody else.

He needs to excuse himself to the bathroom. The cold lager has worked its way through his system and the wine is forcing it further down. But he's worried. He can't shake it.

Ant could panic. He could look away for a moment and then peer back through the window to find that Seth is no longer sitting there. He could see the woman on her own. The woman he is supposed to strangle to death later that night in the bedroom of his own flat. He could worry that Seth has left. He could blow the whole thing. He could run inside the restaurant and shout information that is not for anybody else's ears. He could decide to strangle her right there and then while Seth stands in front of a urinal with his dick in his hand.

It's too much stress for a man who wants to take a piss.

Seth stands up at the table, excuses himself, and looks out of the window for the first time all night. He waits a moment so that he can make eye contact with Ant, hoping the message will get through that he isn't going to disappear; he gestures towards his jacket that is hanging over the back of the chair. He wouldn't leave without it.

Ant's chin lifts slightly, as though he is attempting to look over the window pane to see what Seth is gesturing to. He rests back as though accepting it.

And then he is standing at that urinal, his dick poking out through the zip of his trousers. He's desperate but it won't come. He's too wound up. Another customer walks in and stands at the urinal next to him. He nods at Seth. Seconds later, Seth can hear the guy pissing freely, shutting his eyes and tilting his head back. It's a pleasure that Seth doesn't see coming. He tries not to think about Ant.

The man next to him finishes. He washes his hands then holds them under the drier. Seth uses this opportunity to push hard. Three beads of urine trickle onto the porcelain. Five seconds after the other man exits, Seth starts. And he can't stop. It's the most relaxed he has felt all day.

Back in the restaurant, the next bottle of wine has arrived. His date is still there, alive and drinking. Ant is still outside, watching and waiting. Seth sits back down, relaxed and smiling. He lifts his own drink.

Everything is going to plan.

He peers into the eyes of the woman opposite him.

Not long, now.

154

A friendly, if inebriated, student wobbles past Ant at the bus shelter and politely asks him for the time.

Fuck you, freak.

Can't you see I'm busy?

Get out of here.

Ant didn't say any of those things stumbling around in his busy mind. It was like Seth had told him, 'The best place to hide is in plain sight. By being nothing interesting. Don't make yourself memorable. People remember the extraordinary or the extraordinarily boring.'

'Er,' Ant fumbles for the phone in his pocket. He takes his gaze away from the restaurant window for a moment. 'It's quarter past nine.'

'Thanks. Plenty of time.' And the student walks off, leaving Ant as the solitary bus stop figure.

Plenty of time for drinking. Plenty of time to find drugs. Plenty of time to get laid. Plenty of time to play a prank on a fellow student.

Plenty of time to get back and cram for an exam. Whatever it was, the young scholar seemed more relaxed than Ant could ever be tonight.

He looks up and panics.

Seth and his date have gone.

He looks left and right but nobody is around. Even the student has disappeared around a corner somewhere.

Ant runs across the road without even looking. He is lucky. As he reaches the other side of the road, Seth emerges from the front of the restaurant with his date. Ant is running straight at them. He notices but it is too late, he has committed, he is heading straight for the couple.

Seth is placing his jacket over the woman's shoulders. Ant keeps his eyes on Seth. He doesn't really want to look at her, knowing what he is going to do. He makes sure he steps to the right so that he will hit Seth. They bump shoulders.

'Sorry,' Ant says, his left hand straightening Seth's shirt before he disappears into the restaurant.

'He must really love the cheesecake,' Ant hears him quip as the restaurant door closed.

He watches them cross the road through the window, heading towards a different pub for after-dinner drinks, as planned.

'Good evening, sir. Do you have a reservation?'

Another polite Oxfordian to be unmemorable to.

'I'm sorry?'

'Do you have a dinner reservation for tonight?' The maître d' slows his speech.

Ant looks out the window; they are almost far enough away for him to slink back outside.

'Um, no, I don't. Sorry. I just wondered whether you could fit four of us in at any point, this evening.' He is delaying.

'I'm sorry, we are fully booked and it is late. Maybe a table for two could squeeze in but four would be difficult, I'm afraid.'

Ant knows that. Of course.

'Well, thanks, anyway. I knew it was a long shot.' And he turns. And he leaves. And he waits outside the door until Seth and the blonde woman are walking into the last pub.

He can wait. He's been waiting all night. All his life for this.

Ant gives it another five minutes to be sure. He knows that they are in there having another drink. Seth will be putting the moves on her, closing the deal. Ant wants to hear what that entails. He isn't a closer. He is a cruiser. An automaton. He needs the lesson. But it is too risky after almost knocking them over, he can't go in there now.

'Fuck it,' he says under his breath. Walking past the window, he sees them taking two drinks to a table in the corner. Seth has another pint of lager while she seems to have moved to either a gin or a vodka.

He had to trust that Seth was following through with this.

That he would fulfil the plan.

That he would arrive back at Ant's place that night. With the woman that Ant would be waiting to kill.

155

I'm so drunk.

I want to do something stupid.

I want to fuck.

Red wine usually makes me feel tired. Sunday night, I should be falling asleep on my back with some putrid programme in the background that I've lost interest in but I'm afraid to suggest changing the channel because Seth always gets a little aggravated when I want to switch to the news and I don't know whether he is humouring me or has grown to like these shows.

But I don't feel that way tonight.

I don't want to lie on the sofa. The only way I want to do that is if Seth is down on his knees in front of me. I only want to be lying down on the sofa if my hands are pulling the back of his hair as I get closer to orgasm. I don't want to be lying down on the sofa unless I am lying on my front and Seth is entering me from behind, his full weight down on me, his hand forcing down against the back of my neck.

I feel charged. Alive and excited. Expectant.

I expect sex tonight. It won't go like that. I know how it happens. Seth kisses me next to the bed, his hands hold my face like I'm the only thing he wants to look at, even though his eyes are closed. My fingers run down his back. He does the same. He will undress me. I will try to undress him but have issues with his belt. His hand will move between my legs, touching me softly. Then he will push me playfully onto the bed and remove his own trousers.

He will kiss my neck and my breasts and my stomach and bite at my hips before teasing me around the place I want him to go. I won't let him take me all the way.

'Come here. I want you in me,' I'll say. And he will obey.

He will crawl up my body and ease himself inside. I will pull him close to me because that's where I want him, at first. I want to make love before he fucks me. I want to feel the pressure of him on me.

Then he will straighten his arms and hold his own weight above me. I love looking up at him like that. It's a time when he seems strong. Fit. That's when he will start to move faster. Harder. More forcefully.

And then it will all be over.

That's what I want on my Sunday night. Not my usual drunken slumber on the sofa.

I want closeness and love and sex and spontaneity and my husband to fill me up again.

That's what I want.

And, later, that's what I'm going to get.

156

Deconstructed food made no sense. You have all the ingredients for something. You make it. Then you take it back apart. So, instead of a nice, thick biscuit base with a thick-set cream cheese filling, perhaps a fruit topping, all cut into a perfect triangular wedge with cream, you get a 'deconstruction'. Some kind of sugary cream-cheese sphere with biscuit crumbs sprinkled over the top and a strawberry coulis dotted around the plate with other discs of balsamic vinegar and a sugared basil leaf.

You may as well cook a cheesecake and hit it with a tennis racquet.

That's what Seth had said when his dessert arrived and they'd both laughed about it. Even though it wasn't funny.

And now they're giggling about it in the corner of the pub while Seth gestures something about pouring it on a plate. It was silliness. They were drunk enough to get lost in that.

Seth could smile at her and touch her hand on the table without worrying about her reaction. He could touch her leg underneath the table without smiling and they'd both know exactly where things were heading.

He takes a mouthful of beer and turns on his stool. He can't see Ant. It worries him again. The unpredictability. His enthusiastic immaturity. Seth is left having to assume that there is some degree of self-control and common sense left in Ant and that he is now walking home to wait in the shadows of a bedroom with no light bulb.

Turning back, his date is leaning with her elbows on the table, her face close to his. They look at one another for a moment before Seth makes the move to lean in. He knows that she will kiss him back. It's soft, at first. Then Seth moves his hand to the back of her head to keep her in place, to manoeuvre her where he wants.

They both drink.

'Let's finish these and get out of here.'

He's not asking her whether or not she wants to and he's not forcing her. He's confident and she likes that.

She takes down the last mouthful of her gin and says, 'I'm ready when you are.'

He puts his jacket back over her shoulders and, when they get outside the door and the cold air of the night hits them in the face, amplifying their insobriety, he walks beside her, one arm pinned into his body while her other is rubbed in a gesture of warmth.

Seth has to remember the route back to Ant's flat that he is supposed to pass off as his own.

157

No light bulb. That's what Seth had said to him.

'Unscrew the light bulb from the bedroom.'

Ant hadn't asked any questions. This is how Seth did things. This is how he got away with it. He'd killed three women without so much as a sniff around his London borough; of course Ant was taking notes.

He waited.

In that corner that once had a TV bracket on the wall.

The configuration of the room at the time had called for something that could swing out from the wall and present the picture from the corner. Ant had taken the set down from that position and filled the holes. He had meticulously filled those holes and sanded until you would never believe they had been there. It was a new wall. Untouched. You can't see it, though, because it's so dark in there.

He has no idea how long it will be but now he is in there, he's too afraid to leave. In case they return.

The place smells clean. Not like a clean house, not like somebody who is tidy, there are no bowls of potpourri and there are no scented candles; it's clinical. Not like a hospital but closer to that than it is to a show home.

Ant needs to piss, and that feeling is making him more nervous and uncomfortable. He can feel a wall on each shoulder as he squeezes himself into that corner. He's scared it won't work. That Seth's date's eyes will adjust to the lack of light at some point and she will be able to pick out a figure in the corner of the room.

Then there will be screaming. And Seth might need to silence the cries quickly. And that means he will kill his own date. Ant won't get a look in. He will have another one taken from him. By Seth.

He's sweating. He doesn't want to do that. Not against the wall. He'll have to clean that up after.

He's shaking. He doesn't want to do that. Not while he's so desperate for the toilet. That's something he certainly doesn't want to clear up. His mind couldn't handle that. The smell would always be there to Ant. The memory of a grown man wetting himself. He'd have to replace the carpet.

He's thinking. He shouldn't do that. Hadley Serf's voice on the phone and his friend hanging from that door and almost running into Seth and his date outside the restaurant. And his parents and the numbers he input at work the other day and the photos under the coffee table and whether his mobile phone is charged. It only makes him more anxious. So he shakes more. And then sweats on the wall a little more.

He's waiting. He really doesn't want to do that. Pleasure delay was something for the bedroom but not in this instance. He can see more and more of the room as his eyes adjust to the light. And, as he calms himself and rationalises the scene, the fact that light peeks in through the window and hits the bedframe makes sense, his corner is untouched, though. He is invisible.

Hiding in plain sight.

Like Seth told him.

He breathes. Pure relief.

Then the sound of the door opening.

And voices. One male. One female.

The whisper of a kiss.

The crash of someone being pushed against the wall, passionately.

Then the door opening.

Ant is sweating and shaking and thinking. But he is no longer waiting.

They are here. It's happening. Somebody is about to die.

158

Seth's jacket drops off her shoulders as he pushes her against the wall, her hands held above her head by the wrists in one strong hand, leaving the other free to pull himself into her as they kiss.

The flat is so quiet it makes their kissing seem louder. It's frantic and passionate.

And they both know why they are there.

He puts his hand on the side of her face as they kiss, before moving it behind her head and pulling her hair back to expose more of her neck. He wants to bite her but it's always dangerous to leave that kind of mark, no matter how much bleach you have. He's conditioned himself to not take it that far.

Then he moves his hand down, lifting her leg so that her right knee is up by his waist and works that hand up and down until he grazes between her legs. She makes a noise that tells him she agrees with it.

Then he lets go of her hands on the wall and does the same with the other leg so that she is now clamped around him and he can walk her to the bedroom. Ant's bedroom. Where he waits. Ready to piss his pants.

The bedroom door is ajar and Seth pushes it lightly with his foot.

'Leave the light off,' she tells him.

'Doesn't work, anyway.' He flicks the switch and nothing happens.

They're all on script.

Ant is behind that door. Seth knows this. He's nervous about it but it doesn't affect his arousal.

He walks into that unknown room with a woman wrapped tightly around him. She is kissing him. Her eyes are closed. He kisses back but his eyes are open. He looks towards the corner where he knows Ant is standing. But he can't see him. Not even a partial outline.

To be safe, he moves around to the other side of the bed. The linen smells freshly washed. He stops and puts her down.

He knows exactly what she wants.

He knows exactly what he will do.

They continue to kiss. Lighter, now. It's tender. Too loving for a first date. Seth works at her neck again, feeling her breasts. His hands stroke her back beneath her clothing. He pulls at the bottom of her top and pulls it up over her head. She is wearing a black bra that makes her skin seem so much purer.

More kissing and he works the clasp apart on the bra. Her breasts are real. Firm for a woman of her age. He takes his mouth down, working his tongue around her nipple and then sucking, a little too hard at times but he likes the way she reacts to the pain.

He pushes her lightly, playfully, onto the bed then lies on top of her. He's still fully clothed.

He kisses down her body. Gentle, wet kisses where he licks at the same time and breathes on her enough to tickle her and make her hips thrust subtly.

Down. Down to her stomach. The top two abdominals are strong and visible, even in the dark. It gets a little softer as he works his way down but it's still flat as she lies on her back.

Down. Down to her jeans. He undoes the button and licks slowly across the top of her knicker line. Occasionally flicking his tongue underneath. He teases, pulling down her trousers enough to expose her hip bones. He works his tongue towards them then bites. Nothing that will leave a mark.

She jerks her hips and he smiles. She likes it. He knows she does.

He can smell her, and he likes it. He wants it. He wants his mouth on her.

Down. Down between her legs. He presses his lips against the rectangle of short pubic hair. He runs his tongue down one side and breathes against the place that she wants his tongue to be. He's not going there just yet.

He kisses just the way he would if it was her mouth. His tongue working inside her.

She breathes heavily.

Ant tries not to. He is hard, watching. Listening. Waiting.

Eventually, Seth reaches her clitoris, licking upwards, the texture of his tongue rubbing against her. He repeats the motion. He is slow, deliberate. He doesn't want to take her all the way. Not yet.

He continues. One hand on her stomach, the other pushing a finger inside her and curling it at a faster speed than he licks. He sees some movement in the corner and pulls back.

'Come on. I want you inside me,' she demands.

Seth stands up between her legs and takes his shirt off. Then he unzips his trousers and pulls them down, his erect penis springs upward. He climbs on top of her and she reaches down. Down between his legs, she grips him hard and rubs the tip of his dick around her before easing it inside.

Seth moves himself upwards, pushing everything he has inside of her. His chest rests against hers and he kisses her neck and thrusts himself back and forth, his full weight pressing down on her.

'Fuck me, Seth,' she says in his ear, and he feels himself get excited. He moves faster.

'Harder,' she tells him.

He pushes himself up so that he is looking down on her. He can watch himself disappear inside her. She can look down and see him pounding at her.

He moves faster, harder, beating into her.

She gets louder.

Ant gets more anxious.

Seth pushes his hands against her stomach as he continues to move, her head drops to the side, her tongue pushes out through her mouth and touches her top lip.

Up. Up towards her breasts, he grips them, thrusting, slapping into her.

Up. Up towards her neck. He squeezes slightly as he feels her tightening around him. She likes it. He knows she does.

But that is the signal.

Ant steps out of the shadows.

159

I've had a lot to drink tonight, but I won't forget anything.

Seth lets go of my neck and Ant takes over.

I see his face. I recognise it from earlier when he bumped into us outside the restaurant. I remember him skulking past the pub window. I noticed him when we went for drinks before. And I heard him fidgeting around us while we fucked.

He jumps onto the bed and puts his hands around my throat from the other direction, he is upside down to me. His eyes are wide and his grip is strong.

He's going through with this.

His first kill.

No backing out now.

Seth is still inside me. I wonder whether he will come. He was close. I could feel it.

It's funny, you spend your waking life worrying about all the things you don't have, comparing yourself to others, wondering what you're missing out on, feeling restless and trapped in your situation, unable to change, and, then, when you're faced with death, you think exactly the same thing.

I wanted a child, I think. That's the ultimate connection.

Ant squeezes harder. I see his face, it is pure joy. Like a kid. Like an innocent.

I buck and squirm. Seth comes out of me and falls to the floor.

It's just me and Ant, for now.

I know who he is. I recognise that face.

The entire colour spectrum starts creeping in from the corners of my eyes. I hit at Ant's hands but he hardly moves.

Then, click!

And the tension is released.

Seth is behind Ant. Gun at his head. It has gone exactly how I planned it.

I stand up and look at Ant. I slap him around the face and his cheek smashes into the gun barrel. Then he wets himself.

'Oh, Ant. That is a shame,' I say.

'What the fuck is this? What are you doing, Seth? Who is this crazy woman?'

That's a mistake.

Seth turns Ant around and points the gun at his face. Ant is frozen. I start getting dressed.

'Sit down on the bed. And do not talk about my wife like that.'

'Your wife.'

We both laugh.

'This is very simple. Tell us the password to your computer, so that I can delete those pictures.'

'Is that what this is about?'

'Password.'

'No way. It doesn't matter, there's another printed copy out there. So if anything happens to me...'

'You're not that fucking smart, kid. Now tell me the password.'

I'm covered up and Ant is choking on the barrel of a gun, trying not to gag. It scrapes against his teeth. As he tries to back away, Seth pushes it in harder.

He says something that is muffled. He's looking at me for help.

'What?' Seth asks. I look on.

Ant mumbles the same thing again.

'Password? Your password is password?'

Ant nods. I hear his teeth biting against the metal.

Seth laughs, relaxes his arm for a moment, I see the tension release in Ant's shoulders. He looks right at me.

Then Seth pulls the trigger and Ant's inferior brain sprays out across his perfectly sanded wall. No time to ponder his betrayal. No time to think of his family or friends. No time to consider his mistakes: following Seth home that night; stalking Hadley Serf, watching her die, blackmailing us. No time to reminisce about his travels and the first time he'd ever watched somebody's life drain from their eyes, not doing anything to help. No time to understand that he would never be clean. He would never be anything.

'Password?' I ask. 'All this and it was password. We didn't even need to kill him.'

'Oh, Maeve, we always need to kill them.'

160

Detective Sergeant Pace isn't right.

Detective Sergeant Pace thinks he got lucky.

Detective Sergeant Pace is a tar-filled lung.

It looked like a simple suicide. Cut and dried. The evidence was all there. And the evidence that wasn't there could be overlooked because it would ease the minds of the public to know that this monster was gone and Pace didn't care that it didn't completely add up; his mind could never be eased.

They found the roll of plastic in his flat. The cut at one end tessellated perfectly with the piece that had been taken from Hadley Serf's body. That, alone, was a conviction.

Then there were the pictures on his desktop computer. No password protection. Compromising images of all three girls. That was enough to link him to all three of their murders.

Of course, the Post-it notes he had brought home with him with the names and numbers of emotionally vulnerable and possible future victims made sense after the authorities had spoken with his work colleagues and found out that he also volunteered. They knew from Hadley's phone records that she had called the Samaritans days before her death.

Proof, if it were needed, was mounting against Ant.

Follow-ups with his family would reveal a possible case for post-traumatic stress at the death of his friend.

Pace could look past the lack of a suicide note. He could graze over the fact that there was no powder residue from the gunshot on the hand of the corpse.

And then there was the light bulb. On the bedside table. In perfect working order but taken out of the ceiling light. It had people baffled. That was the intention. To draw focus from what was important. What was missing. In the end, it was decided that the kid was just weird. He was a killer. And now he was dead.

And you shouldn't rejoice in the death of another person but half the country did.

They felt safer.

Detective Sergeant Pace knows it is all bullshit.

Detective Sergeant Pace just wants to go home.

Detective Sergeant Pace is an infection.

It was cut and dried. The photos, the phone calls, the notes, the roll of plastic. This case was over and he could crawl back to London with his giant shadow and his head held low until his sickness spread somewhere else, until it triggered something else.

MONDAY

161

And the phone calls come flooding in.

Hundreds of them, as expected.

People who had recognised Ant from the club on the night in question. One from a drunk young man who thought he had seen him sat at a bus stop that very evening. Fellow volunteers at the Samaritans who are shocked to have been working alongside a three-time murderer. James's mother, who now questions whether her son had committed suicide or it had something to do with his murderous travel companion.

And sandwiched between these and the prank calls and the wastes-of-time and the attentions seekers, is a woman who is worried because her husband has been acting strange recently and has disappeared.

She is worried because he always comes home.

He always comes back to her.

But Detective Sergeant Pace has no time for any of them. Because he is standing in the apartment of the man on the video that went out last night for the country to see. And his brains are sprayed across the wall behind him.

And there's enough evidence in his flat for a conviction that the killer will never have to serve.

And there's another dead body at the foot of the bed.

162

It was the colours in my eyes that had me worried. Wondering.

Why did Seth let it get to that point? Authenticity? I wonder if he wanted to see how far he could take it.

Maybe it had crossed his mind to kill me.

We had used Ant. He was desperate for some kind of rush. And he clearly hated Seth. The psycho thought that Hadley had been taken away from him. Like it should have been his job to either clean her up or kill her himself. He'd been following her.

I knew it was him. When he bumped into us outside the restaurant, he was shielding his face. But that wasn't for my benefit. It was for Seth's. I saw Ant outside the restaurant at the bus stop; I knew he was there, where he was supposed to be. I saw him pass by the window. I saw him lurking in the shadow in the corner of his room. And I saw a halo of colour around him as my husband very nearly allowed him to choke the life out of me.

There was still the opportunity to go along with our original plan, to kill and frame Ant.

My plan.

But, it was the colours.

Seth was getting worse. The incidents were getting closer and closer together. He was chasing the same thing that Ant was. That unattainable feeling of the first kill. That high. That dopamine-fuelled ecstasy.

And, while these incidents were bringing us closer together, they were dragging me down.

I couldn't have that.

It wasn't working.

I remember so vividly the look in Ant's eyes as he realised he had been double-crossed, that Seth was going to kill him. He looked at me like he knew me. I'd told Seth to be quick, to not think about it. To just take the shot.

The haunting disappointment and betrayal was short-lived. Seth did exactly as I instructed him to and Ant's blood flew out through the back of his head before he had a chance to sell me out.

The world lost nothing last night.

And then I said, 'Give me the gun, Seth, we need to get dressed and sort this flat out quickly before we get the hell out of here. It will look like a suicide.'

I was supposed to wipe the gun clean and place it in Ant's hand. The poor boy would look like another misunderstood and lonely male who couldn't deal with the ravages of the real world. Who committed heinous crimes against society then couldn't live with himself.

Seth gave me the gun and I shot him in the chest.

No pause.

There was no time to see the betrayal in his dead eyes.

Then I continued with the plan. My plan. My contingency. It was clean. I was out of it. Maybe they were working together. Maybe Seth was Ant's last kill before he took his own life. Nobody would care because the killing would be over. Sure, the families of the victims wouldn't have closure but I don't care, that's not my problem.

And I thought about bleaching myself off Seth's dick because that was the one thing that would tie me to the scene, but a wash was enough. The only thing I needed to bleach was my hair. So that anybody who remembers seeing Seth in that restaurant will recall him dining with a woman who had been bleached.

So, now, I am dyeing it back. I have already called the police to state my worry about my missing husband. I'm just the lonely wife at home. I know nothing about my partner's infidelity or extracurricular activity. *I just thought he was a hard worker, officer.*

There's only one part left to fulfil. The thing I have wanted since the first news item concerning Daisy Pickersgill's discovery. It will happen today.

So I wait. I drink coffee and I watch the television with my dry, once-again brunette hair, and I wait.

Today, that bell will ring and, when I open the door, the person standing on the other side will be Detective Sergeant Pace.

163

The number of the person that called in, worried about her husband not coming home Sunday night, matched a number on the phone records of each of the victims.

For his late-night project, Seth Beauman had used the home phone to call his would-be suitors. Once he got one to bite, he then started using his burner mobile phones.

The doorbell rings and Maeve races to the door. She wants it to look as though she is anxious. Hopeful that her husband is returning.

When she opens the door, she looks devastated at the figure that darkens her doorway, though it is exactly as she had hoped.

'Oh, I'm sorry, I thought you were going to be someone else. Can I help you?' She sounds a little out of breath.

'Mrs Beauman?' His voice is deep with a crackle that she finds incredibly alluring. Everything about him is so dark he seems to alter the daylight behind him.

'Yes,' she looks sceptical.

'I'm Detective Sergeant Pace, would you mind if I come in a moment to talk?'

'Er, you don't look like a policeman, have you got some kind of identification?'

'Of course, yes.' He fishes around his inside pocket.

'What is this about, officer?'

'You made a call this morning regarding your husband.'

'That's right, is everything okay?'

'Can I come in?'

'Yes, yes, of course. Sorry.'

Maeve ushers the detective over the threshold, shuts the door and leads him into the kitchen.

'Would you like a drink or something? I'm sorry, I've never had the police here before; I feel nervous for some reason. Have you heard from Seth?' She is deliberately fumbling.

'Mrs Beauman, perhaps we could sit down.'

'Yes. It's just through here. You don't want a water or something? Tea?' She gestures him into the lounge. The nights she had been alone and imagined him in that very room with her...

Pace breaks the news to her that Seth is dead. And she cries on cue. And she asks what happened even though she knows everything.

That is the easy part for Pace, telling a wife that her husband has been shot. Next he has to inform her that he was complicit in three brutal murders.

'Don't be so stupid. You don't know Seth. He's just a normal person. He works hard at his job and he comes home. He's level. He doesn't even have extremes of emotion. I can't tell you a time he has raised his voice to me.' She is purposely talking about him as though he is still alive, like she hasn't come to terms with it a week before she pulled the trigger.

Maeve doesn't know how she is doing it. She is so convincing. She is herself but also she is not.

Pace has to ask some routine questions.

'He doesn't have a friend called Ant. I know all of his friends. There really aren't that many.'

'I'm sorry, Mrs Beauman, I know that this is a lot to take in but I assure you it is all true. We can offer you a liaison that will help you through this time...'

She interrupts. 'I don't need a liaison, I just need to know what is going on.'

Pace explains how he sees it. That Seth and Ant were working together. Ant would find the victims through his voluntary position at the Samaritans and they would groom these women, meet them and kill them. Seth was probably responsible for the first two as they were both based in London. There was insufficient evidence at that time to say whether he killed them then took them to Ant in Warwickshire or whether he took them there to be killed, but time would tell.

'I am sorry again to have to ask you this at this time, but is there anything you can tell us that might help piece this together? Perhaps where he might have met Ant or anything he did that seemed suspicious or out of the ordinary.'

Maeve waits. Like she knows something but doesn't want to tell him. But this is exactly where she wants to be.

Silently, she stands up and Pace watches her edge across the room to the other sofa. She slides her arm down the side and pulls out a wad of paper. Seth's special phonebook.

Detective Sergeant Pace cannot believe his luck.

'It was just something he did. He couldn't sleep. He wasn't hurting anyone.'

Pace felt sorry for her. She seems trusting and naïve.

'Thank you for your time, Mrs. Beauman. I know that this will have come as a huge shock to you. The liaison officer will be in touch with you today.'

'I don't know the liaison officer. I'm really not sure who to trust, right now. Could you not be my liaison, Detective Pace?'

'I assure you, she is very trustworthy but I will also check back with you, Mrs Beauman. I'm sure we will have to talk again.'

Maeve had everything she wanted. She was rid of Seth. She was innocent in all of this. And Detective Sergeant Pace was coming back to see her.

The way she felt after seeing him on the television was nothing compared to the high of having him here in her home.

And next time would be even better.

164

It's been a good day.

I made myself a pasta for dinner and now I am lying on the sofa with almost a bottle of white wine inside me.

I look over at the sofa that Seth should be sitting on and I don't miss him; I'm not craving his gaze or his touch.

But I'm not falling asleep like I usually do.

I'm thinking about Detective Pace and it is keeping me awake.

There was some kind of energy when he was here earlier. It was primal and uncomfortable but I liked it. A lot.

I skip through a few channels and Seth is on the news but I really don't have so much of an interest in current affairs, right now. I flick through to a reality show where beautiful but stupid couples are sent away to cheat on their partners. It's idiotic. White noise.

I'm bored. I move over to Seth's old sofa. He doesn't need it anymore. It's just passed ten o'clock. Late, but not too late. I sit on his seat and I think about all the things I did for him: tolerating his moods; watching him decline; paying for more than my share; fucking him; and bleaching all those girls.

I always knew what he was up to. I knew everything he was doing. He was stupid to think that I didn't. I did all those things for him, for us, in spite of everything I knew. And I know that I had to kill him in the end but I'm still not done helping my husband out.

Pace doesn't have everything.

I reach beneath the sofa cushion and pull out a sheet of paper.

There are still a few Taylors left.

I pick up the phone and dial the first number that hasn't been highlighted.

'Hi. This is Maeve. I can't sleep. Want to talk?'

ACKNOWLEDGEMENTS

A few years back, it was suggested that Will Carver was probably dead. So I really need to thank the people that resurrected me.

Karen Sullivan. Holy fuck. A one-off. An absolute force of nature. The hardest-working, most passionate and enthusiastic publisher that a writer could ask for. Courageous. Taking on the books that would scare others. Making them beautiful and getting them read. I knew it would be you from that first time we met.

Tom Witcomb. My beautiful, young and shiny agent. The Runkle I've always wanted. Knowledgeable and brutally honest. Just what I need.

My writer friends. Sarah, who said not to worry, it would happen again. And Tom, whose advice was free, plentiful and usually correct. And I only ignored most of it.

To everyone at Orenda who read and got behind this book. West Camel and Meggy Roussel. What a team. And to Liz for reading it first, passing it on and having excellent taste.

To Phoebe and Coen, my greatest creations. The constant good in my world.

Mum and Brendan for getting me through these years and helping me through the beers.

My real-life friends: Parks, who is there when I need him, and when I don't. Whether it's time or gin or money for my rent. And Tim and Forbes and Bruce for sticking with me when things got shitty.

And to Kel, a great friend who became much more. My new chapter.

Lastly, January David. I'm sorry I didn't get to finish telling your story, man, but I haven't forgotten you, don't worry.